THE GOLDEN GATE

ALISTAIR MACLEAN, the son of a Scots Minister, was brought up in the Scottish Highlands. In 1941 at the age of 18, he joined the Royal Navy; two and a half years spent aboard a cruiser were later to give him the background for HMS *Ulysses*, his first novel, the outstanding documentary novel on the war at sea. He is now the author of twenty-one best-selling novels, of which *Sea Witch* is the most recent; sixteen of them have now sold more than a million copies throughout the world.

Many of his novels have also been filmed – *The Guns of Navarone*, *Where Eagles Dare* and *Breakheart Pass* are mong the most famous – and there are plans to film many more books including *The Golden Gate* and *Force Ten from Navarone*.

ALISTAIR MACLEAN

The Golden Gate

FONTANA/Collins

First published in 1976 by William Collins Sons & Co Ltd
This continental edition first issued in Fontana Book 1977

© Alistair MacLean 1976

Printed in Canada

To MARY MARCELLE

ONE

The operation had to be executed with a surgically military precision marked with a meticulousness that matched, in degree if not in scope, the Allied landings in wartime Europe. It was. The preparations had to be made in total stealth and secrecy. They were. A split-second co-ordination had to be achieved. It was. All the men had to be rehearsed and trained, over and over again until they played their parts perfectly and automatically. They were so trained. Every eventuality, every possible departure from the planned campaign had to be catered for. It was. And their confidence in their ability to carry out their plan, irrespective of reversals and departures from the norm, had to be total. It was.

Confidence was a quality exuded by their leader, Peter Branson. Branson was thirty-eight years old, just under six feet tall, strongly built, with black hair, pleasant features, lips that were curved in an almost perpetual smile and light blue eyes that had forgotten how to smile many years ago. He was dressed in a policeman's uniform but he was not a policeman. Neither was any of the eleven men with them in that disused trucker's garage not far from the banks of Lake Merced, half-way between Daly City to the south and San Francisco to the north, although three were attired in the same uniform as Branson.

The single vehicle there looked sadly out of place in what was, in effect, nothing more than an open-ended shed. It was a bus, but barely, by normal standards, qualified for the term. It was an opulently gleaming monster which above shoulder level was composed, except for the stainless steel cross-over struts, entirely of slightly tinted glass. There was no regular seating as such. There were about thirty swivel chairs, anchored to the floor but scattered seemingly at random, with deep arm-rests and aircraft-type swing-out dining-tables housed in each arm-rest. Towards the rear there was a cloakroom and a remarkably well-stocked bar. Beyond that there was a rear observation deck, the floor of which had for the moment been removed to reveal the cavernous baggage department. This

5

was filled to near capacity but not with baggage. This enormous storage-space, seven and a half feet wide by the same in length, held, among other things, two petrol-driven electric generators, two twenty-inch searchlights, a variety of smaller ones, two very peculiar-looking missile-like weapons with mounting tripods, machine-pistols, a large crated unmarked wooden box and four smaller boxes, wooden but greased and a variety of other items of material, conspicuous among which were large coils of rope. Branson's men were still loading.

The coach, one of six ever made, had cost Branson ninety thousand dollars: for the purposes for which he intended to use it, he considered this figure a trifling investment. He was buying the coach, he had told the Detroit firm, as an agent for a publicity-shy millionaire, who was also an eccentric who wanted it painted yellow. And yellow it had been when it was delivered: it was now a gleaming, translucent white.

Two of the remaining five coaches had been bought by genuine and extrovert millionaires, both of whom intended them for luxurious, personal vacation travel. Both buses had rear ramps to accommodate their mini-cars. Both, presumably, would rest for about fifty weeks a year in their specially-built garages.

The other three buses had been bought by the government. The dawn was not yet in the sky.

The other three white buses were in a garage in down-town San Francisco. The big sliding doors were closed and bolted. In a canvas chair in a corner a man in plain clothes, a sawn-off riot gun held on his lap by flaccid hands, slept peacefully. He had been dozing when the two intruders arrived and was now blissfully unaware that he had sunk into an even deeper sleep because he'd inhaled the single-second squirt from the gas gun without being aware of the fact. He would wake up within the hour almost equally unaware of what had happened and would be extremely unlikely to admit to his superiors that his vigilance had been a degree less than eternal.

The three buses looked undistinguishable from Branson's, at least externally, although the centre one was markedly different in two respects, one visible, the other not. It weighed two tons more than its companions, for bullet-proof glass is a great deal heavier than ordinary plate glass, and those panoramic buses had an enormous glass area. And the interior of the coach was nothing less than a sybarite's dream, which was no less than what one would expect for the private transportation of the country's Chief Executive.

The Presidential coach had two huge facing sofas, so deep, so soft and so comfortable that the overweight man possessed of prudent foresight would have thought twice about ensconcing himself in either of them for regaining the vertical would have called for an apoplectic amount of will-power or the use of a crane. There were four armchairs constructed along the same treacherously voluptuous lines. And that, in the way of seating accommodation, was that. There were cunningly concealed spigots for ice-water, scattered copper coffee tables and gleaming gold-plated vases awaiting their daily consignment of fresh flowers. Behind this section were the washroom and the bar, a bar whose capacious refrigerators, in this particular and unusual instance, were stocked largely with fruit juices and soft drinks in deference to the customs of the President's guests of honour, who were Arabs and Muslims.

Beyond this again, in a glassed-in compartment that extended the full width of the bus, was the communications centre, a maze of miniaturized electronic systems which was constantly manned whenever the President was aboard. It was said that this installation had cost considerably more than the coach itself. Besides incorporating a radio telephone system that could reach any place in the world, it had a small row of differently coloured buttons in a glass case which could be removed only with the aid of a special key. There were five such buttons. To press the first brought instant contact with the White House in Washington: the second was for the Pentagon: the third was for the airborne Strategic Air Command: the fourth was for Moscow and the fifth for London. Apart from the necessity of being in touch with his armed forces all the time, the President was an acute sufferer from telephonitis, even to the extent of an internal phone connecting him with his habitual seat on the bus and the communications compartment at the rear.

But it was not in this coach that the intruders were interested but in the one standing to its left. They entered by the front door and immediately removed a metal plate by the driver's seat. One of the men shone a torch downwards, appeared to locate what he wanted almost immediately, reached up

7

and took from his companion something that looked like a polythene bag of putty to which there was attached a metal cylinder not more than three inches long and one in diameter. This he securely bound to a metal strut with adhesive tape. He seemed to know what he was doing – which he did, for the lean and cadaverous Reston was an explosives expert of some note.

They moved to the rear and went behind the bar. Reston climbed on to a stool, slid back an overhead cupboard door and looked at the liquor contents. Whatever the camp-followers in the Presidential motorcade were going to suffer from, it clearly wasn't going to be thirst. There were two rows of vertically stacked bottles, the first ten to the left, five in each row, being bourbon and scotch. Reston stooped and examined the upside down optics beneath the cupboard and saw that the bottles that interested him in the cupboard were duplicated in the ones below and that those were all full. It seemed unlikely that anyone was going to be interested in the contents of the cupboard for some little time to come.

Reston removed the ten bottles from their circular retaining holes in the cupboard and handed them down to his companion who stacked five of them on the counter and placed the other five in a canvas bag which had evidently been brought along for this purpose, then handed Reston a rather awkward piece of equipment which consisted of three parts: a small cylinder similar to the one that had been fitted forwards, a beehive-shaped device, no more than two inches high and the same in diameter, and a device which looked very like a car fire extinguisher, with the notable exception that it had a plastic head. Both this and the beehive were attached to the cylinder by wires.

The beehive had a rubber sucker at its base but Reston did not seem to have any great faith in suckers for he produced a tube of quick-acting glue with which he liberally besmeared the base of the beehive. This done he pressed it firmly against the forward facing side of the cupboard, taped it securely to the large and small cylinders and then taped the three to the inner row of circular holes which retained the bottles. He replaced the five bottles in front. The device was completely hidden. He slid shut the door, replaced the stool and left the bus with his companion. The guard still slept peacefully. The two men left by the side door by which they had entered and locked it behind them. Reston produced a walkie-talkie. He said: 'PI?'

The amplified voice came through clearly on the fascia-mounted speaker in the bus in the garage north of Daly City. Branson made a switch.

'Yes?'

'Okay.'

'Good.' There was no elation in Branson's voice and no reason why there should have been: with six weeks of solid preparation behind him he would have been astonished if anything should have gone wrong. 'You and Mack get back to the apartment. Wait.'

Johnson and Bradley were curiously alike, good-looking, in their early thirties, almost identical in build and both with blond hair. They also bore a striking resemblance, both in build and coloration, to the two men, newly wakened from sleep, who were propped up in the two beds in the hotel room, gazing at them with an understandable mixture of astonishment and outrage. One of them said: 'Who the hell are you and what the hell do you think you're doing here?'

'Kindly modulate your voice and mind your language,' Johnson said. 'It ill becomes a naval air officer. Who we are doesn't matter. We're here because we require a change of clothes.' He looked at the Beretta he was holding and touched the silencer with his left forefinger. 'I don't have to tell you what those things are.'

He didn't have to tell them what those things were. There was a cold calm professionalism, a chilling surety about Johnson and Bradley that discouraged freedom of speech and inhibited even the very thought of action. While Johnson stood there, gun dangling in apparent negligence by his side, Bradley opened the valise they had brought with them, produced a length of thin rope and trussed up the two men with a speed and efficiency that indicated a long or intensive experience of such matters. When he had finished Johnson opened a cupboard, produced two suits, handed one to Bradley and said: 'Try them for size.'

Not only were the suits an almost perfect fit but so also were the hats. Johnson would have been surprised if they had been otherwise: Branson, that most meticulous of planners, almost never missed a trick.

Bradley surveyed himself in a full-length mirror. He said sadly: 'I should have stayed on the other side of the law. The uniform of a Lieutenant in the US Naval Air Arm suits me very well indeed. Not that you look too bad yourself.'

One of the bound men said: 'Why do you want those uniforms?'

'I thought naval helicopter pilots were intelligent.'

The man stared at him. 'Jesus! You don't mean to stand there and tell us – '

'Yes. And we've both probably flown Sikorskys a damned sight more than either of you.'

'But uniforms? Why steal our uniforms? There's no trick in getting those made. Why do you – '

'We're parsimonious. Sure, we could get them made. But what we can't get made are all the documentation you carry about with you – identifications, licences, the lot.' He patted the pockets of his uniform. 'They're not here. Where?'

The other bound man said: 'Go to hell.' He looked as if he meant it, too.

Johnson was mild. 'This is off-season for heroes. Where?'

The other man said: 'Not here. The Navy regard those as classified documents. They have to be deposited in the manager's safe.'

Johnson sighed. 'Oh, dear. Why make it difficult? We had a young lady stake-out in an armchair by the receptionist's last evening. Redhead. Beautiful. You may recall.' The two bound men exchanged the briefest of glances: it was quite clear that they did recall. 'She'd go on oath in a witness stand that neither of you deposited anything.' He smiled in a wintry fashion. 'A witness stand in court may be the last place on earth she'd want to go near, but if she says it's no deposit, it's no deposit. Let's not be silly. Three things you can do. Tell us. Have your mouths taped and after a little persuasion tell us. Or, if those don't work, we just search. You watch. If you're conscious, that is.'

'You going to kill us?'

'What on earth for?' Bradley's surprise was genuine.

'We can identify you.'

'You'll never see us again.'

'We can identify the girl.'

'Not when she removes her red wig, you can't.' He dug into the valise and came up with a pair of pliers. He had about him an air of gentle resignation. 'Time's a-wasting. Tape them up.'

Both bound men looked at each other. One shook his head, the other sighed. One smiled, almost ruefully: 'It does seem a gesture of useless defiance – *and* I don't want my good looks spoilt. Under the mattresses. At the foot.'

Under the mattresses they were. Johnson and Bradley flicked over the leaves of the two wallets, looked at each other, nodded, extracted the not inconsiderable dollar billfolds in each wallet and placed those by the bedside tables. One man said: 'Couple of crazy crooks you are.'

Johnson said: 'Maybe you'll be needing that more than us pretty soon.' He extracted money from his newly discarded suit and placed it in his uniform while Bradley did the same. 'Our suits you can have. Unthinkable for US officers to be running around the city in their striped underpants. And now, I'm afraid, we have to tape you.' He reached into the valise.

One man, a quick mixture of suspicion and apprehension in his eyes, tried, vainly, to sit up in bed. 'I thought you said – '

'Look, if we wanted to kill you, the noise from those silenced guns wouldn't even be heard in the corridor outside. Think we want you to start hollering the place down the moment we step outside that door? Besides, it would upset the neighbours.'

After they were taped Johnson said: 'And, of course, we don't want to have you jumping and wriggling around and making banging noises on the floor or walls. I'm afraid we can't have any bangs in the next couple of hours or so. Sorry.' He stooped, retrieved what looked like an aerosol can from the valise, and squirted it briefly in the faces of both bound men. They left, hanging up the no disturb notice outside. Johnson double-locked the door, produced his pliers, leaned on the key and snapped it leaving the head jammed in the lock.

Downstairs, they approached the clerk at reception, a cheerful youngster who gave a cheerful good morning.

Johnson said: 'You weren't on last night?'

'No, sir. The management wouldn't believe it but even a desk clerk requires a little sleep now and again.' He looked at them with interest. 'No offence, but aren't you the two gentlemen who're going to ride herd on the President this morning?'

Johnson smiled. 'I'm not sure if the President would care to have you put it quite that way, but yes. It's no secret. We phoned for an alarm call last night. Ashbridge and Martinez. Was it recorded?'

'Yes, sir.' The clerk put his pen through the names.

'Now, we've left one or two – ah – naval things in our room that we really shouldn't have done. Will you make certain that no one goes near our room until we return? Three hours. about.'

'You can depend on me, sir.' The clerk made a note. 'The no disturb sign –'

'We've already done that.'

They left and stopped at the first pay telephone on the street. Johnson went inside with the valise, fished inside and brought out a walkie-talkie. He was immediately through to Branson, waiting patiently in the dilapidated garage north of Daly City. He said: 'PI?'

'Yes?'

'Okay.'

'Good. Get down there.'

The sun was coming up as the six men filed out of their cabin in the hills above Sausalito in Marin County, north across the bay from San Francisco. They made up a non-descript and not particularly attractive group, four of them in overalls and two in faded raincoats that might have been lifted from some unsuspecting scarecrow. They all piled into a rather battered Chevrolet station wagon and headed down to the town. Before them stretched a stunning vista. To the south the Golden Gate and the staggering – if rather Man-hattanized – skyline of San Francisco. To the south-east, lent a slightly spurious glamour by the early rays of the sun, Alcatraz Island, of unhappy history, lay to the north of the Fisherman's Wharf, in line of sight of Treasure Island, the Bay Bridge and Oakland on the far side of the bay. To the east lay Angel Island, the largest in the bay, while to the north-east lay Belvedere Island, Tiburon and, beyond that again, the wide reaches of San Pablo Bay vanishing into nothingness. There can be few more beautiful and spectacular vistas in the world – if such there so be – than that from Sausalito. On the basis that not to be moved by it would require a heart of stone, the six men in the station wagon had between them, it was clear, the makings of a fair-sized quarry.

They reached the main street, travelled along past the immaculate rows of sailing craft and the far from immaculate hodge-podge of boathouses, until eventually the driver pulled off into a side-street, parked and stopped the engine. He and the man beside him got out and divested themselves of their coats, revealing themselves as clad in the uniforms of California State Patrolmen. The driver, a sergeant by the name of Giscard, was at least six feet three in height, burly, red-faced, tight mouthed and, even to the cold, insolent eyes, was the conceptualized epitome of the dyed-in-the-wool tough cop. Policemen, admittedly, were part and parcel of Giscard's life but his frequent acquaintanceships with them he had kept to as limited a nature as possible on the numerous occasions when, hitherto without success, they had attempted to put him behind bars. The other, Parker, was tall, lean and of a nasty appearance and the best that could be said for him was that he might have passed for a cop if one wore myopic or he were viewed at a considerable distance : his habitually wary bitter expression was probably attributable to the fact that he had experienced considerably less success than the sergeant in evading the long arm of the law.

They turned a corner and entered a local police precinct station. Two policemen were behind the counter, one very young, the other old enough to be his father. They looked rather tired and unenthusiastic as was natural for two men who were looking forward to some sleep, but they were polite, courteous.

'Good morning, good morning.' Giscard could be very brisk indeed as only befitted a man who had shown a clean pair of heels to half the police forces on the Coast. 'Sergeant Giscard. Patrolman Parker.' He pulled from his pocket a paper with a long list of names. 'You must be Mahoney and Nimitz?'

'Indeed we are.' Mahoney, a guileless youth, would have found some difficulty in concealing his Hibernian ancestry. 'And how do you know?'

'Because I can read.' The niceties of salon conversation were not for Giscard. 'From this I take it that your station boss didn't advise you we were coming. Well, it's this damned motorcade this morning – and from what I've found out this morning maybe I'm not wasting all that much of my time in making this final check-up. You'd be surprised at the number of policemen in this state who are either illiterate or stone deaf.'

Nimitz was polite. 'If we were to know what we have done wrong, Sergeant – '

'*You* haven't done anything wrong.' He consulted his sheet. 'Just four things. When do the day shift come on? How many? Where are the patrol cars? And the cells.'

'That's all?'

'All. Two minutes. And hurry. I've got to check every place from here across the bridge to Richmond.'

'Eight o'clock. Eight men – twice the usual. The cars – '

'Let me see them.'

Nimitz lifted a key from a board and led the two men round the corner of the block. He opened double doors. The two police cars, as was only proper on this auspicious occasion when a President, a King and a Prince were travelling through their precinct, had the impossible glitter of showroom models.

'Ignition keys?'

'In the ignition.'

Back in the station Giscard nodded to the entrance door. 'Keys?'

'I beg your pardon.'

Giscard was heavily patient. 'I know it's normally never locked. But you might *all* have to leave in a tearing hurry this morning. You want to leave the shop unattended?'

'I see.' Nimitz indicated the keys on the board.

'The cells.'

Nimitz led the way, taking keys with him. They were only a few feet away but round a corner out of sight of the more sensitive citizens who had reluctant occasion to enter the front office. Nimitz entered and Giscard unholstered his pistol and stuck it against his back. 'A dead policeman,' Giscard observed, 'is no good to anyone.' Parker joined them in ten seconds pushing a furious and flabbergasted Mahoney in front of him.

Both captives were gagged and left sitting on the floor, backs to the bars, arms thrust uncomfortably through them and wrists handcuffed. From the baleful expressions on their faces it was as well that they were so securely gagged. Giscard put the keys in his pocket, picked up two other sets from

14

the board, ushered Parker out before him, locked the entrance door, pocketed that key too then went round and opened up the garage. He and Parker backed the cars out and while Giscard locked the doors – and, inevitably, pocketed the keys – Parker went to fetch the other four men from the station wagon. When they appeared they were not, surprisingly, any longer overalled working men but gleaming advertisements for the California State Patrol.

They drove north on the US 101, took the cut-off west to State I, passed by Muir Woods and its pre-Christian stands of two hundred and fifty feet high redwoods and finally stopped in the Mount Tamalpais State Park. Giscard brought out the walkie-talkie that went so well with his uniform and said: 'PI?'

Branson was still patiently waiting in the bus in the abandoned garage. 'Yes?'

'Okay.'

'Good. Stay.'

The forecourt and street outside the luxurious caravanserai atop Nob Hill were, understandably at that hour of the morning, practically deserted. There were, in fact, only seven people in sight. Six of those stood on the steps of the hotel which was that night housing more dollars on the hoof than it ever had remotely had in its long and illustrious career. The seventh of those, a tall, handsome man, aquiline-faced, youthful-looking despite his grey hair and clad in immaculate hounds-tooth, was pacing slowly up and down on the roadway. From the looks exchanged among the six men – two doorkeepers, two policemen and two men in plain clothes whose coats fitted awkwardly under their left armpits – his presence appeared to be giving rise to an increasing degree of vexation. Finally, after a low-murmured conversation among them one of the uniformed men came down the steps and approached him.

He said: 'Morning, sir. No offence, sir, but do you mind moving on. We have a job to do.'

'How do you know I have not?'

'Sir. Please. You must understand we have some very important people in there.'

'Don't I know it. Don't I just know it.' The man sighed, reached inside his coat, produced and opened a wallet. The

15

policeman looked at it, stiffened, unmistakably swallowed and deepened his complexion by two shades.

'I'm very sorry, sir. Mr Jensen, sir.'

'I'm sorry, too. Sorry for all of us. They can keep their damned oil as far as I'm concerned. Dear lord, what a circus.' He talked until the officer relaxed, then carried on his to-and-fro strolling. The policeman returned to the steps.

One of the plain-clothes men looked at him without a great deal of enthusiasm. He said: 'A great crowd mover-on you are.'

'Like to try?'

'If I must give you a demonstration,' he said wearily. He walked down three steps, paused, looked back up. 'He flashed a card at you, didn't he?'

'Sort of.' The policeman was enjoying himself.

'Who?'

'Don't you recognize your own deputy director when you see him?'

'Jesus!' The FBI man's miraculous return to the top step could have been attributed to nothing other than sheer levitation.

'Are you not,' the policeman asked innocently, 'going to move him on?'

The plain-clothes man scowled then smiled. 'From now on, I think I'll leave those menial tasks to the uniformed branch.'

A bell-boy of great age appeared on the top step, hesitated, then went down to the street as Jensen gave him an encouraging wave. As he approached his wizened face was further creased in worry. He said: 'Aren't you taking a helluva chance, sir? FBI man up there.'

'No chance.' Jensen was unperturbed. 'He's California FBI. I'm Washington. Chalk and cheese. I doubt if he'd know the Director-General if he came and sat on his lap. What's the word, Willie?'

'They're all having breakfast in their rooms. No sleepers-in, all on schedule.'

'Let me know every ten minutes.'

'Yes, sir. Gee, Mr Jensen, aren't you taking one godawful chance? The place is swarming with fuzz and not only just inside. Those windows across there – there's a rifle behind a dozen of them and a man behind each rifle.'

'I know, Willie. I'm the man in the eye of the storm. Dead safe.'

'If you're caught – '

'I won't be. Even if I were, you're clear.'

'Clear! Everybody sees me talking to you – '

'Why? Because I'm FBI. I told you that. You've no reason to doubt it. There are six men on the top of the steps who believe the same thing. Anyway, Willie, you can always plead the Fifth Amendment.'

Willie departed. In full view of the six watchers Jensen pulled out his walkie-talkie. 'PI?'

'Yes?' Branson was as calm as ever.

'On schedule.'

'Fine. PI's moving now. Every ten minutes. Right?'

'Of course. How's my twin?'

Branson looked towards the rear of the coach. The bound and gagged man between the aisles bore an uncanny resemblance to Jensen.

'He'll live.'

TWO

Van Effen eased the big coach on to the 280 and headed her north-east up the Southern Freeway. Van Effen was a short, stocky man, with close-cropped blond hair and a head that was almost a perfect cube. His ears were so close to his head that they appeared to have been pasted there, his nose had clearly been at odds with some heavy object in the past, he tended to wear a vacuous smile as if he'd decided it was the safest expression to cope with the numerous uncertain things that were going on in the uncertain world around him and the dreamy light blue eyes, which would never be accused of being possessed of any powers of penetration, served only to reinforce the overall impression of one overwhelmed by the insoluble complexities of life. Van Effen was a very very intelligent person whose knife-like intelligence could cope with an extremely wide variety of the world's problems and, although they had known each other for only two years, he had indisputably become Peter Branson's indispensable lieutenant.

Both men sat together in the front of the coach, both, for the nonce, dressed in long white coats which lent them, as drivers, a very professional appearance indeed: the State Department frowned on Presidential motorcade drivers who opted for lumber jackets or rolled up sleeves. Branson himself generally drove and was good at it but, apart from the fact that he was not a San Franciscan and Van Effen had been born there he wished that morning to concentrate his exclusive attention on his side of the coach's fascia which looked like a cross between the miniaturized flight instrumentation of a Boeing and those of a Hammond organ. As a communications system it could not compare to those aboard the Presidential coach, but everything was there that Branson wanted. Moreover, it had one or two refinements that the Presidential coach lacked. The President would not have considered them refinements.

Branson turned to the man in the seat behind him. Yonnie, a dark, swarthy and incredibly hirsute person who, on the rare occasions he could be persuaded to remove his shirt and approach a shower, looked more like a bear than a human being, had about him the general appearance – it was impossible to particularize – of an ex-pugilist who had taken not one but several hundred punches too many. Unlike many of Branson's associates Yonnie, who had been with Branson since he'd embarked upon his particular mode of life all of thirteen years ago, could not be classed among the intellectually gifted, but his patience, invariable good humour and total loyalty to Branson were beyond dispute.

Branson said: 'Got the plates, Yonnie?'

'The plates?' Yonnie wrinkled the negligible clearance between hairline and eyebrows, his customary indication of immense concentration, then smiled happily 'Yeah, yeah, I got them.' He reached under his seat and brought up a pair of spring-clipped number plates. Branson's coach was, externally, exactly the same as the three in the Presidential motorcade except for the fact that those were Washington DC plates while his were Californian. The plates that Yonnie held in his hand were Washington DC and, even better, exactly duplicated the numbers of one of the three waiting coaches in the garage.

Branson said: 'Don't forget. When I jump out the front door you jump out the back. And fix the *back* one first.'

'Leave it to me, Chief.' Yonnie exuded confidence.

A buzzer on the fascia rang briefly. Branson made a switch. It was Jonson, the Nob Hill stake-out.

'P1?'

'Yes?'

'On schedule. Forty minutes.'

'Thanks.'

Branson closed the switch and flipped another.

'P4?'

'P4.'

'Move in.'

Giscard started up the stolen police car and moved up the Panoramic Highway followed by the second car. They didn't drive sufficiently quickly to attract attention but they didn't linger either and had reached the Mount Tamalpais radar stations in a matter of minutes. Those stations dominated the mountainous countryside for miles around and looked like nothing in the world as much as a couple of gigantic white golf balls. Giscard and his men had the entire lay-out committed to heart and memory and no trouble was envisaged.

Giscard said: 'There'll be no need to lean. We're cops, aren't we? The guardians of the people. You don't attack your guardians. No shooting, the boss says.'

One of them said: 'What if I *have* to shoot?'

'You'll lose half your cut.'

'No shooting.'

Branson flipped another switch.

'P3?' P3 was the code of the two men who had recently booby-trapped one of the motorcade buses.

'P3.'

'Anything?'

'Two drivers, is all.'

'Guards?'

'Okay. No suspicions.'

'Wait.'

Branson flipped a switch as another buzzer rang.

'P5,' the speaker said. 'On schedule. Thirty minutes.'

'Thank you.'

Branson made another switch.

'P2?' The code for Johnson and Bradley.

'Yes?'

'You can go now.'

'We go now.' The voice was Johnson's. He and Bradley, immaculate in their naval air uniforms, were sauntering casually along in the direction of the US Naval Air Station Alameda. Both men were carrying smooth shiny flight bags into which they had transferred the contents of the valise. As they approached the entrance they increased their pace. By the time they reached the two guards at the entrance they were giving the impression of two men who were in a considerable hurry. They showed their cards to one of the guards.

'Lieutenant Ashbridge, Lieutenant Martinez. Of course. You're very late, sir.'

'I know. We'll go straight to the choppers.'

'I'm afraid you can't do that, sir. Commander Eysenck wants you to report to his office at once.' The sailor lowered his voice confidentially. 'The Commander doesn't sound very happy to me, sir.'

'Damn!' Johnson said, and meant it. 'Where's his office?'

'Second door on the left, sir.'

Johnson and Bradley hurried there, knocked and entered. A young petty officer seated behind his desk pursed his lips and nodded silently towards the door to his right. His demeanour indicated that he had no desire whatsoever to participate in the painful scene that was about to follow. Johnson knocked and entered, head down and apparently searching for something in his flight bag. The precaution was needless. In the well-known demoralization ploy of senior officers deepening their intimidation of apprehensive junior officers, Eysenck kept on making notes on a pad before him. Bradley closed the door. Johnson placed the flight bag on the edge of the desk. His right hand was concealed behind it. So was the aerosol gas can.

'So kind of you to turn up.' Eysenck spoke in a flat drawling accent: Annapolis had clearly failed to have any effect on his Boston upbringing. 'You had your strict orders.' He raised his head in what would normally have been a slow and effective gesture. 'Your explanations –' He broke off, eyes widening, but still not suspecting anything untoward. 'You're not Ashbridge and Martinez.'

'No, we're not, are we?'

It was clear that Eysenck had become suddenly aware that there was something very very far untoward. His hand stretched out for a desk button but Johnson already had his thumb on his. Eysenck slumped forward against his desk. Johnson nodded to Bradley who opened the door to the outer office and as he closed it behind him it could be seen that his hand was fumbling in the depths of his bag. Johnson moved behind the desk, studied the buttons below the phone, pressed one as he lifted the phone.

'Tower?'

'Sir?'

'Immediate clearance Lieutenants Ashbridge and Martinez.' It was a very creditable imitation of Eysenck's Boston accent. Branson again called P3, the two watchers by the garage.

'And now?'

'Filling up.'

The three buses inside the garage were indeed filling up. Two of them, indeed, had their complements of passengers and were ready to go. The coach that had been booby-trapped was given over mainly to newspapermen, wire service men and cameramen, among them four women, three of indeterminate age, the other young. On a platform at the rear of the bus were three mounted ciné cameras, for this was the coach that led the motorcade and the cameras would at all times have an excellent view of the Presidential coach which was to follow immediately behind. Among the passengers in this coach were three men who wouldn't have recognized a typewriter or a camera if it had dropped on their toes but who would have had no difficulty whatsoever in differentiating between a Walther, Colt, Biretti, Smith & Wesson and other such paraphernalia generally regarded as superfluous to the needs of the communications media. This was known as the lead coach.

But there was one passenger in this coach who would have recognized a camera if he had seen it – he was, in fact, carrying a highly complicated apparatus – but who would also have had no difficulty at all in differentiating between a Walther, Colt, Biretti and Smith & Wesson, any of which he was legally entitled to carry and not infrequently did. On this occasion, however, he was unarmed – he considered it unnecessary; between them his colleagues constituted a veritable travelling arsenal – but he did carry a most unusual item of equipment, a beautifully miniaturized and transistorized transceiver radio concealed in the false bottom of his camera. His name was Revson and as he had repeatedly proved in the past, in the service of his country although his country knew nothing of this – a man of quite remarkable accomplishments.

The rear coach was also well occupied, again by newspaper men and men with no interest in newspapers, although in this case the ratio was inversed. The greatly outnumbered journalists, although they realized that the Presidential coach would soon, in terms of the realizable assets of its passengers, be nothing less than a rolling Fort Knox, wondered if it were necessary to have quite so many FBI agents around.

There were only three people aboard the Presidential coach, all crew members. The white-coated driver, his 'receive' switch depressed, was waiting for instructions to come through the fascia speaker. Behind the bar, an extraordinarily pretty brunette, who looked like an amalgam of all those 'Fly me' airline advertisements, was trying to look demure and inconspicuous and failing miserably. At the rear, the radio operator was already seated in front of his communications console.

A buzzer rang in Branson's coach.

'P5,' the speaker said. 'On schedule. Twenty minutes.'

A second buzzer rang.

'P4,' the speaker said. 'All okay.'

'Excellent.' For once Branson permitted himself a slight feeling of relief. The take-over of the Tamalpais radar stations had been essential to his plans. 'Scanners manned?'

'Affirmative.'

A third buzzer rang.

'PI?' Johnson's voice was hurried. 'P2. Can we go now?'

'No. Trouble?'

'Some.' Johnson, seated at the helicopter controls, engines still not started, watched a man emerge from Eysenck's office and break into a run, rounding the corner of the building. That could only mean, Johnson realized, that he was going to look through Eysenck's office window and that could only mean that he had failed to open the door which he and Bradley had locked behind them: the key was at that moment in Johnson's pocket. Not that looking through Eysenck's window was going to help him much because he and Bradley had dragged the unconscious Eysenck and petty officer into the windowless washroom leading off the Commander's office. The key of the washroom door was also in his pocket.

The man came into sight round the corner of the building. He wasn't running now. In fact, he stopped and looked around. It wasn't too hard to read what was going on in his mind. Eysenck and the petty officer might well be going about their lawful occasions and he was going to look pretty sick if he started to cry wolf. On the other hand if something had happened and he didn't report his suspicions he was going to make himself highly unpopular with his superiors. He turned and headed in the direction of the Station Commander's office, obviously with the intent of asking a few discreet questions. Half-way towards the office it became clear that his questions weren't going to be all that discreet: he had broken into a run.

Johnson spoke into the walkie-talkie.

'Bad trouble.'

'Hold on as long as possible. Leave in emergency. Rendezvous remains.'

In coach PI Van Effen looked at Branson. 'Something wrong?'

'Yes. Johnson and Bradley are in trouble, want to take off. Imagine what's going to happen if they do, if they have to cruise around ten minutes waiting for us? A couple of hijacked helicopters with the President and half the oil in the Middle East in the city? Everybody's going to be as jittery as hell. They'll take no chances. Panic-stricken. They'll stop at nothing. The choppers will be shot out of the sky. They have Phantoms in a state of instant readiness on that base.'

'Well, now.' Van Effen eased the coach to a stop at the back of the garage which held the motorcade. 'Bad, but maybe not as bad as all that. If they have to take off before schedule, you could always instruct them to fly over the motorcade. It would take a pretty crazy air commander to instruct his pilots to fire machine-guns or rockets at a chopper hovering above the Presidential coach. Bingo – no President, no Arabian oil kings and sheikhs, no Chief of Staff, no Mayor Morrison. Chopper might even crash down on to the top of the Presidential coach. Not nice to be a sacked Rear Admiral without a pension. If, that is to say, he survives the court-martial.'

'I hadn't thought of it that way.' Branson sounded half convinced, no more. 'You're assuming our air commander is as sane as you are, that he would react along your line of thinking. How are we to know that he is not certifiable? Extremely unlikely, I admit, but I have no option other than to accept your suggestion. And we've no option other than to go ahead.'

The buzzer rang. Branson made the appropriate switch. 'PI?'

'Yes?'

'P3.' It was Reston from the garage. 'Lead coach has just moved out.'

'Let me know when the Presidential coach moves.'

Branson gestured to Van Effen, who started up the engine and moved slowly round the side of the garage.

The buzzer rang again.

'P5. On schedule. Ten minutes.'

'Fine. Get down to the garage.'

Again the buzzer rang. It was Reston. He said: 'Presidential coach is just moving out.'

'Fine.' Branson made another switch. 'Rear coach?'

'Yeah?'

'Hold it for a couple of minutes. We've a traffic jam here. Some nut has just slewed his articulated truck across the street. Pure accident, I'd say. But no chances. No panic, no need for anyone to leave their seats. We're coming back to the garage for a couple of minutes till they decide on a new route. Okay?'

'Okay.'

Van Effen drove slowly round to the front of the garage, nosed it past the front door until the first third of the coach was visible to the occupants of the rear coach inside, still parked where it had been. Branson and Van Effen descended unhurriedly from the opposite front seats, walked into the garage: Yonnie, unobserved by those inside, exited via the back door and began to clamp the new number plate on top of the old.

The occupants of the rear coach watched the approach of the two white-coated figures curiously, but without suspicion, for endless frustrating delays were part and parcel of their lives. Branson walked around to the front door opposite the driver's side, while Van Effen wandered, aimlessly as it seemed, towards the rear. Had there been any cause for concern on the part of the occupants, it would have been allayed by the sight of two blue-overalled figures busily doing nothing by the main doors. They were not to know they were Reston and his friend.

Branson opened the front left-hand door and climbed up two steps. He said to the driver: 'Sorry about this. It happens. They're picking out a new route, a safe route, for us to go up to Nob Hill.'

The driver looked puzzled, no more. He said: 'Where's Ernie?'

'Ernie?'

'Lead coach driver.'

'Ah! That's his name. Taken sick, I'm afraid.'

'Taken sick?' Suspicion flared. 'Only two minutes ago –'

The driver twisted round in his seat as two minor explosions occurred in the rear of the coach, less explosions than soft plops of sound, to the accompanying sounds of breaking glass and a hiss as of air escaping under pressure. The rear of the coach was already enveloped in a dense, billowing and rapidly mushrooming cloud of grey smoke, so dense that it was impossible to see the now closed rear door and the figure of Van Effen leaning against it and making sure it stayed that way. Every man in the bus – or those who were still visible – had swung round in his seat, reaching for a gun in an automatic but useless reaction for there was nothing to be seen to fire at.

Branson held his breath, threw two of the grenade-shaped gas bombs in rapid succession – one in the front aisle, one at the driver's feet – jumped to the garage floor, slammed the door and held the handle, a somewhat pointless precaution as he knew, for the first inhalation of that gas produced immediate unconsciousness. After ten seconds he left, walked round the front of the bus where he was joined by Van Effen. Reston and his companion had already closed and bolted the main entrance. Now they were stripping off their overalls to reveal the conservative and well cut suits beneath.

Reston said: 'Over? So soon? Just like that?' Branson nodded. 'But if one whiff of that can knock a man out, surely it's going to kill them – if they keep on sitting there, I mean, inhaling the stuff all the time?'

They left via the side door, not too hurriedly, locking it behind them. Branson said: 'Contact with oxygen neutralizes the gas inside fifteen seconds. You could walk inside that bus now and be entirely unaffected. But it will be at least an hour before anyone in that bus comes to.'

Harriman stepped out of a taxi as they came round to the garage front. They boarded the coach – now the new rear coach of the motorcade – and Van Effen headed for Nob Hill. Branson made a switch in the fascia.

'P2?'

'Yes.'

'How are things?'

'Quiet. Too damned quiet. I don't like it.'

'What do you think is happening?'

'I don't know. I can just see someone on the phone asking for permission to launch a couple of guided missiles at us.'

'Permission from whom?'

'The highest military authority in the country.'

'Could take time to contact Washington.'

'Take damn-all time to contact Nob Hill.'

'Oh, my God!' Momentarily, even Branson's habitual massive calm was disturbed. The highest military authority in the country was, indeed, in the next suite to the Presi-

26

dent in the Mark Hopkins hotel. General Cartland, Chief of Staff and adviser extraordinary to the President, was indeed participating in that day's motorcade. 'You know what happens if they do contact him?'

'Yes. They'll cancel the motorcade.' Chief of the Armed Forces though the President might be, he could be over-ruled in matters of security by his Chief of Staff. 'Hold it a minute.' There was a pause then Johnson said: 'One of the guards at the gate is on the telephone. This could mean anything or nothing.'

Branson was conscious of a slight dampness in the region of his neck collar. Although he had given up the habit of prayer even before he'd left his mother's knee, he prayed it was nothing. Perhaps the call to the guard was perfectly innocuous: perhaps the outcome of the call might be innocuous: if it were not, the many months and the quarter million dollars he'd spent in preparation for this *coup* was so much irrecoverable water under the bridge.

'P1?'

'Yes?' Branson was dimly aware that his teeth were clamped tightly together.

'You're not going to believe this but tower has just given us permission to lift off.'

Branson remained silent for a few moments while someone lifted the Golden Gate Bridge off his back. He was not one much given to brow-mopping but this, if ever, seemed a warranted occasion. He refrained. He said: 'Never look a gift horse in the mouth. How do you account for this?'

'The guards must have said that they'd checked our identity papers and that they were in order.'

'Start up, will you? I'd like to find out if I can hear you over the racket of the rotors.'

Twin lines of security men, back to back at a distance of about six feet and facing outwards, formed a protective lane for the short distance between the hotel and the waiting Presidential coach, which seemed rather superfluous as the streets had been barricaded off from the public for a hundred yards all around. The visiting dignitaries from the Persian Gulf seemed to be in no way put out by this nor to be suffering from any claustrophobic sense of imprisonment: in their own homelands, where the fine art of assassination had reached peaks as yet undreamed of in the United States, this was part and parcel of their everyday lives: not only would they have felt naked without this overt show of protection, they would have been offended if not humiliated by the very concept that they were sufficiently unimportant not to merit the massive security precaution.

The President led the way, looking almost wistfully from side to side as if disappointed that there was no one there for him to wave at. He was a tall, rather portly figure, immaculately attired in a tan gaberdine suit, with a patrician face vaguely reminiscent of one of the better-fed Roman emperors and a splendid head of the purest silver hair which was widely supposed to be his especial pride and joy. One had but to look at him to appreciate that he had been doomed from the cradle to end up in the Oval office: that anyone else should aspire to be – or be – the Chief Executive was quite unthinkable. Better brains there might be on Capitol Hill, but that magnificent presence was unique. As far as politicians went he was a man of the utmost probity – the fact that he was a multi-millionaire may have helped him in this – intelligent, humorous and was loved, liked, admired or held in genuine affection to an extent that had been achieved by no other President in the previous half century, a remarkable but far from impossible achievement. As always, he carried a stout cane, a relic from that occasion when he had required it for almost two days after tripping over the leash of his Labrador. That he had no need of the cane was quite indisputable. Perhaps he thought it rounded off his image, or lent him a slightly Rooseveltian aura. Whatever the reason, he was never seen in public or private without it.

He reached the coach, half-turned, smiled and bowed slightly as he ushered the first of his guests aboard.

Precedence and pride of place went inevitably to the King: his vast kingdom held as much oil as the rest of the world put together. He was a tall, imposing figure, a king from the floor-sweeping skirts of his dazzling white robes to the top of the equally dazzling burnous. He had an aquiline dark face, with a splendidly trimmed white beard and the hooded eyes of a brooding eagle. Supposedly the wealthiest man in all history, he could easily have been a tyrant and despot but was neither: against that his autocratic rule was absolute and the only laws he obeyed were those he made himself.

The Prince came next – his small sheikhdom had never rated and never had had a king. While his territorial holdings came to less than five per cent of the King's, his influence was almost as great: his sheikhdom, an arid and barren expanse of some of the world's most inhospitable sands, was literally afloat on a sea of oil. An extrovert and flamboyant personality, who owned a Cadillac for every four miles of his principality's hundred miles of road – it was said with some authority that if one of his cars had the slightest mechanical trouble it was regarded as obsolete and never used again, a fact which must have given some small satisfaction to General Motors – he was an excellent pilot, a remarkably gifted race-car driver and an assiduous patron of many of the most exclusive nightclubs in the world. He went to considerable lengths to cultivate his reputation as an international playboy, an exercise which deceived nobody: behind the façade lay the computerized mind of an outstanding businessman. He was of medium height, well built and wouldn't have been seen dead in the traditional Arab clothes. He was Savile Row's best customer. 'Dapper' was the only word to describe him, from the pointed crocodile shoes to the almost invisible hairline moustache.

They were followed by Sheikh Iman and Sheikh Kharan, the oil ministers respectively of the King and the Prince. They looked remarkably alike and were rumoured to have the same grandfather, which was not at all impossible. Both wore Western clothes, both were plump, smiling almost to the point of beaming and extremely shrewd indeed. The only way to tell them apart was while Iman sported a tiny black goatee beard Kharan was clean-shaven.

The next to board was General Cartland. Although wearing civilian clothes – an inconspicuous blue pin-stripe – he was unmistakably what he was. If he had been wearing only a bath towel he would still have been immediately recognizable as a general. The erect bearing, the precise movements, the clipped speech, the cool blue eyes that never asked a question twice – everything marked him out for the man he was. Even his grey hair was shorn. Although Cartland had more than a peripheral interest in oil – he did, after all, require some form of fuel for his ships, tanks and planes – he was not along because of any special expertise in the oil business. He was along primarily because the President refused to cross the street without him. The President – and he made no bones about it – was heavily dependent on Cartland for his advice, far-ranging width of experience and solid common sense, a fact which had given and still gave rise to considerable if wholly misplaced jealousy in Washington. Cooler judgements in that city regarded him as being virtually irreplaceable as Presidential adviser, and although this duty left him with less and less time to run his army, navy and air force Cartland seemed to cope with both tasks effortlessly. He would have made an excellent politician or statesman but had unfortunately been cursed from birth with an unshakable incorruptibility and moral integrity.

The next man to board was Hansen, the President's energy czar. He was the latest appointee to the post and as yet a largely unknown quantity. His qualifications for the post were impeccable but his experience so far slight. Energy was one thing he appeared to possess in abundance. He was a darting, nervous, volatile individual, painfully thin, whose hands and dark eyes were never still. He was reputed to have a first-class brain. This was his biggest – indeed almost his only – confrontation with great oil barons and his awareness of being on trial was painful.

Muir went next. He was a very rubicund man, almost bald, and the number of his chins varied from two to four according to the angle of his neck. Unlike most fat men he had a permanently doleful expression. He had a positively bucolic appearance about him, an unsuccessful farmer who concentrated less on the production than the consumption of what he grew on his farm. This proposed deal with the Arab nations could raise as many political as physical problems, which was why Under-Secretary of State Muir was along. Although it was almost impossible to believe he was unquestionably the country's leading expert on the Middle East.

The President waved the last man aboard but John Morrison, waving his hand in turn, declined. The President acknowledged the gesture, smiled and preceded him up the steps. Morrison, a burly, genial man of unquestionably Italian ancestry, was not along for his energy expertise. Energy concerned him but not to the extent of causing him sleepless nights. He was along partly as a guide, partly because he conceived it to be his duty to accept the Presidential invitation. Although the President was the official host to his guests, this was Morrison's parish and here he was both host and king. He was the Mayor of San Francisco.

In the rear coach, some fifty yards away, Branson saw the Presidential coach door close. He made a switch.

'P2?'

'Yes?' Johnson.

'We go now.'

'Now it is.'

The motorcade moved off, led by a police car and motor cycle outriders. They were followed by the lead coach, the Presidential coach, the rear coach, a second police car and two more outriders. There was no attempt to make any scenic tour of the town, that had been attended to the previous afternoon soon after Air Force One had landed at the International Airport. This was strictly a business trip. The motorcade went along California, right down Van Ness, left along Lombard, angled right up Richardson Avenue and so into the Presidio. From this point onwards the roads had been closed that morning to all normal traffic. They took the Viaduct Approach, curving right and to the north until at last, dead ahead, loomed the immensity of the Golden Gate Bridge.

THREE

The Golden Gate Bridge is unquestionably one of the engineering wonders of the world. To San Franciscans, inevitably, it is *the* engineering wonder of the world and as bridges go it must be at once the most spectacular and graceful in existence. To see the two great brick-red – or orange or ochre, according to the quality of the light – towers emerging from the dense banks of fog that so frequently billow in from the Pacific is to experience a profound sense of unreality and when the fog disperses completely the feeling changes to one of disbelief and a benumbment of the senses that men had not only the audacity to conceive of this epic poem in mechanical grandeur but also the technical expertise to bring it into being. Even while the evidence of the eyes is irrefutable it still remains difficult for the mind to accept that it actually is there.

That it is there at all is not, in fact, due to man but to one man, a certain Joseph B. Strauss, who, in the pig-headed fashion of considerable Americans, despite seemingly unsurmountable and political difficulties and the assurances of his architectural colleagues that his dream was a technical impossibility, just went ahead and built it anyway. The bridge was opened in May 1937.

Until the construction of the Varrazano-Narrows Bridge in 1964, it was the longest single-span suspension bridge in the world. Even now, it is only about twenty yards shorter. The two massive towers that support the bridge soar seven hundred and fifty feet above the waters of the Golden Gate: the bridge's total length is just under one and three-quarter miles. The cost of construction was $35,000,000: to replace it today something in the region of $200,000,000 would be needed.

The one sombre aspect about the bridge is that for Americans who find the burdens of life intolerable to bear this is unquestionably the most favoured point of departure. There have been at least five hundred known suicides: probably as many again have gone undetected. There have been eight known survivors. Among the rest, the possibility of survival seems extremely remote. If any did indeed survive the shattering impact of the two hundred foot drop to the water, the surging tides and vicious currents of the Golden Gate would swiftly have completed what the jump itself failed to do. Those dangerous tides and currents make their effect felt for some distance on either side of the bridge. Three miles to the east lies what used to be the forbidding prison-fortress of Alcatraz Island. No precise figures of those who attempted escape by swimming are available: but it is believed that only three of those who tried it ever survived.

It is idle to speculate upon the choice of the bridge as a springboard to eternity. Psychiatrists would have it that it is a spectacular and attention-riveting finale to a drab and unspectacular life dragged out in a grey anonymity. But it would seem that there is nothing either eye-catching or spectacular in jumping into the darkness in the middle of the night.

The procession made its stately way under the first of the giant towers. In the upholstered luxury of the Presidential coach, the King, Prince and their two oil ministers gazed around them with a carefully controlled degree of regal and vice-regal appreciation, for although there was a marked absence of Golden Gate Bridges in their dusty homelands and, indeed, no need for them – it would not have done to admit that there were some things better done in the West than in the Middle East. Nor did they enthuse overmuch about the scenery, for although a million square miles of drifting sands might not be without its attractions for a homesick Bedouin, it could hardly be said to compare with the lush and fertile greenery of the farm land and forest land that stretched ahead of them across the Golden Gate. Indeed, the whole of the Bay Area could not have looked better than it did on that splendid June morning, with the sun already climbing high to their right in a cloudless sky and sparkling iridescently off the blue-green waters below. It was the perfect story-book setting for a day which, the President and Hansen, his energy czar, devoutly hoped would have a story-book ending.

The Prince looked around the coach, this time in open admiration, for he was very much a man of his own generation and possessed of a passion for all things mechanical and said in his clipped Oxford accent: 'My word, Mr President, you do know how to travel in style. I wish I had one of those.'

'And so you shall,' the President said indulgently. 'My country would be honoured to present you with one such, as soon as possible after your return to your homeland. Equipped to your own specifications, of course.'

The King said drily: 'The Prince is accustomed to ordering his vehicles by the round dozen. No doubt, Achmed, you would like a couple of those to go with it.' He pointed upwards to where two naval helicopters were hovering overhead. 'You do take good care of us, Mr President.'

The President smiled non-committally. How could one comment upon the obvious? General Cartland said: 'For decorative purposes only, your Highness. Apart from your own security men waiting on the other side and an occasional police car, you will see nothing between here and San Rafael. But the security is there all the same. Between here and San Rafael the motorcade will be under heavily armed surveillance literally every yard of the way. There are crack-pots everywhere, even in the United States.'

'Especially in the United States,' the President said darkly.

In mock seriousness the King said: 'So we are safe?'

The President regained his smiling composure. 'As in the vaults of Fort Knox.'

It was at this point, just after the lead coach had passed the half-way mark across the bridge, that five things happened in almost bewilderingly rapid succession. In the rear coach Branson pressed a button on the console in front of him. Two seconds later a small explosion occurred in the front of the lead coach, almost beneath the driver's feet. Although unhurt, the driver was momentarily shocked, then swore, recovered quickly and jammed his foot on the brake pedal. Nothing happened.

'Sweet Jesus!' It took him all of another second to realize that his hydraulic lines were gone. He jammed his hand-brake into the locked position and changed down into first gear. The coach began to slow.

Branson abruptly lifted his right arm, as abruptly lowered it again to reinforce the left in bracing himself against the fascia. Behind him his men did the same, outstretched arms, slightly bent at the elbows as they had learnt in frequent practices, braced against the backs of the seats in front: nobody sat in the front seats. Van Effen slipped the gear into neutral and kicked down on the brake pedal as if he were trying to thrust it through the floor.

The fact that Van Effen had recently and with malice aforethought seen fit to de-activate his rear brake lights did little to help the plight of the hapless driver of the police car behind. The motorcade was travelling slowly, about twenty-five miles an hour, and the rear police car was trailing the coach by about the same number of feet. The driver had no reason to suspect that anything might be amiss, for the bridge was closed to all traffic except the motorcade: there was no earthly reason to expect anything should interfere with the smooth and even tempo of their progress. He may even have spared a momentary side glance to admire the view. However it was, when he first realized that all was not what it should have been the distance between them had halved. An incredulous double-take cost him another few feet and, skilled police driver though he was, his reactions were no faster than those of the next man and by the time his foot had hit the brake the gap between himself and the now stationary coach had lessened to not more than five feet. The effect of a car's striking a solid and immovable object at twenty miles an hour has a less than humorous effect on the occupants of that car: the four officers in the car were no exception.

At the moment of impact Branson touched a second button on the fascia. The lead coach, slowing only by its hand-brake, was now doing no more than ten miles an hour when another small explosion occurred in the drinks cabinet at the rear, an explosion followed immediately by a pronounced hissing as if caused by compressed air escaping under very high pressure. Within seconds the entire compartment was filled with a dense, grey, obnoxious and noxious gas. The coach, almost immediately out of control as the driver slumped forward over the wheel, slewed slowly to the right and came to a rest less than two feet from the side of the road. Not that it would have mattered particularly if it had struck the safety barriers on the side of the bridge which were of a nature to withstand the assaults of anything less than a Chieftain tank.

The Presidential coach came to no harm. The driver had seen the lead coach's brake warning lights come on, braked, pulled left to avoid the slewing coach ahead and came to a rest beside it. The expressions of the twelve occupants of the coach expressed varying degrees of unhappiness but not, as yet, of alarm.

The police car and two motor-cycle outriders leading the motorcade had been curiously slow to observe the confusion behind them. Only now had they spotted the slewed coach and were beginning to turn.

In the rear coach everything was taking place with the clockwork precision that stemmed from a score of practice runs that had covered all conceivable potentialities. Van Effen jumped down from the left-hand door, Yonnie from the right, just as the two motor-cycle outriders pulled up almost alongside. Van Effen said: 'You better get in there fast. Looks like we got a stiff on our hands.'

The two patrolmen propped their machines and jumped aboard the coach. They could now no longer be seen by the returning lead police car and outriders so it was safe to take swift and efficient action against them, which was done with considerable ease not least because their attention had immediately been caught up by the sight of the bound figure lying sprawled on the floor in the rear aisle.

Seven men emerged swiftly from the doors of the coach. Five of those joined Van Effen and Yonnie and ran towards the other coaches. Two more ran back towards the crashed police car. Two others inside the coach swung wide the rear door and mounted what appeared to be a relatively harmless length of steel tubing on a tripod stand. Branson and Jensen remained where they were: the bound man on the floor, whose identity Jensen had taken over, regarded them all severally with a baleful expression but, beyond that, the options open to him were rather limited.

The two men who had run back towards the crashed police car were called Kowalski and Peters. They didn't look like criminals, unless a couple of prosperous young commuters from the stockbroker belt could be called criminals. Yonnie apart, none of Branson's associates bore any resemblance whatever to the popular concept of those who habitually stepped outside the law. Both men, in fact, had killed a number of times, but then only legally – as far as the term 'legal' could be interpreted – as members of a highly specialized Marine comando unit in Vietnam. Disillusioned with civilian life they'd found their next best panacea with Branson, who

36

had a splendid eye for the recruitment of such men. They had not killed since. Branson approved of violence if and when necessary: killing was not permitted except as a last resort. In his thirteen years of upsetting law officers in the United States, Canada and Mexico, Branson had not yet had to have recourse to the last resort. Whether this was due to moral scruples or not was unclear: what was clear was that Branson regarded it as bad business. The degree of intensity of police efforts to catch robbers as opposed to murderers differed quite appreciably.

The windows of both front doors of the car were wound down – obviously they had been so at the moment of the crash. The four uniformed men seated inside had not been seriously injured but clearly had been badly shaken and had suffered minor damage, the worst of which appeared to be a broken nose sustained by the man in the front seat next to the driver. For the most part they were just dazed, too dazed, in any effect to offer any resistance to the removal of their weapons. Working in smooth unison Kowalski and Peters wound up the front windows. Peters closed his door while Kowalski threw in a gas bomb and closed his in turn.

None of any of this action had been witnessed by the returning police car's crew or the motor-cycle outriders. The policemen left their cars and machines and were cautiously approaching the lead coach when Yonnie and Van Effen with the five others came running up. All had guns of one kind or another in their hands.

'Quickly!' Van Effen shouted. 'Take cover! There are a couple of crazy bastards back in that coach there, one with a bazooka, the other with a Schmeisser. Get behind the bus!'

Given time to consider the matter the policemen might have queried Van Effen's statements but they weren't given the time and the instinct for immediate if irrational self-preservation remains always paramount. Van Effen checked quickly to see if they were hidden from the view of the Presidential coach. They were. Not that he feared anything from that source, he just wanted to be spared the chore of blasting open the lock of the door that would be surely locked against them if their actions were observed.

He nodded to Yonnie and walked away with another man towards the rear of the bus. Whatever might be said, and had unkindly been said, about Yonnie's cerebral limitations, this was the situation he had been born for, a basically elemental one in which action took precedence over thoughts. Long training had even given the vocabulary appropriate to the occasion. He said: 'Let's kinda put our hands up, huh?'

The six men turned round. Their expressions ran through the gamut of astonishment, anger and then resignation. Resignation was all that was left them. They had, with reason enough, not yet thought it time to produce their own weapons, and when the wise man is confronted at point-blank range with a pair of submachine-pistols he does what he is told and just kinda puts his hands up. Yonnie kept them covered while another man relieved them of their pistols. The remaining two men began to run back towards the rear coach as soon as they saw Van Effen and another climb aboard the Presidential coach.

The reaction of those aboard this coach had, so far, amounted to no more than an amalgam of perplexity and annoyance, and even that was slight enough. One or two were making the customary laborious effort to rise when Van Effen mounted the steps.

'Please relax, gentlemen,' he said. 'Just a slight delay.' Such is the authority of even a white coat – in a street accident a crowd will make way for a man in a butcher's apron – that everybody subsided. Van Effen produced an unpleasant-looking weapon, a double-barrelled 12-bore shotgun with most of the barrel and stock removed to make for easier transport, if not accuracy. 'I am afraid this is what you might call a hold-up or hi-jack or kidnap. I don't suppose it matters very much what you call it. Just please remain where you are.'

'Good God in heaven!' The President stared at Van Effen's moonface as if he were a creature from outer space. His eyes, as if drawn magnetically, went to the King and the Prince, then he returned his incredulous, outraged gaze to Van Effen. 'Are you insane? Don't you know whom I am? Don't you know you're pointing a gun at the President of the United States?'

'I know. You can't help being what you are any more than I can help being what I am. As for pointing guns at Presidents, it's a long if not very honourable tradition in our country. Please do not give any trouble.' Van Effen looked directly at General Cartland – he'd had him under indirect observation from the moment he had entered the coach.

'General, it is known that you always carry a gun. Please let me have it. Please do not be clever. Your .22 can be nasty enough if it is accurate enough: this whippet will blast a hole the size of your hand through your chest. You are not the man, I know, to confuse courage with suicide.'

Cartland smiled faintly, nodded, produced a small, black, narrow automatic and handed it across.

Van Effen said, 'Thank you. I'm afraid you will have to remain seated for the moment at least. You have only my word for it, but if you offer no violence you will receive none.'

A profound silence descended. The King, eyes closed and hands folded across his chest, appeared to be communing either with himself or with the All-powerful. Suddenly he opened his eyes, looked at the President and said: 'Just how safe are the vaults in Fort Knox?'

'You'd better believe me, Hendrix,' Branson said. He was talking into a hand-held microphone. 'We have the President, the King and the Prince. If you will wait a minute or two I'll have the President himself confirm that to you. Meantime, please don't attempt anything so stupid or rash as to try to approach us. Let me give you a demonstration. I assume you have some patrol cars near the south entrance and that you are in radio contact with them?'

Hendrix didn't look like anyone's conception of a Chief of Police. He looked like a professorial refugee from the campus of the near-by university. He was tall, slender, dark, slightly stooped and invariably immaculately groomed and conservatively dressed. A great number of people temporarily or permanently deprived of their freedom would have freely if blasphemously attested to the fact that he was very very intelligent indeed. There was no more brilliant or brilliantly effective policeman in the country. At that moment, however, that fine intelligence was in temporary abeyance. He felt stunned and had about him the look of a man who has just seen all his nightmares come true.

He said: 'I am.'

'Very well. Wait.'

Branson turned and made a signal to the two men at the rear of the coach. There was a sudden explosive whoosh from the recoil-less missile weapon mounted at the rear. Three seconds later a cloud of dense grey smoke erupted between the pilons of the south tower. Branson spoke into the microphone. 'Well?'

'Some kind of explosion,' Hendrix said. His voice was remarkably steady. 'Lots of smoke, if it is smoke.'

'A nerve gas. Not permanently damaging, but incapacitating. Takes about ten minutes' time before it oxidizes. If we have to use it and a breeze comes up from the north-west, north or north-east – well, it will be your responsibility, you understand.'

'I understand.'

'Conventional gas-masks are useless against it. Do you understand that also?'

'I understand.'

'We have a similar weapon covering the northern end of the bridge. You will inform police squads and units of the armed forces of the inadvisability of attempting to move out on to the bridge. You understand that too?'

'Yes.'

'You will have been informed of the presence of two naval helicopters hovering over the bridge?'

'Yes.' The rather hunted look had left Hendrix's face and his mind was clearly back into top gear. 'I find it rather puzzling, I must say.'

'It needn't be. They are in our hands. Have an immediate alarm put through to all local army and naval air commanders. Tell them if any attempt is made to dispatch fighters to shoot down those helicopters they will have very unpleasant effects on the President and his friends. Tell them that we shall know immediately whenever any such plane does lift off. The Mount Tamalpais radar stations are in our hands.'

'Good God!' Hendrix was back to square one.

'He won't help. They are manned by competent radar operators. No attempt will be made to retake those stations whether by land or airborne assault. If such an assault is made we are aware that we have no means of preventing it. However, I do not think that the President, King or Prince would look kindly upon any individual who was responsible for depriving them of, say, their right ears. Please do not think that I am not serious. We shall deliver them, by hand, in a sealed plastic bag.'

'No such attempt will be made.' Captain Campbell, a burly,

sandy-haired, red-faced and normally jovial character whom Hendrix regarded as his right-hand man, regarded Hendrix with some surprise, not because of what he had just said but because it was the first time he had ever seen Hendrix with beads of sweat on his brow. In an unconscious gesture Campbell reached up and touched his own forehead, then looked with a feeling of grave disquiet at the dampened back of his hand.

Branson said: 'I hope you mean what you say. I will contact you shortly.'

'It will be in order if I come down to the bridge? It would appear that I have to set up some kind of communications headquarters and that seems the most logical place for it to be.'

'That will be in order. But do not move out on to the bridge. And please prevent any private cars from entering the Presidio. Violence is the very last thing we want but if some arises I do not wish innocent people to suffer.'

'You are very considerate.' Hendrix sounded, perhaps justifiably, more than a little bitter.

Branson smiled and replaced the microphone.

The gas inside the lead coach had vanished but the effect it had had on the occupants had not. All were still profoundly unconscious. Some two or three had fallen into the aisle without, apparently, having sustained any injuries in the process. For the most part, however, they just remained slumped in their seats or had fallen forward against the backs of the seats in front of them.

Yonnie and Bartlett moved among them but not in the capacity of ministering angels. Bartlett, at twenty-six, was the youngest of Branson's men, and looked every inch a fresh-faced college boy which he every inch was not. They were searching every person in the coach, and searching them very thoroughly indeed, those who were being subjected to this indignity being in no position to object. The lady journalists were spared this but their handbags were meticulously examined. It said much for the standards that Branson imposed that none of the several thousand dollars that passed through the hands of Yonnie and Bartlett found its way into either of their pockets. Robbery on a grand scale was big business: robbery on a small scale was petty larceny and not

41

to be tolerated. In any event, they weren't looking for money, they were looking for guns. Branson had reasoned, and correctly as it turned out, that there would be several special agents in the journalists' coach, whose assignment would be not the direct protection of the President and his guests but the surveillance of the journalists themselves. Because of the world-wide interest aroused by the visit of the Arabian oil princes to the United States, at least ten of those journalists aboard were from abroad – four from Europe, the same from the Gulf States and one each from Nigeria and Venezuela, countries which might well be regarded as having a pressing interest in any transactions between the major oil states and the United States.

They found three such guns and pocketed them. The three owners of the guns were handcuffed and left where they were. Yonnie and Bartlett descended and joined the man who was guarding the six still largely uncomprehending policemen who were handcuffed together in single file. Another man was seated behind one of the bazooka-like missile firers that was guarding the north tower. Here, as at the southern end, everything was completely under control, everything had gone precisely as Branson had meticulously and with much labour planned over the preceding months. Branson had every reason to be feeling agreeably pleased with himself.

Branson, as he stepped down from the rear coach, looked neither pleased nor displeased. Things had gone as he had expected them to and that was that. His followers had often remarked, although never in his hearing, on Branson's almost staggering self-confidence: on the other hand they had to admit that he had never, as yet, failed to justify his utter trust in himself. Of Branson's permanent nucleus of eighteen men, nine of them had spent various times in various penitentiaries up and down the country reflecting upon the vagaries of fortune. But that was before they had been recruited by Branson. Since then not one of the eighteen had even got as far as a court-room far less the prison walls: when it was taken into account that those included such semi-permanent guests of the United States Government as Parker this record could be regarded as an achievement of no little note.

Branson walked forward to the Presidential coach. Van

Effen was standing in the doorway. Branson said: 'I'm moving the lead coach ahead a bit. Tell your driver to follow me.'

He moved into the lead coach and with Yonnie's help dragged clear the slumped driver behind the wheel. He slid into the vacant seat, started the engine, engaged gear, straightened out the coach and eased it forward for a distance of about fifty yards, bringing it to a halt with the use of the hand-brake. The Presidential coach followed, pulling up only feet behind them.

Branson descended and walked back in the direction of the south tower. When he came to the precise middle of the bridge – the point at which the enormous suspension cables were at their lowest – he looked behind him and again in front of him. The fifty yards of the most central section of the bridge, the sections where the helicopter rotors would be most unlikely to be fouled by the cables, even if subjected to the unseen and unforeseen vagaries of wind, was clear. Branson walked clear of the area and waved to the two machines chattering overhead. Johnson and Bradley brought their naval helicopters down easily and with the minimum of fuss. For the first time in its long and august history the Golden Gate Bridge was in use as a helipad.

Branson boarded the Presidential coach. Everyone there was instinctively aware that he was the leader of their kidnappers, the man behind their present troubles, and their reception of him did not even begin to border on the cordial. The four oil men and Cartland looked at him impassively: Hansen, understandably, was more jittery and nervous than ever, his hands and eyes for ever on the rapid and almost furtive move: Muir was his usual somnolent self, his eyes half-closed as if he were on the verge of dropping off to sleep: Mayor Morrison, who had won so many medals in the Second World War that he could scarcely have found room for them even on his massive chest, was just plain furious: and so, indisputably, was the President: that expression of kindly tolerance and compassionate wisdom which had endeared him to the hearts of millions had for the moment been tucked away in the deep freeze.

Branson said without preamble but pleasantly enough: 'My name is Branson. Morning, Mr President. Your Highnesses. I would like – '

'*You* would like!' The President was icily angry but he had

43

the expression on his face and the tone in his voice under control: you don't have two hundred million people call you President and behave like an unhinged rock star. 'I suggest we dispense with the charade, with the hypocrisy of empty politeness. Who are you, sir?'

'I told you. Branson. And I see no reason why the normal courtesies of life should not be observed. It would be pleasant if we were to begin our relationship – an enforced introduction on your side, I agree – on a calmer and more reasonable basis. It would make things so much more pleasant if we behaved in a more civilized fashion.'

'Civilized?' The President stared at him in a genuine astonishment that swiftly regressed to his former fury. 'You! A person like you. A thug! A crook! A hoodlum! A common criminal. And you dare suggest we behave in a more civilized fashion.'

'A thug? No. A crook? Yes. A hoodlum? No. A common criminal? No. I'm a most uncommon criminal. However, I'm not sorry you adopt this attitude. Having you express yourself with such hostility to me doesn't mean that it eases my conscience in what I may have to do to you. I don't have any conscience. But it makes life that much simpler for me. Not having to hold your hand – I don't speak literally, you understand – makes it all that much easier for me to achieve my ends.'

'I don't think you'll be called upon to hold any hands, Branson.' Cartland's voice was very dry. 'How are we to regard ourselves? As kidnapees? As ransom for some lost cause you hold dear?'

'The only lost cause I hold dear is standing before you.'

'Then hostages to fortune?'

'That's nearer it. Hostages to a very large fortune, I trust.' He looked again at the President. 'I genuinely do apologize for any affront or inconvenience caused by me to your foreign guests.'

'Inconvenience!' The President's shoulders sagged as he invoked his tragic Muse. 'You don't know what irreparable damage you have done this day, Branson.'

'I wasn't aware that I had done any yet. Or are you referring to their Highnesses here? I don't see what damage I can have caused there. Or are you referring to your little trip to San Rafael today – I'm afraid we'll have to postpone that for a bit – to inspect the site of what will be the biggest oil refinery in the world?' He smiled and nodded towards the oil princes. 'They really have you and Hansen over a barrel there, don't they, Mr President – an oil barrel? First they rob you blind over oil sales, accumulate so much loot that they can't find homes for all of it, conceive the bright idea of investing it in the land of the robbed, come up with the concept of building this refinery and petro-chemical complex on the West Coast and running it themselves – with your technical help, of course – on their own oil which would cost them nothing. The foreseeable profits are staggering, a large portion of which would be passed on to you in the form of vastly reduced oil prices. Bonanzas all round. I'm afraid international finance is beyond my scope – I prefer to make my money in a more direct fashion. If you think your deal is going to slip through because of the offence now being given to those Arabian gentlemen you must be an awful lot more naïve than a President of the United States has any right to be. Those are not gentlemen to be swayed by personal considerations. They have tungsten steel where their hearts should be and IBM computers for brains.' He paused. 'I'm not being very polite to your guests, am I?'

Neither the King nor Prince Achmed were quite so impassive now: their eyes, as they looked at Branson, were expressive of a distinct yearning.

Cartland said: 'You seem to be in no great hurry to get on with whatever you intend to get on with.'

'How right you are. The need for speed has now gone. Time is no longer of the essence except that the longer I spend here the more profitable it is going to be for me. That I shall explain later. In the meantime, the longer you remain here the more time it will give both you and your peoples both here and in the Gulf States to appreciate just what a pretty pickle you find yourselves in. And, believe me, you are in a pickle. Think about it.'

Branson walked to the rear of the coach and spoke to the blond young soldier who was manning the massive communication complex. 'What's your name?'

The soldier, who had heard all that had gone on and obviously didn't like any of it, hesitated, then said grudgingly: 'Boyann.'

Branson handed him a piece of paper. 'Get this number,

please. It's just local.'

'Get it yourself.'

'I did say "please".'

'Go to hell.'

Branson shrugged and turned. 'Van Effen?'

'Yes?'

'Bring Chrysler here.' He turned to Boyann. 'Chrysler has forgotten a great deal more about telecommunications than you've learnt so far. You think I hadn't anticipated meeting up with young heroes?' He spoke again to Van Effen. 'And when you bring him take Boyann here out and have him thrown over the side of the bridge into the Golden Gate.'

'Right away.'

'Stop!' The President was shocked and showed it. 'You would never dare.'

'Give me sufficient provocation and I'll have you thrown over the side too. I know it seems hard but you've got to find out some way, some time, that I mean what I say.'

Muir stirred and spoke for the first time. He sounded tired. 'I think I detect a note of sincerity in this fellow's voice. He may, mark you, be a convincing bluffer. I, for one, wouldn't care to be the person responsible for taking the chance.'

The President bent an inimical eye on the Under-Secretary but Muir seemed to have gone to sleep. Cartland said in a quiet voice: 'Boyann, do what you are told.'

'Yes, sir.' Boyann seemed more than happy to have had the decision taken out of his hands. He took the paper from Branson who said: 'You can put it through to the phone by that chair opposite the President's?' Boyann nodded. 'And patch it in to the President's?' Boyann nodded again. Branson left and took his seat in the vacant armchair.

Boyann got through immediately: clearly, the call had been awaited.

'Hendrix,' the voice said.

'Branson here.'

'Yes. Branson. Peter Branson. God, I might have guessed!' There was a silence then Hendrix said quietly: 'I've always wanted to meet you, Branson.'

'And so you shall, my dear fellow, and much sooner than you think. I'd like to speak to you later. Meantime, I wouldn't be surprised if the President didn't want to have a word with you.' Branson stood up, not without difficulty, and offered both the telephone and seat to Morrison who in turn struggled to his feet and accepted the offer with alacrity.

The President ran true to the form of any President who might have been so unfortunate as to find himself in his position. He ran through the whole gamut of incredulity, outrage, disbelief and horror that not only the Chief Executive but, even more important, foreign potentates should find themselves in a situation so preposterous as to be, in his opinion, without parallel in history. He laid the blame, predictably, entirely at Hendrix's door – security cover, as the President knew all too well, was arranged by Washington and the local police forces did precisely what they were told to do, but the President's memory, logic and sense of justice had gone into a state of shock – and ended up by demanding that Hendrix's duty was to clear up the whole damnable mess and that he should do something about it immediately.

Hendrix, who had a great deal longer time to consider the situation, remained admirably calm. He said: 'What do you suggest I do about it, sir?'

The incoherent splutterings that followed were indication enough that constructive suggestions were at that moment some light years away from the President's mind. Morrison took advantage of the momentary hiatus.

'Bernard? John here.' Morrison smiled without meaning to. 'The voters aren't going to like this, Bernard.'

'All one hundred and fifty million of them?'

Again the same smile. 'If we must think nationally, yes.'

'I'm afraid this is going to turn into a national problem, John. In fact, you know damn well it already is. And on the political side it's too big for either of us.'

'You cheer me greatly, Bernard.'

'I wish someone would cheer me. Do you think our friend would let me speak to the General?'

'I'll ask.' He asked and Branson nodded amiably enough. The other occupants of the coach eyed one another with a mounting degree of suspicion and apprehension, both directed against Branson. The man was too utterly sure of himself. And, as matters stood at that moment, there seemed to be little reason why he shouldn't be. He just didn't hold all the aces in the pack – he held a pack full of aces.

Hendrix said: 'General Cartland? Hendrix. The way I see it, sir, this is going to be as much a military operation as a police one. Much more so, if I'm any judge. I should call in the senior military officers on the coast?'

'Higher than that.'

'The Pentagon?'

'At once.'

'Local action?'

'Damn all. Wait until the situation stabilizes itself – and we find out what this madman wants.' Branson smiled politely but as usual the smile never touched his eyes. 'According to what he says himself – if you can believe a word he says – time is not of the essence. I think he wants to talk to you.'

Branson took the phone from Cartland and eased himself comfortably into the armchair. 'One or two questions and requests, Hendrix. I think I am in the position to expect answers and compliance with whatever I want. Wouldn't you agree?'

'I'm listening.'

'Has the news been broken yet?'

'What the hell do you mean broken? Half of San Francisco can see you stuck out on that damned bridge.'

'That's no way to speak of my favourite bridge. Nationwide is what I mean.'

'It'll get around fast enough.'

'See that it gets around now. The communication media, as those people term themselves nowadays, are going to be interested. I am prepared to allow, no, that's wrong, I insist that you put a helicopter, no, two helicopters at the disposal of some of the hundreds of news cameramen who will wish to record this historic event. The Bay Area is thick with suitable machines, both military and civilian.'

There was a silence then Hendrix said: 'What the devil do you want those for?'

'Obviously, surely. Publicity. The maximum exposure. I want every person in America and indeed every person in the world who is within reach of a television set to see just what a predicament the President and his Arabian friends are in. And they are in a predicament, wouldn't you say?'

Another silence. 'This publicity, of course, you will use as a lever to get public opinion on your side, to help you obtain what you want, whatever that might be?'

'What else?'

Hendrix said heavily: 'You wouldn't like me to send a coach-load of reporters on to the bridge, would you?'

Branson smiled into the telephone. 'A coach-load of reporters I wouldn't mind but I don't much fancy a coach-load of FBI men armed to the teeth and disguised as reporters. No, I think we'll pass that one up. Besides, reporters we have, our own coach-load.'

'What's to prevent me from loading those helicopters up with troops, maybe paratroopers?'

Branson sighed. 'Only your own common sense. We've got hostages, or had you forgotten? A bullet can reach the President far more quickly than a paratrooper ever could.' Branson glanced at the President, whose expression indicated that he clearly didn't care to be used as a bargaining counter.

'You wouldn't dare. You'd defeat your own ends. You'd have nothing left to blackmail us with.'

'I'd still have a king and a prince. Try me and see. You're whistling in the dark and you know it. Or do you want to go down in history as the man responsible for the deaths of a president, a king and a prince?' Hendrix made no reply. It was clearly not a role he envisaged for himself. 'However, it hasn't escaped me that there might be some death-or-glory hotheads who would stop at nothing in taking blind gambles, so I've got my second request to make now. This area is crammed with military stations—the Presidio itself, Fort Baker, Treasure Island, Forts Funston, Miley and Mason, Fort Barry, Cronkite—you name them, they're around and all within easy reach of here by road. I'd be very surprised if between them they can't rustle up the two mobile self-propelled rapid-fire anti-aircraft guns which I want on the bridge within the hour. Plenty of ammunition, of course—and the army will test them out first. You know how some of that hardware gets afflicted with all kinds of jinxes.'

'You're quite mad.'

'A divine sort of madness. Instructions now.'

'I refuse.'

'You refuse? General Cartland?'

Cartland heaved himself upright and walked heavily down the coach. He took the phone and said quietly: 'Do what the madman asks. Don't you recognize megalomania when you hear it?'

'That was very unkind, General.' Branson smiled and retrieved the phone. 'You have the message, Hendrix?'

'I have the message.' Hendrix sounded as if he were being strangled.

'My third request. Call up a couple of squads of army engineers. I want two sets of steel barriers built on the bridge, one under either tower. They are to be strong enough to stop a tank and high enough – barbed at the top, of course – to prevent anyone from climbing over. The north barrier is to be unbroken, the south with a hinged central section, wide enough to permit the passage of a jeep, and capable of being opened from the inside – our side – only. The barriers will be anchored to the sides of the bridge by bolting or welding and secured to the roadway by pneumatically driven spikes. But the army will know a great deal more about such things than I do. I shall supervise the operations personally.'

Hendrix seemed to be having some difficulty with his breathing. Finally he said: 'Why?'

'It's those nasty fogs that come rolling in from the Pacific all the time. More often than not they cover the bridge – in fact I can see one coming in right now.' Branson sounded almost apologetic. 'It would be too easy to rush us under fog cover.'

'And why the hinged section in the south barrier?'

'I thought I told you. To permit the passage of a jeep. For such things as negotiating committees, a doctor if need be and the transport of the best food and drink in town.'

'Jesus! You have your nerve, Branson.'

'Nerve?' Branson was hurt. 'This humanitarian consideration of the well-being of my fellow man? You call that nerve? Kings and presidents are not accustomed to going hungry. Among other things you don't want to go down in history as, Hendrix, includes, I'm sure, being the man responsible for starving kings and presidents to death. Think of the verdict of history.'

Hendrix was silent. He may or may not have been thinking about the verdict of history.

Branson went on: 'And we must not forget the delicate sensibilities of royalty. Before the barriers are in place we'd like to have a couple of mobile latrine vans in position.

Equipped, of course, to the very highest standards – and that does not include being loaded to the gunwales with FBI agents. You have all that, Hendrix?'

'It's been recorded.'

'Then set the wheels in motion. Or must I call in General Cartland again?'

'It will be done.'

'Now?'

'Now.'

Branson cradled the phone on his knee and looked at it wonderingly. 'And he didn't even tell me I couldn't get off with it.' He lifted the phone again. 'Last request, Hendrix, but the most important one. The President is temporarily incapacitated. How can one talk to the leader of a leaderless nation?'

'The Vice-President is already in Chicago. He's on his way to O'Hare airfield now.'

'Splendid. Splendid. Co-operation without even asking for it. But I'm afraid I'll also have to ask for the co-operation of one or two other senior ministers of the government. I know it's asking for a lot but I feel –'

'Spare me your schoolboy humour, Branson.' There was an edge to Hendrix's voice now but it was a tired edge. 'I suppose you have some people in mind?'

'Just a couple, that's all.' Branson had a gift for sounding eminently reasonable when making the most unreasonable demands.

'And if you get them and the Vice-President together here I suppose you'll make all three of them hostages too.'

'No. You've only got my word for it, of course, but no. You're losing whatever grip you had, Hendrix. You don't kidnap negotiators. If you did you'd have to negotiate with someone else and so on down the line until we came to someone like you.' Branson awaited for comment but Hendrix appeared to be beyond comment. 'I want the Secretary of State.'

'He's on his way.'

'A mind-reader, no less! From where?'

'Los Angeles.'

'How very convenient. How come he was there?'

'An IMF meeting.'

'IMF? Then that means –'

Branson replaced the receiver. 'Well, well, well. Little Peter Branson *vis-à-vis*, the Secretary of the Treasury. What a *tête-à-tête* this should be. I thought the day would never come.'

'Yes,' Hendrix said wearily. 'The Secretary of the Treasury was there. He's flying up with him.'

FOUR

Paul Revson surfaced slowly, almost reluctantly, to a state of consciousness. His eyelids felt leaden, his head fuzzy and he thought that he had gone slightly deaf. Otherwise he felt no after-effects from having been gassed – he knew he must have been gassed but everything had happened so quickly after the explosion under the driver's feet that he had no clear recollection of what had happened. As his eyesight cleared he looked around him. By his side a girl with a mop of blonde hair was huddled forward against the back of the seat before her, her neck twisted at an uncomfortable angle. Some people, he saw, were lying in the aisle, apparently asleep. A score of others were still in their seats, all resting at the most uncomfortable angles: some of them, like himself, were just beginning to stir. He peered through the coach window, blinked unbelievingly, then stared again. As a born and bred San Franciscan it took him nothing flat to realize that their coach was halted almost squarely in the middle of the Golden Gate Bridge. It was a circumstance, he felt, which called for some explanation.

He turned his immediate attention to the girl at his side. She was worth anyone's attention. She was possessed of a slight figure, hardly strong enough, one would have thought, to lug around the heavy ciné camera which, shoulder-slung, accompanied her everywhere. The blonde hair was so bleached – naturally, Revson thought – that it almost qualified for the description of platinum, and she was quite beautiful with a very pale skin that the sun never appeared to touch. She was, she had given him to understand, a fashion photographer for one of the major TV companies and as the official party of this Presidential trip was exclusively male it was rather difficult to understand just why she was there. It didn't make sense, but then, again, neither did most Presidential trips. Her name was equally preposterous. April Wednesday, she called herself, and her press card bore this out. Revson could only assume that she had been born of singularly unimaginative parents who, as christening day approached, had seized upon the birth date as the easy way out.

He put his hands on her shoulders and gently pulled her upright. The blonde head lolled against his shoulder. He had no idea how to revive people who had suffered from some form of gas poisoning. Should he shake her, slap her cheek gently or just let her sleep it off? He was spared the resolution of this problem when she stirred, shivered for some reason or other – although she was clad in only a thin and markedly abbreviated green silk dress, the temperature in the bus must have been in the eighties – then opened her eyes and gazed unblinkingly at Revson's.

In a face not noticeably lacking other commendable features, those eyes were by far the most remarkable feature. They were huge, clear, of a startling deep sea-green and were possessed of an odd quality of purity and innocence. Revson wondered idly just how devious she was: any young woman who toted a camera for a TV company must have lost her innocence quite some time ago, assuming she was possessed of any in the first place.

She said, not taking her eyes from his: 'What happened?'

'At a guess, some joker must have let off a gas bomb. The instant effect variety. How do you feel?'

'Punch-drunk. Hung-over. You know what I mean?' He nodded. 'Why would anyone want to do a thing like that?'

'Why a lot of things.' He looked at his watch. 'Why, after an hour and ten minutes, are we still stranded in the middle of the Golden Gate Bridge?'

'What!'

'Look around you.'

She looked around her, slowly acknowledging the reality of the surroundings. Suddenly she stiffened and caught hold of the hand that was still around her shoulders.

'Those two men across the aisle.' Her voice had dropped to a whisper. 'They're wearing handcuffs.'

Revson bent forward and looked. The two large and still sleeping men were undoubtedly wearing handcuffs.

'Why?' Again the whisper.

'How should I know why? I've just come to myself.'

'Well, then, why aren't we wearing them?'

'How should – we are among the blessed.' He looked over his shoulder and saw the Presidential coach parked just behind them. 'Excuse me. As a good journalist I think the odd probing question is in order.'

'I'm coming with you.'

'Sure.' She stepped into the aisle and he followed. Instead of moving directly after her he lifted the coat lapel of the nearest of the sleeping men. An empty shoulder holster was much in evidence. He followed the girl. At the front door he noticed that the driver, still sound asleep, was propped against the right-hand front door, quite some distance from his seat: obviously, he hadn't made it there under his own steam.

He joined the girl on the bridge. A very large and extremely ugly policeman – Yonnie had the kind of face that would have given any force a bad name – was pointing a machine-pistol at them. That a policeman should be pointing a gun at them was peculiar enough. That a policeman should be armed with a machine-gun was even more peculiar. Most peculiar of all, however, was the spectacle of six scowling and clearly unhappy policemen standing in a line, each attached to the other by a pair of handcuffs.

April Wednesday stared at them in astonishment, then looked at Revson. He said: 'I agree. This would seem to call for some kind of explanation.'

'You'll have it.' Branson, walking easily, talking easily, had just appeared round the front of the Presidential bus. 'What's your name?'

'Revson.'

'Sorry about this. You too, young lady.'

'Helicopters!' she said.

'Yes, they are, aren't they? Explanations will be forthcoming but not severally. When your friends have all come to then we'll have a little talk.' Branson walked away towards the rear coach. His step was almost jaunty and he did not seem too displeased with life. He looked at the bank of cloud moving in slowly, very slowly, from the west. If it troubled him he did not show it. He reached the crashed police car and spoke to the man standing guard. 'Have our four friends recovered, Chrysler?'

'Yes, sir. I wouldn't say they're in very high spirits, though.' Chrysler was a lean, dark, intelligent-looking young man and it only required the addition of a brief case to see him as an up-and-coming attorney. He was indeed, as Branson had told Boyann, a tele-communications expert. He was also very good with combination locks and frightening people with guns.

'I dare say. Let them stay in the car. Easier than getting them out and handcuffing them. When the four FBI men – at least from the fact that they were armed I assume they were FBI men – in the lead coach have come to, take a couple of the boys and escort them, along with the six cops up front, the four here and the two inside our coach half-way towards the south tower. Sixteen in all and any one a potential menace if we keep them here. Half-way there take off whatever handcuffs there are – very useful things, handcuffs, you never know when we may need them again – then let them walk off the bridge under their own steam. Okay?'

'It's done.' He pointed to the west, to the slowly advancing bank of cloud. 'Do you like that, Mr Branson?'

'Could have done without it. We'll cope when it comes. Looks as if it may well pass under the bridge anyway.'

'Mr Branson.' It was Jensen, beckoning urgently from the front door of the rear coach. 'Mount Tamalpais. Urgent.'

Branson ran into the coach, seated himself in front of the console and lifted the microphone. 'Branson.'

'Giscard. We've picked up a blip. Coming from the south – well, a bit east of south. Light plane, looks like. Maybe eight miles out.'

'Thank you.' Branson made another switch. South and a little east. That could only be San Francisco International Airport. 'Chief of Police Hendrix. At once.'

Hendrix was on the phone in seconds. 'What now?'

'I told you to keep a clear air-space. Our radar's picked up a blip, airport direction – '

Hendrix interrupted. His voice was sour. 'You wanted to see Messrs Milton and Quarry, didn't you?' Milton was the Secretary for State, Quarry the Secretary of the Treasury. 'They came in from Los Angeles fifteen minutes ago and are flying up direct by helicopter.'

'Where are they landing?'

'In the Military Reservation in the Presidio. Two, three minutes by car.'

'Thanks.' Branson made the switch to Mount Tamalpais. Giscard acknowledged. Branson said: 'No sweat. Friends. But watch that scanner – the next one may not be a friend.'

'Will do, Mr Branson.'

Branson rose, made to leave the coach then stopped and looked at the bound man in the rear of the aisle. He said to

Jensen, who had taken the place of the bound man: 'You can get back to calling yourself Harriman again. Untie Jensen here.'

'Sending him off the bridge?'

For once Branson hesitated and didn't like the feeling at all. Hesitation was not in his nature. Whether he arrived at decisions intellectually or instinctively he almost invariably did so immediately: the few mistakes he'd made in his life had invariably been associated with hesitation. He made up his mind.

'We'll keep him. He might come in useful, I don't know how yet, but he just might. And he *is* deputy director of the FBI. He's no minnow to have in our net. Tell him the score but keep him here until I give the word.'

He left and walked towards the lead coach. At least a score of people were lined up outside the coach under the watchful eyes and guns of Yonnie and his two colleagues. They had, understandably, a general air of bafflement about them. Branson saw that included among them were four handcuffed men. He looked inside the coach, saw that it was empty, and turned to Peters.

'Take those four gentlemen with the handcuffs and the six policemen down to Chrysler. He'll know what to do with them.'

He turned to look at the oncoming fog. Close up, it was coming in a deal faster than it had seemed at a distance. But it was a low bank: with luck it would pass under the bridge. Even if it didn't, he imagined that they could cope by using suitable threats against the President and his friends, but he wouldn't feel really happy about those intermittent fogs until the steel barriers were in position at either end of the bridge.

He turned and looked at the correspondents. There were four women among them but only one of them, the green-eyed blonde with Revson, could truthfully have claimed to have been a post-war baby – World War Two, that was.

'You can all relax,' Branson said. 'No harm is going to come to any of you. In fact, when I have finished you'll be given a free choice – to walk off the bridge in safety or stay aboard the bridge, equally in safety.' He smiled his generous empty smile. 'I somehow fancy that most of you will elect to stay. When I have finished you will realize, I hope, that a story like this does not fall into your laps every week.'

When he had finished, not one of those frantically scribbling and furiously camera-clicking journalists and photographers was under any doubt whatsoever: a story like this fell into their laps once in a lifetime, if they had the luck to have a very long life, that was. Physical violence would have been required to remove any of them from the Golden Gate Bridge. They were slap bang in the middle of an unprecedented episode in criminal history and one that bade fair to become part of the more general history of their times.

The fog had reached the bridge now, but not enveloped it. Thin wisps of it drifted over the top but the main body of the fog rolled by twenty feet below the bridge: the effect was to produce an odd feeling of weightlessness, of suspension in space, as if the bridge was afloat on the insubstantial bedrock of water vapour.

Branson said: 'You have elected to remain so you must accept some guide rules. In the rear coach there are three telephone lines to town. Those are for my own personal and emergency use but you will be allowed to use them once — to contact your photographic services, newspapers, wire services or whatever to arrange for a representative to be stationed at the southern end of the bridge to pick up your dispatches and photographs. This can be done three times a day at times yet to be arranged. Markers will be arranged in an oblong around the Presidential coach and no one will cross those without permission. No one will interview any person inside the Presidential coach without my permission or the consent of the party concerned: it would be more satisfactory all round and fairer to all concerned if, say, the President were to hold a press conference out here, but that I cannot and will not force anyone to do. The helicopters will be similarly cordoned off and that will also be forbidden territory. Twenty yards south of my coach and twenty yards north of yours white lines will be painted across the bridge. Those will be your demarcation limits. Five yards beyond those lines will be a guard with a machine-pistol and his orders will be not to warn but to shoot anyone who steps over those lines. Finally, you will be confined to your coach during the hours of darkness: this rule will only be relaxed if some particularly newsworthy happening occurs. I will be the judge of what is newsworthy. Anyone unwilling to abide by those ground rules may leave now.'

Nobody left.

'Any questions?' Branson watched the fog roll eastwards, obscuring Alcatraz Island, as the newsmen conferred among themselves. Two men took a step forward. Both were middle-aged, dressed in well-cut, conservative suits, one almost completely bald, the other with grizzled hair and beard, both inordinately bushy. The bald man said: 'We have.'

'Your names?'

'I'm Grafton – AP. This is Dougan – Reuters.'

Branson regarded them with an interest that was pointless to conceal. Those two could reach more newspapers worldwide than all the rest put together. 'And the question?'

'We would be right in saying, Mr Branson, that you didn't exactly got up this morning and say "This would be a fine day for kidnapping the President of the United States"?'

'You would.'

Dougan said: 'This operation bears all the hallmarks of long and meticulous planning. Without condoning your actions one has to admit that you appear to have left nothing to chance and have foreseen every eventuality. How long did the planning take?'

'Three months.'

'That's not possible. The details of this itinerary were released only four days ago.'

'The details were known in Washington three months ago.'

Grafton said: 'On the evidence before us we have to believe you. Why do you think this was kept under wraps so long?'

'In order to obviate the possibility of people like me doing exactly what I have done.'

'How did you get the advance information?'

'I bought it.'

'How? Where?'

'In Washington, as in many other places, thirty thousand dollars buys a lot of information.'

Dougan said: 'Would you care to name names?'

'That's a stupid question. Any others?'

A dark-suited lady of indeterminate years said: 'Yes. Here we have all the signs of a highly experienced professionalism. We can assume that this is not your first foray outside the law?'

Branson smiled. 'You may assume what you like. What's past is prologue.'

She persisted. 'Do you have a criminal record, Mr Branson?'

'I have never been in court in my life. Anything else?'

'Of course.' It was Dougan. 'The thing that we all want to know. Why?'

'That you will find out in the course of a press conference I shall be holding within two hours. At the conference will be a TV camera and crew representing the three main companies. Also present will be the Secretary of State and the Secretary of the Treasury. Vice-President Richards we expect later but not in time for the conference.'

Experienced newsmen and newswomen though they were they appeared to be at a temporary loss for words. Finally Dougan said carefully: 'Would it be true to say of you that you subscribe to the belief that if a thing is worth doing it's worth doing well?'

'A pragmatic philosophy, but it works. You may now use the telephones in my coach. Three at a time.'

Branson turned away and took a step towards the Presidential coach when Yonnie's voice stopped him.

'Jesus!' Yonnie, mouth inelegantly agape, was staring out to the west. 'You see what I see, Mr Branson?'

Branson saw what he saw. Not much more than half a mile away the fog-bank came to an abrupt end as if it had been sliced off by a cleaver. Less than a mile beyond that again could be seen the superstructure of a very large vessel indeed. Although the hull of the vessel was still hidden by the fogbank there was, from what could be seen of it, very little doubt as to its identity. Branson stood still for a second or two, ran for the Presidential coach, entered, hurried down the aisle oblivious to curious stares of the seated men and said quickly to Boyann: 'Hendrix. Hurry!' He indicated a phone in a recess beside the console. 'That one.'

Hendrix was on the line immediately. When Branson spoke his voice was cold, almost savage, a marked departure from the norm: even Branson had defences that could be breached.

'Hendrix. Want I should send the President's ears now?'

'What the hell do you mean?'

'What do *you* mean? Or is that little paddleboat just out there by happenstance? Call it off.'

'God's sake, call what off?'

Branson spoke his words clearly and spaced them distinctly.

'There is a very large battleship approaching the Golden Gate Bridge. I don't want it to approach. I don't know what you have in mind but I don't think I would like it. Call it off!'

'I just don't know what you're talking about. Hold on.' While the line was silent Branson beckoned to Van Effen, who approached down the aisle.

Branson said quickly: 'There's a battleship approaching the bridge. Trouble? I don't know. What I do know is I want everybody under cover at once, the press in their own coach, our men in ours. Doors to be closed. Then come back at once.'

Van Effen nodded to where a red-haired young man was standing by the driver's seat, his hand resting on a pistol that was stuck in his belt. 'Think Bradford can manage?'

Branson pulled out his own pistol and laid it in the telephone recess. 'I'm here too. Hurry.' He was vaguely disappointed in Van Effen. Bradford could have carried out his warder duties just as effectively by going outside and standing near the door but for the creation of the properly threatening climate of menace and intimidation it was better that he remain in the full view of the captives. Then Hendrix was on the phone again.

'That is the battleship USS *New Jersey*. San Francisco is her home base for several months of the year. This is one of her regular fuel and food reprovisioning returns to base. She's coming at this particular time because she can only get under the bridge at low tide.'

That much, Branson knew, was true. The tide, he had observed, was out and it seemed highly unlikely that the authorities could whistle up a battleship at such short notice – less than two hours. And it was difficult to see what use could be made of it – certainly they were unlikely to blow up the bridge with the President on it. But Branson had a profound distrust of his fellow man, which was one of the reasons he had survived so long. He said: 'Stop it. It's not to come under the bridge. Want I should throw one of your oil boys on to its bridge as it passes beneath?'

'For God's sake, are you a nut, a complete madman?' Branson smiled to himself, the sharp edge of anxiety in Hendrix's voice was unmistakable. 'We're trying to raise him.'

Correspondents and guards alike were crowding the western

side of the bridge fascinated by the approach of the giant battleship. Although reason said that there was no danger in the battleship's passing under the bridge there was a growing degree of tension among the spectators. The superstructure towered so high that it seemed certain that some sections of it must inevitably strike the bridge and this feeling existed in spite of the elementary reasoning which would have reassured them that the ship must have made the same passage many times in the past and the Navy was not in the habit of putting at risk some hundred million dollar battleship in a let's-try-it-and-see effort.

One person showed no apparent interest in the approach of the *New Jersey*. Revson, alone in the front coach, was intent on securing a considerable length of green cord, so slender as to be hardly more than the thickness of a stout thread, to a black cylinder about eight inches in length and one in diameter. He thrust both cylinder and cord into the capacious pocket of his bush jacket, left the bus, took a bearing on the approaching superstructure of the battleship and wandered casually round to the right-hand side of the coach. As he did so he could see Van Effen hurrying across to the far side of the bridge where the spectators were grouped. What Van Effen's purpose was he couldn't be sure but there was an urgency behind his half-trot that told Revson that the time at his own disposal might be very short.

He forced himself not to hurry but sauntered towards the east side of the bridge. No one took any notice of him because there was no one there to do so. He leant casually against the side and as casually withdrew cylinder and cord from his pocket. He glanced, seemingly aimlessly, around him, but if he were arousing cause for suspicion no one was giving any indication of this. Swiftly, without moving either hands or elbows, he let some hundred feet slide through his fingers then secured the cord to a strut. He trusted his estimate of length was reasonably accurate then dismissed the thought: what was done was done. He returned leisurely to the coach, took his seat and transferred what was left of the green cord to the bottom of April Wednesday's carry-all. If his dangling cord were discovered and a search of their personal belongings carried out he would rather that the cord be discovered elsewhere than in his possession. Even if it were found in her bag he doubted whether she would come to any harm. She'd been on the other side of the bridge since the *New Jersey* had first appeared behind the bank of cloud and there would be sufficient witnesses to attest to that: April Wednesday was the sort of person whose absence would not go lightly unremarked. Even if she were to find herself in trouble that he could bear with fortitude: he didn't care who came under suspicion as long as it was not himself.

'You have to believe me, Branson.' Hendrix's voice could hardly have been said to carry a note of pleading, an alien exercise to a man of his nature, but there was no questioning the earnestness, the total sincerity in the tone. 'The *New Jersey*'s captain has heard no news of what happened and he thinks it all an elaborate joke at his expense. You can't blame him. He sees the damned bridge standing safe and sound as it's stood for forty years. Why should anything be wrong?'

'Keep trying.'

Van Effen entered and closed the door of the Presidential coach securely behind him. He approached Branson.

'All safely corralled. Why?'

'I wish I knew. Almost certainly Hendrix is right and this is just sheer coincidence. But on the one chance in a hundred that it isn't? What would they use? Not shells, no kind of high explosive. Gas shells.'

'No such things.'

'Wrong. There are. They wouldn't mind temporarily knocking out the President and a few oil sheikhs if they could saturate the centre of the bridge with some knock-out gas and lay us all low. Then the troops and police, like enough with gas-masks, could come and take us at their leisure. But the insulation is tight in those air-conditioned coaches.'

'It's pretty far-fetched.'

'And what *we* are doing is not? Wait.' Hendrix was on the phone again.

'We've tried, Branson, and at last he agrees with us. But he refuses to do anything. Says he has too much way on and to try to take turning or reversing action at this stage would endanger both the battleship and the bridge. And he says his money would be on the *New Jersey* if it hit a tower. A forty-five-thousand-ton battering ram takes a lot of stopping.'

'You'd better pray, Hendrix.' Branson hung up and moved towards the centre of the coach, Van Effen behind him, and peered through the right-hand windows, waiting for the battle-ship's superstructure to reappear from under the bridge.

The President's voice was nothing if not testy. 'Just what is happening, Branson?'

'You know. The USS *New Jersey* is passing beneath us.'

'So? Doubtless going about its lawful occasions.'

'You'd better hope so. You'd better hope the captain doesn't start throwing things at us.'

'At us?' The President paused and pondered the pos-sibility of an awful lese-majesty. 'At *me*?'

'We all know you're the Commander-in-Chief of the Armed Forces. At the moment, however, you're a bit isolated from the lower echelons. What happens if the captain considers it his duty to act upon his own initiative? Anyway, we'll soon find out. Here he comes now.'

The superstructure of the *New Jersey* had moved into view. All nine of the seated captives struggled to their feet and crowded close to the right-hand windows. One of them crowded very closely indeed on Branson who suddenly became aware of something, obviously metallic, jabbing painfully into his left kidney.

'Initiative, you said, Mr Branson.' It was Sheikh Iman, the one with the beard, and he was still beaming. 'Your own gun. Tell your men to drop theirs.'

'Good man!' There was triumph in the President's voice and an element of vindictiveness that the voters wouldn't have liked at all.

Branson said patiently: 'Put that gun away. Don't you know when you're dealing with professionals?'

He turned around slowly and Iman proved Branson's implied point that he was not a professional by letting Branson hold his gaze for all of a second. A gun boomed, Iman shrieked in pain, dropped his gun and clutched a shattered shoulder. Sheikh Kharan stooped swiftly to retrieve the gun from the floor and cried out in agony as Branson's heel crushed his hand against the metal: a peculiar crackling splintering sound left no doubt that several of Kharan's fingers had been broken. Branson picked up his gun.

Van Effen was apologetic but not unduly so. 'Had to, I'm afraid, Mr Branson. If I'd warned him – well, I didn't want any gunfight in the OK corral with all those nasty ricochets from the bullet-proof glass. He might have done himself an injury.'

'Quite right.' Branson looked through the window again. The *New Jersey* was now almost a half mile away and its captain was obviously not in a belligerent mood. Branson turned away and spoke to Bradford.

'Go to our coach and fetch the first-aid box. Bring Peters.'

'Peters, Mr Branson?'

'Used to be field corpsman. Take your seats, gentlemen.' Unhappily, they took their seats: the President, in particular, looked especially deflated. Branson wondered briefly just how hollow a man he might be then dismissed the line of thought as unprofitable. 'I don't think I have to warn you not to try anything so silly again.' He went to the communications console and picked up the phone. 'Hendrix?'

'Here. Satisfied now?'

'Yes. Warn the harbour-master or whoever the responsible official is that there is to be no more traffic under the bridge. Either way.'

'No more traffic? You'll bring the entire port to a standstill. And the fishing fleet –'

'The fishing fleet can go fish in the bay. Send an ambulance and a doctor and do it quickly. A couple of men here have gotten themselves hurt, one badly.'

'Who? How?'

'The oil ministers – Iman and Kharan. Self-inflicted injuries, you might say.' As he spoke Branson watched Peters hurry into the coach, approach Iman and start scissoring away the sleeve of his coat. 'There will be a TV van coming to the bridge soon. Let it through. I also want some chairs brought on to the bridge – forty should do.'

'Chairs?'

'You don't have to buy them,' Branson said patiently. 'Confiscate them from the nearest restaurant. Forty.'

'Chairs?'

'Things you sit on. I'm going to hold a news conference in an hour or so. You don't stand around at news conferences. You sit around.'

Hendrix said carefully: 'You're going to hold a news conference and you're going to televise it live?'

'That's it. Nation-wide.'

'You're out of your mind.'

'My mental health is my concern. Milton and Quarry there yet?'

'You mean the Secretary and the Secretary of the Treasury?'

'I mean Milton and Quarry.'

'They've just arrived and are with me now.'

Hendrix looked at the two men who were with him then inside the big mobile communications van. Milton, the Secretary of State, was a tall, thin, dyspeptic character with no hair, rimless steel-legged glasses and an enviable reputation in Foreign Offices around the world: Quarry, white-haired, plump and cheerful, had a kindly avuncular air about him which many men, even some very highly intelligent ones, had taken to be a reflection of the true personality of the man: his reputation as a banker and economist stood as high as that of Milton in his field.

Milton said: 'It would be easy to say "he's quite crazy, of course". Is he?'

Hendrix spread his hands. 'You know what they say. Crazy like a fox.'

'And violent, it would seem?'

'No. Violence he uses only as a last resort and even then only when pushed into a corner. Iman and Kharan must have made the mistake of pushing him into a corner.'

Quarry said: 'You would seem to know a fair bit about him?'

Hendrix sighed. 'Every senior police officer in the States knows about him. And in Canada, Mexico and God knows how many South American countries.' Hendrix sounded bitter. 'So far he has spared Europe his attentions. It's only a matter of time, I'm sure.'

'What's his speciality?'

'Robbery. He robs trains, planes, armoured cars, banks and jewellers. Robbery, wherever possible, as I say, without violence.'

Quarry was dry. 'I gather he is quite successful?'

'Quite successful! To the best of our knowledge he has been operating for at least a dozen years and the lowest estimate of his takings in that time is twenty million dollars.'

'Twenty million!' For the first time there was a note of respect in Quarry's voice, the banker and economist in him surfacing. 'If he's got all that money, why does he want more?'

'Why do Niarchos and Getty and Hughes want more – after all, they too are comfortably off? Maybe he's just a business-man in the way that they are businessmen and he's hooked on his job. Maybe he finds it a stimulating intellectual exercise. Maybe it's sheer greed. Maybe anything.'

Milton said: 'Has he ever been convicted?'

Hendrix looked pained. 'He's never even been arrested.'

'And that has something to do with the fact that neither of us has ever heard of him?'

Hendrix gazed through the van window at the magnificent sweep of the Golden Gate Bridge. There was a far-off look of yearning in his eyes. He said: 'Let us say, sir, that we do not care to advertise our failures.'

Milton smiled at him. 'John and I' – he nodded at the Secretary of the Treasury – 'frequently suffer from the same bashfulness and for the same reasons. Infallibility is not the lot of mankind. Anything known about this man – apart from what is known about his criminal activities?'

Hendrix said sourly: 'It wouldn't be hard to know more about him than we do about his life of crime. Pretty well documented background, really. A WASP from out east. Comes from what they call a good family. Father a banker and when I say banker I mean he owned – still does, I believe his own bank.'

'Branson,' the Treasury Secretary said. 'Of course. Know him. Not personally, though.'

'And something else that will interest you, sir – profession-ally. Branson took a degree in economics and went to work in his father's bank. While he was there he took a PhD – and no coffee-grinder diploma school either – genuine Ivy League. Then for his post-graduate course he took up the subject of crime – something to do with having worked in his old man's bank, maybe.' Hendrix looked gloomy. 'I suppose we could say that he has graduated in that subject now too – *summa cum laude*.'

Milton said: 'You seem to have almost a degree of admira-tion for this person, Hendrix?'

'I'd give my pension to see him behind bars. Both as a man and a policeman he outrages whatever passes for my sensibilities. But one can't help respecting sheer professionalism, no matter how misused.'

'My sentiments too, I'm afraid,' Milton said. 'He's not a particularly retiring person, this Branson of yours?'

'I wish he were mine. If you mean does he suffer from our bouts of bashfulness, no, sir, he does not.'

'Arrogant?'

'To the point, perhaps, of megalomania. At least, that's what General Cartland says, and I wouldn't care to dispute what the General says.'

'Few would.' Milton spoke with some feeling. 'Speaking of self-opinionated characters, where art thou at this hour, my James?'

'Sir?'

'What other self-opinionated character is there? I refer to Mr Hagenbach, the self-opinionated head of our FBI. I would have thought he would have been the first man hot-foot to the scene.'

'Washington says they don't know where he is. They're trying every place they can think of. I'm afraid he's a very elusive man, sir.'

'Man's got a mania for secrecy.' Milton brightened. 'Well, if he's watching his TV in an hour or so he should be considerably enlightened. What a perfectly splendid thought – the head of our FBI the last man in America to know about this.' He thought for a moment. 'Branson's insistence on maximum publicity – TV, radio I'll be bound, newsmen, photographers – has he ever declared himself publicly like this before? I mean, before or during any of his criminal activities?'

'Never.'

'The man must be terribly sure of himself.'

'In his place, so would I.' Quarry appeared distracted. 'What can we do to the man? As I see it, he's in an impregnable, quite unassailable position.'

'I wouldn't give up hope, sir. We have one or two experts looking for an answer. Admiral Newson and General Carter are in our HQ now working on this.'

'Newson. Carter. Our twin geniuses of finesse.' Quarry seemed more discouraged than ever. 'Never use one hydrogen bomb where two will suffice. Someone should send our Arabian oil friends word that they're about to become involved in a nuclear holocaust.' He gestured through his window towards the bridge. 'Just look at it. Just think of it. A totally impossible situation – if it weren't for the fact that we can see now that it's all too possible. Total, absolute isolation, completely cut off from the world – and in the full view of everybody in San Francisco – everybody in the world, for that matter, as soon as those TV cameras start turning. A figurative stone's throw away – and they might as well be on the moon.' He sighed heavily. 'One must confess to a feeling of utter helplessness.'

'Come, come, John.' Milton was severe. 'Is this the spirit that won the West?'

'The hell with the West. I'm thinking about me. I don't have to be very clever to know beyond any doubt that I am going to be the man in the middle.'

Hendrix said: 'Sir?'

'Why else do you think this ruffian had summoned the Secretary of the Treasury to his royal presence?'

Hands in pockets, as if deep in thought, Revson wandered along the east side of the bridge, stopping frequently to gaze at, and presumably admire the panorama stretched out before him – to his left the tip of Belvedere beyond Fort Baker, Tiburon and Angel Island, the largest in the Bay; to his right the city itself and straight ahead Alcatraz Island and beyond it Treasure Island: between the two the rapidly diminishing shape of the *New Jersey* was heading for its berth at Alameda. He made frequent stops, as if peering over the side. On one of those occasions he reached casually for the green cord he'd attached to the strut and hefted it. It was weightless.

'What are you doing?'

He turned unhurriedly. April Wednesday's big green eyes, if not exactly alive with curiosity, held a certain puzzlement.

'You do have flannel feet. I thought I was the only person within miles – well, yards.'

'What are you doing?'

'When I look at this marvellous view here and then at you I really don't know which I prefer. I think you. Have any people ever told you that you're really rather beautiful?'

'Lots.' She caught the green cord between finger and thumb and started to lift it then made a muffled sound of pain as his hand closed none too gently over hers.

'Leave that alone.'

She rubbed her hand, looked around her and said: 'Well?'

'I'm fishing.'

'Not for compliments, that's for sure.' She massaged her knuckles tenderly, then looked at him with some uncertainty. 'Fishermen tell tall tales, don't they?'

'I've done it myself.'

'Tell me one.'

'Are you as trustworthy as you're beautiful?'

'Am I beautiful? And I'm not fishing. Honest.'

'You are.'

'Then I'm trustworthy too.' They smiled at each other and he took her arm. 'A really tall one?'

'Yes, please.'

'Why ever not?' They walked slowly away together.

Hendrix replaced the receiver in its cradle. He looked at Milton and Quarry. 'You are ready, gentlemen?'

'Act One, Scene One, and all the world's a stage. That's wrong somehow.' Milton rose and looked critically at Quarry. 'The shirt's wrong too, John. White shows up badly on TV. Should be blue – like me – or the President. Blue shirts are all he has: you never know when a TV camera is lurking round the next corner.'

'Oh, shut up.' Quarry turned morosely towards the rear door of the van then stopped as a motor-cycle policeman drew up with a suitably dramatic screeching of tyre and smell of burning rubber, dismounted, propped his machine and hurried to the rear steps of the van. He held up his hand to Hendrix. 'For you, sir.'

Hendrix took the eight-inch-long narrow cylinder. 'It's got my name on it, all right. Where did you get it from?'

'The pilot boat brought it in from the *New Jersey.* The captain – of the *New Jersey,* that is – thought it might be very urgent.'

FIVE

The centre section of the Golden Gate Bridge was fast assuming the appearance of an embryonic town, sprawling, inchoate and wholly disorganized as those burgeoning settlements tend to be, but none the less possessed of a vitality, a feverish restlessness that augured well for its expansive future. The fact that all the buildings were on wheels and that all the village elders, seated in solemn conclave, were immaculately dressed and had clearly never done a single day's physical toil in their collective lives, did little to detract from the curious impression that here were the pioneers pushing forwards the limits of the wild frontier.

There were three coaches and three police cars – the third had just brought Hendrix, Milton and Quarry. There were two large, glaze-windowed vehicles which bore the euphemistic legend 'Rest Room'. painted in becoming red and yellow stripes they had been borrowed from an itinerant circus currently stopped-over in the city. There was an ambulance, which Branson had commandeered for purposes best known to himself, a large side-counter wagonette which had provided hot meals, a very large TV camera truck with its generator placed at a discreet hundred yards distance and, finally, a van that was unloading blankets, rugs and pillows to help ease the new settlers through the rigours of their first night.

There were, of course, the discordant, even jarring items. The helicopters, the tracked anti-aircraft guns, the patrolling armed men, the army engineers at a distance on either side busily erecting steel barricades – those did tend to project a disturbing hint of violence to come. And yet they were not entirely alien there: so bizarre were the circumstances that the normal would have tended to look sadly out of place. The unreality of it all, when matched up against the outside world, had its own strange reality in this particular point in time and place. And for those participating in the scene, the reality of their situation was all too self-evident. No one smiled.

The cameras were in position, so were the hostages, the three newly arrived men and, behind them in the second row, sat the journalists. The photographers had taken up positions best suited to themselves, none of them more than a few feet distant from an armed guard. Facing them, in solitary splendour, sat Branson. Close by him on the ground lay a peculiar object, a length of heavy canvas with cone-shaped objects embedded in it: beside it lay a heavy metal box, its lid closed.

'I will not detain you unnecessarily, gentlemen,' Branson said. Whether or not he was enjoying his moment of glory, the knowledge that he held some of the most powerful men in the world at his complete mercy, the consciousness that a hundred million people were looking at and listening to him, was quite impossible to say. He was calm, relaxed, unnervingly confident of and in himself, but displaying no other visible emotion. 'You will have guessed why we all find ourselves here and why I am here.'

'The reason why I'm here, I take it,' Quarry said.

'Exactly.'

'You will bear in mind that, unlike you, I am not a law unto myself. The final decision is not mine.'

'Appreciated.' Branson could have been conducting some urbane seminar in an Ivy college. 'That comes later. First things first, don't you think, Mr Quarry?'

'Money.'

'Money.'

'How much?' Quarry's reputation for disconcerting bluntness had been easily earned.

'One moment, Mr Secretary.' The President had his weaknesses no less than the two hundred million people for whom he was the elected head of state and high on the list was an almost pathological dislike of being upstaged. 'What do you want this money for, Branson?'

'What's that got to do with it – supposing it's any of your business?'

'It is my business. I must state categorically if you want it for any subversive activities, for any evil practices whatsoever, and especially for any anti-American activities – well, I tell you here and now that you can have my body first. Who am I compared to America?'

Branson nodded approval. 'Stoutly spoken, Mr President, especially considering the fact that you have left your speechwriters behind. I hear the voice of our founding fathers, the clarion call of the conscience that lies at the grass-roots of America. The Grand Old Party are going to love you for that. It should be worth another two million votes come November. However, quite apart from the fact that you don't mean a word you say, I have to reassure you that this money is required for purely apolitical purposes. It's for a private trust, in fact. Branson Enterprises, Inc. Me.'

The President wasn't a man to be easily knocked off stride – if he were he wouldn't have been President. 'You have just mentioned the word "conscience". You have none?'

'I don't honestly know,' Branson said frankly. 'Where money is concerned, none. Most of the really wealthy men in the world are moral cripples, basically criminally-minded types who maintain a façade of spurious legality by hiring lawyers as morally crippled as they are themselves.' Branson appeared to muse. 'Multi-millionaires, politicians, lawyers – which of them lies furthest beyond the moral pale? But don't answer that – I may unintentionally be putting you in an invidious position. We're all rogues, whether under the hypocritical cover of legalism or out in the noon-day sun, like me. I just want some fast money fast and I reckon this is as good a way as any of getting it.'

Quarry said: 'We accept that you are an honest thief. Let us come to cases.'

'My reasonable demands?'

'The point, Mr Branson.'

Branson surveyed the Arabian oil barons – now without Iman who was in hospital – and the President. 'For this lot, on the hoof, in prime condition and no haggling about pennies – three hundred million dollars. That's a three followed by eight nothings.'

To the many million viewers throughout America it was immediately obvious that there had been a sound transmission breakdown. The silence, however, was more than compensated for by the wide and interesting variety of expressions registered on the faces of those on the screen, which ranged from total outrage through total incomprehension through total incredulity to total shock: indeed, in those few imperishable moments, sound would have been an unforgiveable intrusion. Predictably, in view of the fact that he was accustomed to dealing with figures which contained large numbers of zeros, Secretary of the Treasury Quarry was the first to recover.

'You did say what I thought I heard you say?'

'Three zero zero, comma, zero zero zero, comma, zero zero zero period. If you give me a blackboard and some chalk I'll write it out for you.'

'Preposterous! Lunatic! The man's mad, mad, mad.' The President, whose now puce colour showed up rather well on colour television, clenched his fist and looked round in vain for a table to bang it on. 'You know the penalty for this, Branson – kidnapping, blackmail, extortion under threats on a scale –'

'A scale quite unprecedented in the annals of crime?'

'Yes. On a scale quite – shut up! The death penalty can be invoked for treason – and this is high treason – and if it's the last thing I do –'

'That might be any moment. Rest assured, Mr President, that you won't be around to pull the switch. You better believe me.' He produced his pistol. 'As a token of my intent, how would you like a hundred million viewers to see you being shot through the knee-cap – then you really would need that cane of yours. It's a matter of indifference to me.' And in his voice there was a chilling indifference that carried far more conviction than the words themselves. The President unclenched his fist and seemed not so much to sink into his chair as to deflate into it. The puce was assuming a greyish hue.

'You people have to learn to think big,' Branson went on. 'This is the United States of America, the richest country in the world, not a banana republic. What's three hundred million dollars? A couple of Polaris submarines? A tiny fraction of what it cost to send a man to the moon? A fraction of one per cent of the gross national product? If I take one drop from the American bucket who's going to miss it – but if I'm not allowed to take it then a lot of people are going to miss you, Mr President, and your Arabian friends.

'And to think what you are going to lose, you and America. Ten times that, a hundred times that? To start with the San Rafael refinery deal will fall through. Your hopes of becoming a most favoured nation receiving oil at rock-bottom prices are gone for ever. In fact, if their Highnesses fail to return to their homeland it is certain that a total oil embargo would be placed on the States which would send the country into a bottomless recession which would make 1929 look like a Sunday afternoon picnic.' He looked at Hansen, the energy czar. 'You would agree, Mr Hansen?'

Clearly, the last thing that Hansen wanted to do was to agree with anyone. His nervous tics were rapidly assuming the proportions of a St Vitus's Dance. Head darting, he looked around for succour in his hour of need. He swallowed, he coughed into his hands, he looked imploringly at the President and seemed almost on the point of breaking down when the Secretary of the Treasury came to his rescue.

Quarry said: 'I would read the future the same way.'

'Thank you.'

The King raised his hand. 'A word, if you will.' The King was a man of a very different calibre to the President. As one who had to remove, permanently more often than not, quite a number of his closest relatives in order to get his crown, the rough and tumble of life was hardly a new experience for him: he had lived with violence all his life and would very probably die with or because of it.

'Of course.'

'Only the blind have their eyes closed to reality, I am not blind. The President will pay.' The President had no comment to make on this generous offer: he was staring down at the roadway like a fortune teller peering into his crystal ball and not wanting to tell his client what he sees there.

'Thank you, your Highness.'

'You will of course be hunted down and killed afterwards no matter where you may seek to hide in the world. Even if you were to kill me now your death is already as certain as to-morrow's sun.'

Branson was unconcerned. 'As long as I have you, your Highness, I have no worries on that score. I should imagine that any of your subjects who as much as endangered your life far less being responsible for your losing it would find himself rather precipitately in paradise – if regicides go to paradise, which I don't think should be allowed. And I hardly think you're the type of man to run to the side of the bridge now and jump over in order to incite the faithful to come after me with their long knives.'

'Indeed.' The hooded eyes were unblinking. 'And what if I were not the sort of person you think I am?'

'If you were to jump – or try to?' Again the chilling indifference. 'Why do you think I have a doctor and ambulance here? Van Effen, if anyone is as misguided as to make a break for it – what are your instructions?'

Van Effen matched the indifference. 'Chop his foot off with my machine-pistol. The doctor will fix him up.'

'We might even – eventually – provide you with an artificial foot. You're worth nothing to me dead, your Highness.' The hooded eyes had closed. 'Well, the ransom figure? Agreed? No objectors? Splendid. Well, that's for starters.'

'Starters?' It was General Cartland speaking and one could almost see the firing squad mirrored in his eyes.

'To begin with, that means. There's more. Two hundred million dollars more. That's what I want for the Golden Gate Bridge.'

This time the state of traumatic shock did not last quite so long – there is a limit to how much the human mind can take. The President raised his eyes from the depths of the bottomless pit he was scanning and said dully: 'Two hundred million dollars for the Golden Gate Bridge?'

'It's a bargain. At the price, practically a give-away. True, it cost only forty million to build and the asking price of two hundred million just exactly represents the five-fold inflation over the past forty years. But, money apart, think of the fearful cost of replacing it. Think of the noise, the dust, the pollution, the disruption to all the city traffic as all those thousands of tons of steel have to be brought in, of the tourists who will cripple the city's economy by staying away in their tens of thousands. Beautiful though San Francisco is, without the Golden Gate it would be like Mona Lisa without her smile. Think – and this is for a period of at least one year, perhaps two – of all those Marin County motorists who couldn't get to the city – it's a long long way round by the San Rafael bridge – or, come to that, the city motorists who couldn't get to Marin County. The hardship would be intolerable for everyone – except for the owners of the ferry-boat companies who would become millionaires. And who am I to grudge the entrepreneur the making of an honest dollar? Two hundred million dollars? Philanthropy, that's what it is.'

Quarry, the man accustomed to thinking in rows of noughts, said: 'If we do not accede to this monstrous request, what do

76

you intend to do with the bridge? Take it away and pawn it somewhere?'

'I'm going to blow it up. A two-hundred-foot drop – it should be the most almighty splash the West Coast has ever seen.'

'Blow it up! Blow up the Golden Gate Bridge!' Mayor Morrison, whose normal boiling point was just above freezing, was on his feet, his face suffused with ungovernable anger and had launched himself at Branson before anyone realized what was happening, certainly before Branson had realized. In tens of millions of American homes they saw Branson being knocked backwards off his seat, his head striking heavily against the roadway as Morrison, all two hundred and twenty pounds of him, followed him down and struck at his face with berserker fury. Van Effen stepped forward and brought the butt of his machine-pistol down on Morrison's neck. He immediately swung round to cover the seated men with his gun but the precaution was superfluous, no one was showing any inclination to follow Morrison's example.

It was a full twenty seconds before Branson could sit up, and then only groggily. He accepted a pad of medical gauze and dabbed at a smashed lip and a very bloody nose. He looked at Morrison, then at the doctor.

'How is he?'

The doctor carried out a brief examination. 'He'll be all right, he's not even concussed.' The doctor glanced at Van Effen without enthusiasm. 'Your friend seems to be able to judge those things to a nicety.'

'Practice,' Branson explained thickly. He accepted another gauze pad in place of the already blood-saturated one and rose unsteadily to his feet. 'Mayor Morrison doesn't know his own strength.'

Van Effen said: 'What shall I do with him?'

'Leave him be. It's his city, it's his bridge. My fault – I just trod on a man's dreams.' He looked at Morrison consideringly. 'On second thoughts you'd better handcuff him – behind the back. Next time he might knock my head off my shoulders.'

General Cartland came to his feet and walked towards Branson. Van Effen levelled his gun menacingly but Cartland ignored him. He said to Branson: 'You fit to talk?'

'I'm fit to listen, anyway. He didn't get round to my ears.'

'I may be Chief of Staff but to trade I'm an army engineer. That means I know explosives. You can't blow up the bridge and you should know it. You'd require a wagon-load of explosives to bring down those towers. I don't see any wagon-load of explosives.'

'We don't need them.' He pointed to the thick canvas strap with the conical mounds embedded in it. 'You're the expert.'

Cartland looked at the strap, then at Branson, then at the seated watchers, then back at the strap again. Branson said: 'Suppose you tell them. My mouth hurts, I can't imagine why.'

Cartland took a long look at the massive towers and the cables suspended from them. He said to Branson: 'You have experimented?' Branson nodded. 'Successfully – or you wouldn't be here?' Branson nodded again.

Reluctantly, almost, Cartland turned to the seated hostages and journalists. 'I was wrong. I'm afraid Branson can indeed bring the bridge down. Those cones you see embedded in the canvas strap contain some conventional explosives – TNT amatol, anyway something of the requisite power. Those cones are called "bee-hives", and because of their concave bases are designed to direct at least eighty per cent of their explosive value inwards. The idea, I should imagine, is to wrap one of those canvas straps with its hundredweight or whatever of high explosive round one of the suspension cables, probably high up near the top of a tower.' He looked at Branson again. 'I should imagine you have four of those.' Branson nodded. 'And designed to fire simultaneously.' He turned back to the others. 'I'm afraid that would be it. Down it all comes.'

There was a brief silence, which must have been very nail-biting for TV watchers, a silence caused by the fact that Branson understandably didn't feel very much like speaking and the others couldn't think of very much to say. Cartland said eventually: 'How can you be sure they all go off together?'

'Simple. Radio wave that activates an electric cell that burns the wire in a mercury fulminate detonator. Up goes the primer and up goes the bee-hive. One's enough. The others go up by sympathetic detonation.'

Quarry said heavily: 'I suppose that ends your demands for the day?'

'Not quite.' Branson turned a palm up in an apologetic

gesture. 'But it's only a trifle.'

'One wonders what *you* might consider a trifle.'

'A quarter of a million dollars.'

'Astonishing. By your standards, a grain of sand. And what might that be for?'

'My expenses.'

'Your expenses.' Quarry breathed deeply, twice. 'My God Branson, you are the piker to end all pikers.'

'I'm used to people calling me names.' He shrugged. 'I don't hurt so easily any more and one learns to take the rough with the smooth. Now, as to payment – you are going to pay me, aren't you?'

No one said whether they were going to pay him or not.

'I have to make arrangements with a friend in New York who has friends in certain European banks.' He looked at his watch. 'It's noon now so it's either eight or nine o'clock in Central Europe and all good Central European bankers knock off at six precisely. So I'd be greatly obliged if you'd let me have your decision by seven o'clock in the morning.'

Quarry said cautiously: 'What decision?'

'As to the availability of the funds and the form that they will take. Not that I care very much what they are, anything from Euro-dollars to stock in suitably selected off-shore funds. You, of all people, should find little problem in handling such things with a certain amount of discretion – witness, for instance, the hundreds of millions of dollars you've funded such organizations as the CIA for subversive activities overseas without the poor taxpayer being any the wiser. A childishly simple routine for your Treasury. Not that I care whether those funds are traceable or not: just as long as they are convertible.

'When my New York friend has informed us that those funds have all arrived at their several destinations – and that shouldn't take more than another twenty-four hours, say until noon the same day – we shall take our farewells of you. Our hostages will, of course, accompany us.'

'And where are you taking us?' Cartland demanded.

'You I'm not taking anywhere. The armed services may regard you as invaluable but your value to me as a bargaining counter is zero. Besides, you're the only man here who could conceivably cause me trouble. Not only are you a man of action but you're far too lean – let me have men about me that are fat and all that bit. The President and his three remaining oil friends. There's no harm in telling you that I have a friend in the Caribbean who is the President of an island that doesn't and never will have an extradition treaty with the United States. He's willing to put us up, bed and breakfast, for a million dollars a night.'

No one had anything to say to this. In terms of the sums of money that Branson had so recently been bandying about, it seemed a reasonable enough charge.

'One point,' Branson said. 'I did not mention that as from noon the following day – day after tomorrow that is – there will be a penalty clause, an escalation charge you might call it, for every hour's delay in the reported lodgment of the funds. Two million dollars an hour.'

'You do place a certain value on your time, don't you, Mr Branson,' Quarry said.

'If I don't, who will? Would there be any more questions?'

'Yes,' Cartland said. 'How do you propose to get to this island paradise of yours?'

'Fly there. How else? A ten-minute flight in our helicopters to the International Airport and we board our plane there.'

'You have all this arranged? You have a plane standing by?'

'Well, it doesn't know it's standing by but it will soon enough.'

'What plane?'

'Air Force 1, I believe you call it.'

Even Cartland was shaken out of his habitual reserve. 'You mean you're going to hi-jack the Presidential Boeing?'

'Be reasonable, General. You surely can't expect your President to judder his way down to the Caribbean in a clapped-out DC3? It's the logical, the only way of transporting world leaders who are accustomed to the ultimate in luxury travel. We'll show them the latest films. Brief though their incarceration may be we'll make it as comfortable as possible for them. We might even get some more new films when we fly them back to the States again.'

'We?' Cartland said carefully.

'My friends and I. I feel it only right – no, more than that, our bounden duty – that we should see them safely back again. How any man of any sensitivity can bear to live in that monstrosity they call the White House I don't know but, after all, there's no place like home.'

Milton was equally careful. 'You mean you're going to set foot on American soil again?'

'My own, my native land. Why ever not? You disappoint me, Mr Milton.'

'I do?'

'You do. Apart from the Supreme Court and the Attorney General I would have thought that the Secretary of State would know as much about our law and constitution as any other man in the land.' There was silence. Branson looked around but there was still silence so he addressed himself to the Secretary again. 'Or don't you know that bit where it says that no man who has been granted a full and free pardon by the State for any crime, actual or alleged, can ever again be arraigned on that same charge?'

It took at least ten seconds for the full implications to dawn and it was then that the Potomac, in the person of the Chief Executive, burst its banks. It was also then that the President lost twice the number of the putative votes he might have gained from his earlier statement that he would sacrifice himself for America. He could hardly be blamed. Devious some politicians may be and others are armoured in pachydermal hides; but never had the President encountered such Machiavellian effrontery. Even Presidents may be forgiven the odd earthy turn of phrase within the privacy of their own four walls but they customarily abjure such phraseology when addressing the electorate. But, momentarily, the President had totally forgotten the fact that he was, in effect, addressing the electorate; he was appealing to a mindless heaven for justice. And it was in that direction that his anguished face was lifted as he stood there, arms rigidly outstretched and fists clenched, his face assuming a peculiarly purplish hue.

'Half a deleted billion dollars! *And* a deleted full and free pardon! God al-deleted-mighty!' He lowered his gaze from the cloudless sky and turned the full fury of his wrath on Branson who, disappointingly, had not been struck down by a bolt from heaven.

Branson murmured to the doctor: 'You have your cardiac arrest unit handy?'

'This is not funny.'

The President warmed to his theme. 'You evil twisted deleted bastard! If you imagine –'

Cartland, belatedly, reached his side, touched his arm and whispered urgently: 'You're on television, sir.'

The President, cut off in mid-expletive, looked at him, screwed his eyes shut in sudden comprehension, opened them again, looked the camera squarely in the eye and addressed it in measured tones.

'I, as the elected representative and Chief Executive of the American people, will not stand for this vile blackmail, the machinations of this evil and amoral man. The American people will not stand for it. Democracy will not stand for it. Come what may we shall fight this cancer in our midst – '

'How?' Branson asked.

'How?' The President tried manfully to control his blood pressure at the thought of this but full rationality had not yet returned to him. 'The entire resources of every investigative agency in those United States of ours, the entire weight of the armed forces the full majesty of law and order will be brought to bear – '

'You're not up for re-election for six months yet. How?'

'When I have consulted with the senior members of my cabinet – '

'You're through with consulting anyone, except on my say-so, A full and free pardon. If not, your stay on this tropical island may be indefinitely extended. Most of the island, as I say, is pretty close to paradise: but there's a small stockaded section in one corner of the island that's been modelled rather closely on the Devil's Island that used to be. The Generalissimo has to have some place for his political dissidents, and as he doesn't care for them overly much the majority of them never emerge again. It's a combination of hard labour, fever and starvation. I somehow don't see the King here with a pickaxe in his hand. Nor yourself for that matter.

'And instead of waffling on about the nation's moral rectitude, you might give thought to another possible predicament of your guests here. It is no secret that both the King and Prince have trusted Government ministers and relatives who are just yearning to try their thrones for size. If your friends' stay in the Caribbean were to be unduly prolonged, one rather suspects that they would have neither kingdom nor sheikhdom to return to. You appreciate, of course, that American opinion would never let you deal with their usurpers – especially as you would be the one held to blame for it. Bang goes November. Bang goes San Rafael. Here comes either redoubled oil prices or a total embargo and, in either case, a disastrous recession. You won't even rate a footnote in history. At best, if they ever get round to compiling a list of history's most stupid and disastrous national leaders, then you have a fair chance of making the *Guinness Book of Records*. But history itself? No.'

'You have quite finished?' The President's anger had seemingly evaporated and he had attained a curious sort of resigned dignity.

'For the moment.' Branson motioned to the TV cameramen that the performance was over.

'May I have a word with the King, Prince, my governmental colleagues and the Chief of Police?'

'Why not? Especially if it helps you to arrive at your decision more quickly.'

'In privacy?'

'Certainly. Your coach.'

'In the strictest privacy?'

'The guard will remain outside. As you know, the coach is sound-proof. The strictest privacy, I promise you.'

They moved away, leaving Branson alone. He beckoned Chrysler, his tele-communications expert.

'Is the bug in the Presidential coach activated?'

'Permanently.'

'Our friends are having a top-level secret discussion in there. Wouldn't you care to have a rest in our coach? You must be tired.'

'Very tired, Mr Branson.'

Chrysler made his way to the rear coach and sat by the driver's seat in front of the console. He made a switch and lifted a single ear-phone. Apparently satisfied with what he heard he replaced the ear-phone and made another switch. A tape recorder started humming.

April Wednesday said to Revson: 'Well, what did you make of that?'

'I'd love to see the Nielsen ratings when they re-run that later in the day.' They were walking to and fro along the western or deserted side of the bridge. 'What a cast. Rehearsals would have ruined it.'

'You know I don't mean that.'

'I know. He's quite a boy, our Peter Branson. Highly intelligent – but we know that already – all the angles figured, every eventuality taken care of far in advance, he'd have made an excellent general. You could – at least I could – almost like and admire the guy, except for the fact that, the odd half billion apart, he plainly does this for kicks, he's a moral vacuum and the ordinary standards of right and wrong just do not hold good for him, they simply don't exist. There's something strangely empty about him.'

'His bank-book isn't going to be. But I didn't mean that either.'

'I know that too. In answer to your unspoken question, yes he has us helpless.'

'Do you intend to do anything about it?'

'Intentions are one thing, achievements another.'

'Well, you just can't walk up and down there doing nothing. After what you told me this morning – '

'I know what I told you this morning. A little respectful silence, if you please. Can't you see I'm thinking?'

After some little time he said: 'I've thought.'

'I can't wait.'

'Have you ever been sick?'

She lifted her brows which had the effect of making the huge green eyes larger than ever. With those eyes, Revson reflected, she could wreck a cardinals' council in nothing flat. To keep his mind on the work on hand, he looked away. She said: 'Of course I've been sick. Everybody's been sick some time.'

'I mean really sick. Hospital. Like that.'

'No. Not ever.'

'You're going to be very soon. In hospital. Sick. If you're still prepared to help, that is.'

'I've told you that already.'

'Asperity ill becomes a lovely lady. There's quite an element of risk. If you're caught, Branson would make you talk. Half a billion dollars is a lot of money to have at stake. You'd talk very quickly.'

'Even more quickly than that. I'm not one of your wartime resistance heroines and I don't like pain. Caught at what?'

'Delivering a letter for me. Leave me alone for a few minutes, will you.'

Revson unshipped his camera and took some still shots, of

84

the coaches, helicopters, anti-aircraft guns and guards, trying as much as possible to keep the southern tower and the San Franciscan skyline in the background, clearly a dedicated craftsman at work. He then turned his attention and lens towards the ambulance and the white-jacketed doctor leaning against it.

The doctor said: 'Instant fame for me, is it?'

'What else? Everyone wants to be immortalized.'

'Not this doctor. And an ambulance you can film anywhere.'

'You need psychiatric help.' Revson lowered his camera. 'Don't you know that it's positively anti-social in this country not to want to hog the camera lens? My name's Revson.'

'O'Hare.' O'Hare was youthful, cheerful, red-haired and his Irish ancestry lay no more than a generation behind him.

'And what do you think of this lovely little set-up?'

'For quotation?'

'I'm a cameraman.'

'Aw, hell, quote me if you want. I'd just love to belt smarty-pants's ears off.'

'It figures.'

'What?'

'The red hair.'

'I'd feel the same if I were black, blond or bald as a coot. Arrogant smoothies do something to me. And I don't like the way he needles the President and publicly humiliates him.'

'You're a President man, then?'

'Hell, he's a Californian, I'm a Californian. I voted for him last time and I'll do so next time. Okay, so he's stuffy and over-does the kindly uncle bit but he's the best we have. Not that that says a great deal – but, well, he's really a decent old stick.'

'Decent old stick?'

'Don't blame me, I was educated in England.'

'Would you like to help him?'

O'Hare looked at Revson thoughtfully. 'Funny question. Sure I would.'

'Would you help me to help him?'

'How can you help him?'

'I'll try and I'll tell you how – if you say "yes", that is.'

'And what makes you think you can help more than anyone else?'

'Special qualifications. I'm a Government employee.'

'So what's with the camera, then?'

'And I always thought it took a fair amount of intelligence to qualify as a doctor. What do you expect me to be carrying – a foot-wide plaque on my chest saying "I am an FBI agent"?'

O'Hare smiled, but only faintly. 'Well, no. But the story is that all the FBI men were left asleep in a down-town garage. Except for a few on the press coach who were rousted out and marched off the bridge.'

'We don't put all our eggs in one basket.'

'And agents don't usually disclose their identity either.'

'Not this agent. I'd disclose my identity to anyone if I were in trouble. And I'm in trouble now.'

'As long as it's not unethical – '

'I wouldn't bring a blush to the Hippocratic cheek. That guaranteed, would you consider it unethical to help put Branson behind bars?'

'Is that guaranteed too?'

'No.'

'Count on me. What do you want done?'

'We have a lady photographer with us who is young, rather beautiful, by the unlikely name of April Wednesday.'

'Ha!' O'Hare brightened considerably. 'The green-eyed blonde.'

'Indeed. I want her to take a message ashore, if that's the word, for me and bring me back an answer within a couple of hours. I propose to code this message, film it and give you the spool. It's about half the size of a cigarette and I'm sure you can easily conceal it in one of the many tubes and cartons you must carry about with you. Anyway, no one questions a doctor's integrity.'

'Don't they, now?' O'Hare spoke with some feeling.

'There's no hurry. I'll have to wait till Messrs Milton, Quarry and Hendrix have been escorted off the bridge. By which time, too, I expect that the trusty Mr Hagenbach will have arrived from wherever he has been lurking.'

'Hagenbach? You mean this old twister – '

'You are referring to my respected employer. Now, this is just an ambulance. Apart from your usual medical kit, heart unit, oxygen kit to stitch together the misguided who step out of line, I don't suppose you carry anything much more sophisticated.' O'Hare shook his head.

'So you don't have any radiological gear or clinical investigative equipment and most certainly not operational facilities, even if you did have an anaesthetist, which you haven't. I suggest then that, when Miss Wednesday takes most painfully ill in about an hour or so, you diagnose something that may demand, or may not demand – doctors can't take chances – immediate hospital diagnosis and possible surgery. Something like a grumbling appendix or suspected peritonitis or such-like. Don't ask me.'

'I wouldn't.' O'Hare looked at Revson with some disfavour. 'You seem to be unaware that even the rawest intern, no matter how damp behind the ears, can diagnose appendicitis with his hands, figuratively, in his pockets.'

'I am aware. But I'm damned if I could do it. And I'm pretty certain that no one else on this bridge could do it either.'

'You have a point. Right. But you'll have to give me fifteen to twenty minutes' notice – before I call in Branson or whoever. The odd job or two to induce the proper symptoms. No danger.'

'Miss Wednesday has just informed me that she is allergic to pain.'

'She won't feel a thing,' O'Hare said in his best dentist's voice. 'Besides, it's for the homeland.' He looked at Revson consideringly. 'I believe you gentlemen of the press are handing your stuff over at the south barrier in two hours' time. Couldn't it wait till then?'

'And get my answer back by carrier pigeon next week. I want it this afternoon.'

'You *are* in a hurry.'

'During the war – World War Two, that is – Winston Churchill used to annotate all instructions to his military and governmental staff with just three scribbled words: "Action this day". I am a great admirer of Sir Winston.'

He left the slightly bemused O'Hare and returned to April Wednesday. He told her that O'Hare had okayed his request and her first question was: 'Want I should bring back a miniaturized transceiver radio?'

He gave her a kind look. 'Thoughtful, but no. Electronic surveillance of all kinds can hardly be your province. Such a transceiver I have, screwed into the base of my camera. But that little revolving disc above the villains' coach means only one thing – they have an automatic radio-wave scanner. They'd pick me up in five seconds. Now listen carefully and I'll tell you exactly what I want you to do and how I want you to behave.'

When he had finished she said: 'Understand. But I don't much care for the thought of the kindly healer there running amok with his hypodermic.'

'You won't feel a thing,' Revson said soothingly. 'Besides, it's for the fatherland.'

He left her and walked casually across to the press coach. The imperial conference in the Presidential coach was still in full plenary session, and though the speech inside was wholly inaudible from where Revson stood it was clear from the gestures and expressions of those inside that all they had succeeded in reaching so far was a marked degree of difference in opinion. Their problem, Revson reflected, was hardly one susceptible to the ready formation of a consensus of opinion. Branson and Chrysler were up front in the rear coach, apparently dozing, which they probably weren't – though it wouldn't have mattered very much if they were, for alert guards were very much in evidence patrolling between the freshly-painted boundary lines on the bridge. Members of the various news media stood around in groups, wearing an air of almost hushed anticipation as if expecting the next momentous occasion to happen along any second now, which seemed as likely as not.

Revson entered the press coach. It was deserted. He made his way to his own seat, unshipped his camera, produced a pad and felt pen and began, quickly and without hesitation, to write what was apparently pure gibberish. There were those who were lost without their code-books but Revson was not one of them.

SIX

Hagenbach, the chief of the FBI, was a burly and formidable character in his middle sixties, with short-cropped grey hair, short-cropped grey moustache, slightly hooded light blue eyes which never appeared to blink and a face possessed of a total non-expression which it had taken him years of hard work to acquire. It was said that among the upper echelons of his FBI there was a sweepstake as to the day and date when Hagenbach would first be seen to smile. The sweepstake had been running for five years.

Hagenbach was a very able man and looked it. He had no friends and he looked that too. Men with a consuming passion seldom do and Hagenbach was a man with a consuming passion. As was said of one of his illustrious predecessors, he was alleged to have a file on every senator and congressman in Washington, not to mention the entire staff of the White House. He could have made a fortune in blackmail but Hagenbach was not interested in money. Nor was he interested in power, as such. Hagenbach's total dedication lay in the extirpation of corruption, whenever and wherever he might encounter it.

He looked at Admiral Newson and General Carter, the former plump and rubicund, the latter tall and lean and looking disconcertingly like his superior, General Cartland. Both men he had known, and well, for almost twenty years and had not once called either by his first name. That anyone should address Hagenbach by his Christian name was unthinkable. It would also have been extremely difficult as no one seemed to know it. He was the type of man who didn't need a first name.

Hagenbach said: 'So those are the only tentative proposals for action you have come up with so far?'

'The situation is unprecedented,' Newson said. 'Carter and I are fundamentally men of direct action. To date, direct action seems out of the question. Let's hear your ideas.'

'I've only just arrived. Have you any *immediate* proposals for the moment?'

'Yes. Await the arrival of the Vice-President.'

'The Vice-President is a nincompoop. You know that. I know that. We all know that.'

'Be that as it may, he's the only man in the United States who can approve and authorize any course of action we may eventually decide to make. Also, I think we had first better wait and consult Mr Milton, Mr Quarry and Chief Hendrix when they're released.'

'If they're released.'

'Hendrix is certain they will be and Hendrix knows far more about Branson than we do. Besides, he has to negotiate with somebody.' He picked up the message that had arrived from Revson via the *New Jersey*. 'How much reliance do you place on this?'

Hagenbach took the note and read it aloud.

' "Please wait. No precipitate action. No violence – especially no violence. Let me evaluate the situation. Cannot use transceiver – the bandits have an automatic radio-wave scanner in constant use. Will communicate with you this afternoon." '

Hagenbach laid down the paper. 'Quite a bit, actually.'

Carter said: 'What's he like, this Revson of yours?'

'Ruthless, arrogant, independent, dislikes authority, a loner who consults superior officers only under duress and even then goes his own way.'

Newson said: 'That doesn't sound very encouraging. What's a hot-head like that doing along on a trip like this?'

'He's no hot-head. His mind is as near ice-cold as any man's can be. I also forgot to say that he's highly intelligent, very ingenious and extremely resourceful.'

'Then he's a hand-picked man?' Newson said. Hagenbach nodded. 'You hand-picked him?' Again the nod. 'So he's the best in the business?'

'I can't say. You know the size of our organization. I can't possibly know all the field agents. He's just the best I happen to know.'

'Is he good enough to cope with Branson?'

'I don't know because I don't know Branson. What's for sure, for once Revson is going to depend heavily on outside help.' There was a degree of satisfaction in Hagenbach's voice.

Carter said: 'And how in hell is he going to communicate with us this afternoon?'

'I have no idea.' Hagenbach nodded to Revson's note. 'He got that through, didn't he?' There was a brief pause as the Admiral and General respectfully contemplated the note. 'Would either of you gentlemen have thought of that?' They shook their heads. 'Me neither. Resourceful is what I said.'

Branson walked up and down the bridge between the rear and Presidential coaches. No nervous pacing, no signs of strain or tension, he could have been taking a pleasant saunter in the afternoon sun, and, indeed, the afternoon was extremely pleasant. The skies were cloudless, the view all around came straight from the pages of a fairy-tale book and the waters of the Golden Gate and the Bay sparkled in the warm sun. Having had his fill of the view, Branson consulted his watch, strolled unhurriedly towards the Presidential coach, knocked on the door, opened it and stepped inside. He surveyed the occupants and the sound of voices stilled.

Branson said pleasantly: 'You have arrived at a decision, gentlemen?' There was no reply. 'Am I to take it, then, that you have arrived at an impasse?'

The President lowered the very large gin and martini with which he had been sustaining himself.

'We require more time for our deliberations.'

'You've had all the time you're going to have. You could sit here all day and get no further. If all your minds weren't so devious and at the same time so closed to the facts of life, you'd recognize this for the painfully simple issue it is. Pay up or else. And don't forget the escalation penalty clause.'

The President said: 'I have a proposal to make.'

'Let's hear it.'

'Permit the King, Prince and Sheikh Kharan to go. I shall remain as hostage. The situation would remain the same. You would still have the President of the United States. For that matter I can't see why you don't let *all* the hostages in this coach go.'

Branson was admiring. 'My heavens, what a perfectly splendid gesture. Noble, I should say. Why, do that, and the electorate would demand that they re-alter the constitution and let their hero run for another three terms instead of one.' He smiled and went on without a change in tone. 'No way, Mr President. Apart from the fact that I shudder at the very thought of you being in the White House for the next thirteen years I've always dreamt of holding a hand of cards with four aces in it. Here I've got four. One is not enough. And has it ever occurred to you that if you *were* to be the only hostage left on the Golden Gate Bridge the Government, in the person of your Vice-President who would just love to sit behind that table in the Oval Office, might be sorely tempted to achieve some sort of immortality by wiping out this monstrous band of criminals who have kidnapped you and your Arabian friends? Nothing drastic of course – nobody who destroyed this bridge could ever hope to be President. A single supersonic fighter-bomber from Alameda would do the job nicely. And if one of his rockets went off course slightly – well, that's just bad luck, an Act of God and pilot's error.'

The President spilt a considerable amount of his gin and martini on the carpet.

Branson looked at Quarry, Milton and Hendrix in turn, said: 'Gentlemen', and left the coach. The three men followed. The President carefully didn't watch them go. He appeared to have found something of profound interest in the depths of what remained of his drink.

Outside, Branson spoke to Van Effen. 'Get that TV van and crew back here again. Make sure the TV companies are notified.'

Van Effen nodded. 'It would be wrong of you to let the nation suffer this agonizing suspense. Where are you going?'

'To the south end with those three gentlemen.'

'As guaranteed escort for their safety? Can't they take the word of a gentleman?'

'Not that. I just want to inspect the progress being made on the barrier. Saves the walk, that's all.'

The four men climbed into the police car and drove off.

Still alone in the press coach, Revson watched them go then returned his attention to the three small sheets of notepaper on his knees. Each was smaller than the average postcard and all three were covered with small, neat and incomprehensible writing. He focused his camera and photographed each three times – Revson always covered his bets. He then took each paper in turn, set fire to it and crushed the blackened remains in his ash-tray. It was a very curious paper for it gave off no smoke. He then wound off the camera spool, sealed it and wrapped it in a very thin lead foil; as he had promised O'Hare, the completed result was no larger than half a cigarette.

He reloaded his camera and went outside. The atmosphere of suspense and excitement had markedly heightened. He spoke to a near-by newspaperman – understandably, he knew none of them by name.

'Something new afoot?'

'Branson's just sent for the television van again.'

'Do you know why?'

'No idea.'

'Nothing very important, probably. Maybe he's always had a yen to appear on TV. Maybe he's just wanting to keep the pressure on the nation and the government – and the Arabian governments too, for this time the big three companies will be geared for action, the satellites will be ready and waiting and so will be all the Persian Gulf. The executives of the big companies will be hard put to it to shed crocodile tears for the plight of their beloved President and at the same time refrain from jumping for joy. The biggest show on earth and all for free. What's the odds Branson won't be putting on a late show about two in the morning?'

Revson shot about a dozen other pictures. The chances of its being discovered that he had taken no pictures at all were remote in the extreme, but then again Revson always covered his bets. He drifted casually across to where O'Hare was leaning against his ambulance and shook a cigarette from its pack.

'Light, doctor?'

'Sure.' O'Hare produced a lighter and lit it. Revson cupped the flame in his hands to shield it from the very slight breeze and as he did so he slid the spool into O'Hare's palm.

'Thanks, Doc.' He looked idly around. There was no one within earshot. 'How long to hide?'

'One minute. I have the place for it.'

'Two minutes and you'll have your patient.'

O'Hare went into the ambulance while Revson sauntered half-way across the bridge where April Wednesday was prudently standing alone, a circumstance normally very difficult for her to achieve. She looked at him, wet her lips and tried to smile at him. It wasn't a very successful effort.

Revson said: 'Who's that solid dependable-looking character standing by the engine of the ambulance?'

'Grafton. United Press. A nice man.'

'Go and collapse gracefully against him. Discretion is of the essence. We don't want any undue fuss. But first let me get to the other side of the bridge. I want to be at a safe distance when you're taken ill.'

When Revson reached the far side of the bridge he turned and looked back. April had already begun to head in the direction of the ambulance. Her gait seemed a little unsteady but not markedly so. She may be scared, he thought – and she unquestionably was – but she can act.

She was about fifteen feet distant from Grafton when he first saw her or, more precisely, when she first attracted his attention. He regarded her slightly wavering approach with curiosity, a curiosity which quickly turned to concern. He took two quick steps forward and caught her by the shoulders. She leaned gratefully against him, lips and eyes compressed as in pain.

'April Wednesday,' he said. 'What's the matter, girl?'

'I've a terrible pain. It just hit me now.' Her voice was husky and she was holding herself with both hands. 'It – it feels like a heart attack.'

'How would you know?' Grafton said reasonably, his tone reassuring. 'And wherever your heart is, it's not on the right-hand side of your tummy. Don't misinterpret me, but some people have all the luck.' He took her firmly by the arm. 'There's a doctor only five yards from here.'

From the far side of the bridge Revson watched them vanish round to the rear of the ambulance. As far as he could reasonably tell, he had been the only person to observe the brief by-play.

Branson walked unhurriedly away from the half-completed southern barrier, apparently well satisfied with the progress of the work in hand. He reached the rear coach and swung up to sit beside Chrysler.

'Any more sensational revelations?'

'No, Mr Branson. It's all become a bit repetitive and boring. You can have a play-back or transcript if you like but it's not worth it.'

'I'm sure it's not. Tell me.'

'Can I switch off, Mr Branson? They're really not worth listening to.'

'They never were. Well?'

94

'Same old story. About the payment. Still arguing.'

'But they're going to pay.'

'No question. It's whether to pay now or stall. Latest opinion poll has four for, two undecided, two against. The King, the Prince and Kharan are all for the money being handed over now – Treasury money, of course. Mayor Morrison is of the same mind.'

'That's understandable. He'd pay a billion dollars within the hour to ensure the safety of his beloved bridge.'

'Cartland and Muir have no preference either way, the only difference being that General Cartland is willing to fight us to the death. The President and Hansen are very much against immediate payment.'

'Again understandable. Hansen's never made a decision in his life and the President would stall for ever, hoping for a miracle to happen, hoping to save the nation the loss of a half billion for which, rightly or wrongly, he would probably be blamed, hoping to save face and his Presidential image. Let them stew in their own juice.' He turned as Peters appeared in the doorway. 'Something wrong?'

'Nothing that affects us, sir. Seems Dr O'Hare has some medical problem on his hands. He'd like to see you as soon as possible.'

When Branson entered the ambulance he found April lying on the hinged side bed, a discreet six inches of her midriff showing, her face chalk-white. Branson did not much care for finding himself in the presence of sick people and this was obviously a sick person. He looked enquiringly at O'Hare.

O'Hare said: 'I've a very sick young lady on my hands, here, Mr Branson. I want her removed to hospital immediately.'

'What's wrong?'

'Look at her face.'

It was indeed ashen, an effect easily achieved by the application of an odourless talcum.

'And at her eyes.'

They were opaque with enormously dilated pupils, the effect of the first of the two jabs that O'Hare had given her. Not that the eyes hadn't been big enough to begin with.

'Feel her pulse.'

Reluctantly, Branson lifted the slender wrist and dropped it almost immediately.

'It's racing,' he said. And indeed it was. O'Hare had probably been a little too thorough there. The rate of the pulse when she had entered the ambulance had already been so high as to render the second injection unnecessary.

'Would you care to feel the distension on the right-hand side of the abdomen?'

'No, I would not.' Branson was emphatic.

'It could be a grumbling appendix. It could be a threatened peritonitis. The signs are there. But I have no proper diagnostic equipment, no X-ray facilities, no way of carrying out abdominal surgery and, of course, no anaesthetist. Hospital, and pretty damn quick.'

'No!' April had sat up in bed, fear in her face. 'No! Not hospital! They'll cut me up! Surgery! I've never even *been* in a hospital in my life.'

O'Hare put his hands on her shoulders, firmly and not bothering to be gentle, and pressed her back down again.

'And if I'm not that sick? If it's only a tummy-ache or something? Mr Branson wouldn't let me back. The only scoop of my life. And I'm scared!'

O'Hare said: 'It's more than a tummy-ache, lassie.'

'You can come back,' Branson said. 'But only if you do what the doctor and I say.' He nodded towards the door and stepped down. 'What do you think really is the matter with her?'

'A doctor doesn't have to discuss a patient with a layman.' O'Hare was showing every symptom of losing his patience. 'And I can tell you this, Branson. Make off with half a billion dollars and you'll probably end up as some kind of folk hero. It's happened often before, although not, admittedly, on this scale. But let this girl die because you denied her access to medical care and you'll become the most hated man in America. They'll never stop till they get you. To start with, the CIA will find you wherever you are in the world – and they won't bother to bring you to trial.'

Branson showed no signs of losing his patience. He said mildly: 'You don't have to threaten me, Doctor. She'll get her medical care. I'm just asking as a favour.'

'In confidence?' Branson nodded. 'You don't have to be a doctor to see that she's a pretty sick kid. But there are more than one way of being sick. Is she threatened with appendicitis or peritonitis? I don't think so. She's an excitable, intense, highly-strung kid who lives on her nerves. Under pressure, as of now, those could produce an emotional trauma or psychosomatic disorders which are capable of causing the symptoms we've just seen. It's rare, but it exists. In medicine, there's a condition called the Malthusian syndrome where a person can actually will himself into producing – faking, if you want to call it that – symptoms of a non-existent disease. Not in this case – if it is what I think it is, it's involuntary. But you see my position – I can't take chances. She may require intensive medical diagnosis or psychiatric evaluation. The first I can do myself, but I need hospital equipment. The second I can't – I'm not a psychiatrist. Either way I must get to hospital. We're wasting time.'

'I won't keep you long. Do you mind if we search your ambulance?'

O'Hare stared at him. 'What the hell for? What do you think I'm carrying? Bodies? Narcotics – well, quite a lot, really. What do you think I would be taking off this bridge that I didn't bring on to it? I'm a doctor, not an FBI agent.'

'We'll forget it. Another question. Do you mind if we send a guard along – for observation purposes?'

'Send half a dozen. They'll get damned little observation done.'

'What's that supposed to mean?'

'It means that Harben – he's chief of surgery – cherishes his unit like a new-born baby. He wouldn't give a damn about you and your bridge. If any of your men tried to force their way into emergency reception of the emergency theatre he'd have a dozen sharp-shooters there in ten minutes. I'm not joking – I've seen him do it.'

'We'll forget that, too. It's unimportant.'

'One thing that is important. Will you phone, ask them to have the emergency operating theatre ready and Dr Huron standing by.'

'Dr Huron?'

'Senior psychiatrist.'

'Right.' Branson smiled faintly. 'Do you know that a Presidential route is always laid out so that it's never more than a few minutes from the nearest hospital? Just in case. Convenient, isn't it?'

'Very.' O'Hare turned to the driver. 'Start the siren.'

As the ambulance moved towards the south tower they were

passed by a TV van and generator truck coming the other way. Immediately, cameramen, photographers and reporters began moving into what they assumed would be the same TV arena as before. Some cameramen were so overcome by the occasion that they began wasting film on the forthcoming truck as if this were an unprecedented spectacle in itself.

Revson was not one of those who joined in the surge forward. He moved in the opposite direction and regained his seat in the deserted press coach. He unclipped the base of his camera, removed the miniaturized transceiver, slipped it into a side pocket, reached into his carrier bag and fed spare film into the base of his camera. He was just reclipping the base of his camera when he became aware of being watched. He looked up. Blue eyes under blond hair, a head the approximate shape of a sugar cube and a vacuous smile. Revson believed in that vacuous smile the way he believed in Santa Claus. Branson would have settled for nothing less than an exceptional man when picking his lieutenant.

'Revson, isn't it?'

'Yes. Van Effen, I believe.'

'Yes. Why aren't you out there with the others, recording this historical moment for posterity?'

'First, what is there to record yet? Second, the big eye of TV can do a damned sight better job of posterity-recording than I can do. Third, if you'll excuse the hackneyed phrase, what I'm after is the human interest angle. Fourthly, I prefer to load in the shadow.'

'That looks a most exceptional camera.'

'It is.' Revson permitted himself a small proprietary smile that almost bordered on a smirk. 'Hand-made and assembled. Swedish. A rare species. The only camera in the world that can take colour stills, black and white stills and is a ciné camera at the same time.'

'May I have a look? I'm a bit of a camera buff myself.'

'Certainly.' The battery-powered air-conditioning in the coach, Revson thought, was falling down on the job.

Van Effen examined the camera with the eye of a connoisseur. Inadvertently, as it seemed, his hand touched the spring clip at the base. A dozen cassettes and spools tumbled on to the seat beside Revson.

'I *am* sorry. It would seem that I'm not all that much of a camera buff.' He inverted the camera and looked with admiration at the recessed base. 'Very very ingenious.' While Revson sat, acutely conscious of the slight bulge caused by the transceiver in his side pocket, Van Effen meticulously replaced cassettes and spools in the base, closed the flap and handed the camera back to Revson. 'Excuse my curiosity.'

'Well, you went to the right finishing school, anyway.'

'It always shows.' Van Effen gave him his vacuous smile and left.

Revson did not mop his brow for it was a gesture alien to his nature. Had he been a brow-mopper, he would have done so. He wondered if Van Effen had noticed the two tiny spring clips in the base. He probably had. Had he realized their significance? Equally probably not. They could have been the retaining clips for any number of esoteric attachments.

Revson turned in his seat. The hostages were descending from their coach, the President manfully substituting for his black scowl a calm, resolute and statesmanlike expression. Even Van Effen, Revson saw, had his eyes on them. Revson left the coach by the door opposite the driver's so that he was on the blind side of all the spectators and participants. He leaned his elbows in brief contemplation on the outer rail, then opened his right hand, the one that held the transceiver. He had read somewhere that it took a solid object, accelerating at thirty-two feet per second, only three seconds to fall from the bridge to the Golden Gate and he gravely doubted whether the man responsible for those figures could count. Nobody had noticed anything amiss. Revson had covered his bets again.

He made his unhurried and silent entry into the coach again, closed the door quietly behind him and emerged, much less quietly, from the opposite door. Van Effen turned, smiled vaguely, then turned back his attention to the circus on hand.

As before, Branson had everything stage-managed to perfection, hostages and newsmen seated in their proper places, ciné and still cameramen strategically positioned although, this time, there was one minor but significant difference from the previous occasion. This time Branson had two TV cameras instead of one. Without further ado Branson, calm, relaxed and as assured as ever, re-embarked upon his psychological warfare. Apart from being a born general and a born stage manager, he could also have been a born anchor-man on TV.

He divided his attention fairly evenly between the TV lens and those seated beside him. After a wholly unnecessary introduction of himself, the President, the King and the Prince, his first reference, not unsurprisingly, was to cameras.

'We have, this afternoon, two television cameras with us. One for the illustrious company you are now viewing, the other facing the other way towards the south or San Franciscan shore. The second one is a tracking camera with a telephoto zoom lens, that, up to half a mile, can give the clarity of resolution that one would expect at the distance of ten feet. As there is no trace of fog this afternoon it should be able to perform its function admirably. Its function is as follows.'

Branson lifted the canvas cover from a large, rectangular box then, microphone in hand, went and sat in a specially reserved vacant chair by the President. He gestured towards the object he had just unveiled.

'A courtesy gesture towards our assembled guests. A rather splendid colour TV set. No better obtainable anywhere. American, of course.'

The President had to make himself heard. After all, most of the so-called civilized eyes in the world were upon him. He said, with heavy sarcasm and a cold distaste: 'I'll wager you haven't paid for your TV set, Branson.'

'That's hardly relevant. The point is that I don't want to make you and your guests feel like second-class and deprived citizens. All the world will be able to see in close detail how we are going to attach the first of our explosive charges to one of the cables by the south tower and I feel it would be unjust to deprive you of the same privilege. After all, at a distance of over two thousand feet and an elevation of over five hundred feet, it would be difficult for even the keenest-eyed to appreciate the finer points of this operation. But the box here will show you everything you want.' Branson smiled. 'Or don't want. Now, please direct your attention to the vehicle descending the ramp from the rear coach.'

They so directed their attention. What they saw could also be seen on the TV set before them. The vehicle looked like a stripped-down, miniaturized golf-cart. It was self-propelled but silent, clearly electrically powered. The driver, Peters, stood on a tiny platform at the rear immediately over the batteries. On the flat steel platform before him was a large coil of very thin rope and, at the very front, a small, double-drummed winch.

At the foot of the ramp, Peters stopped the vehicle. Four men appeared from the rear of the coach. The first two were carrying an obviously very heavy canvas strap of explosives – similar to the one that Branson had earlier demonstrated on TV. This they deposited, very carefully indeed, on the vehicle's platform beside the rope. The other two men carried objects about eight feet in length: one was a boat-hook, the other an H-sectioned steel beam with butterfly screw clamps at one end and a built-in pulley at the other.

'The tools of our trade,' Branson said. 'You should be able to guess what they're all for but in any event this will be explained to you when they are put to use. Two things are of particular interest: the explosives and the rope. That strap of explosives is ten feet long and contains thirty bee-hives of high explosive, each five pounds in weight: the rope, which is a quarter of a mile long, looks, and is, thinner than the average clothes-line, but, as it is made of steel-cored nylon, has a breaking strain of eight hundred pounds which is exactly five times as much as will be required of it.' He gestured to Peters, who nodded, eased open the circular control wheel and trundled off in the direction of the south tower. Branson looked directly at the TV lens.

He said: 'For those of you who don't know, and apart from the citizens of San Francisco there will be many who will not know, those towers are something less than solid structures.' On the TV set before him and on countless millions of sets throughout the world, the south tower came into sharp, close focus. 'These towers consist of steel framework boxes called cells. Each is about the size of a phone booth, but twice as high, riveted together and connected by manholes. Each tower consists of over five thousand such cells. They contain elevators and ladders – a rather staggering twenty-three miles of them.'

He reached under his seat and brought up a manual.

'As you will appreciate, it would be very easy for the inexperienced to get lost inside this labyrinth. Once, when they were building this bridge, two men spent the entire night inside the north tower trying to find their way out and, indeed, Joseph Strauss, the designer and builder of this bridge, was capable of getting completely lost inside the tower. It was with this in mind that Strauss produced this twenty-six-page manual – well, not this one, this is a facsimile I was fortunate enough to come by – instructing inspectors how to find their way about inside the towers.

'At this moment, two of my men, each with a copy of this manual – although they hardly need them, they're using the elevator – are at, or nearing, the top of the east tower there, the one facing towards the bay. They are carrying with them nothing except a fifteen-pound weight, the purpose of which you will shortly discover. May we observe the progress of our electric truck, please?'

The telephoto TV camera obligingly descended and closed on Peters, travelling along the wrong side of the bridge. Even as they watched, it slowed and came to a halt almost directly under the lowest of the four massive cross-struts of the south tower.

Branson said: 'Elevation, please.'

Again the telephoto camera focused on the saddle – the curved steel housing over which the cable passed – on the bayside tower. Almost immediately two men came into sight by the saddle, tiny figures for those directly observing from the middle of the bridge, close-up for those looking at the TV screens.

'On cue, on time,' Branson said with some satisfaction. 'In those matters, co-ordination is of the essence. I dare say that not one in ten thousand of you would care to be where those two men are now. Quite frankly, neither would I. One misstep and it's over seven hundred and fifty feet down to the Golden Gate: only a seven-second fall but at a hundred and seventy miles an hour hitting water is no different from hitting solid concrete. But those two are as safe as you would be in a church pew. Spidermen, they're called – the workers you can see standing on girders a thousand feet above the streets of New York or Chicago when they're building a new skyscraper.'

The camera closed on Peters again. He produced a pistol, unusual as to both length of barrel and width of muzzle, took brief aim upwards and fired. Neither camera could track nor eye see the nature of the missile ejected: what the camera did show, four seconds after firing, was that Bartlett, one of the men by the saddle, had a green cord safely in his hands. He reeled this in swiftly. At the end of the cord was a leather-hung pulley, which in turn was attached to one end of the rope. Two and a half minutes elapsed before the rope was in Bartlett's hands.

He held this securely while his partner, Boyard, undid both cord and pulley. Bartlett reeled in about another dozen feet, cut this section off with a knife and handed it to Boyard, who secured one end to a strut and another to the strap of the pulley. The rope was then passed through the pulley, through a hole at its top, to a pear-shaped lead weight which the men had brought up with them. Both weight and rope were then released and sank swiftly down to bridge level again.

Peters caught the weight, undid the knot that secured the rope but did not withdraw the rope. Instead he passed it through the pulley in the steel beam and a ring at the end of the boat-hook and secured all three together. He took a few turns of the other end of the rope round one of the drums of the winch and started up the electric motor.

The winch, though small, was powerful and fast. From bridge to saddle took less than a minute and a half. There was a gentle breeze blowing from the north, apparently freshening as the altitude increased, and the rope and its burden swayed quite noticeably, striking each of the cross-struts, at times quite forcibly, on the way up. Peters seemed unconcerned, his gaze fixed on Bartlett. As the rope and its cargo neared the top Bartlett made a horizontal waving motion of his arm. Peters eased the winch drum to a crawl. Bartlett made a slow upwards beckoning motion with his arm then stretched it out horizontally. Peters unwound the rope after stopping the winch, leaving only one turn on the drum.

Bartlett and Boyard pulled in the beam and boat-hook, detached them along with the lead weight, passed the rope through the pulley and resecured the lead weight. They then eased out the H-beam for a distance of about six feet then clamped the inner end to a strut, tightening the butterfly nuts to their maximum. Bartlett signalled Peters who took the last turn off the drum. Weight and rope sank rapidly downwards.

Two minutes later the rope was on its way up again, this time with the canvas strap of explosives which dangled at its full length, fastened to the rope by two heavy metal buckles at one end of the strap. Unlike the previous occasion Peters now moved with great caution, the drum moving very slowly and occasionally stopping altogether. General Cartland commented on this to Branson.

'Your winchman is trying to eliminate all sway?'

'Yes. We don't want that strap of explosives to bang against one of the cross-struts.'

'Of course. I'd forgotten how sensitive fulminate of mercury detonators are.'

'The detonators are in Bartlett's pocket. But the primers can be temperamental too. That's why we have that extended beam up top – to give clearance. Also, it's asking a bit much for even two strong men to haul a hundred and sixty pounds – not a hundredweight as you estimated, General – over five hundred feet vertically upwards.'

They watched the explosive safely negotiate the second top cross-strut. Cartland said: 'So it's one strap there, one on the opposite cable and the other two at the north tower?'

'No. We've changed our minds on that. We suspect that the suspension cables – and don't forget that there are over twenty-seven thousand spun wires inside that steel sheath – may be considerably stronger than the mock-up we used for the test. So we're going to use all four explosive straps at the south tower, a pair on each cable. That will leave no margin for doubt. And if the south end of the bridge falls into the Golden Gate it seems reasonable to expect that the north end will follow suit. Whether the north tower – don't forget it will then be bearing most of the weight of the four-thousand-two-hundred-feet span – will be pulled down too we haven't been able to determine but it seems pretty close to a certainty.'

Van Effen took two quick steps forwards and clicked off the safety catch on his machine-pistol. Mayor Morrison, half out of his seat, slowly subsided back into it but his fists were still tightly clenched, his eyes still mad.

By now, Bartlett and Boyard had the boat-hook round the rope and were steadily, cautiously and without too much trouble, overhanding the explosives in towards themselves. Soon it disappeared out of the range of the telephoto TV camera. So, immediately afterwards, did all of Bartlett except for head and shoulders.

'Inserting the detonators?' Cartland asked. Branson nodded and Cartland gestured to the section of the cable nearest them. At that point, in the centre of the bridge, the cable dipped until it.was almost within arm's length. 'Why go to all that immense labour? Wouldn't it have been easier just to fix the charges here?'

'Easier, yes, but there's no guarantee that severing the cables in mid-bridge would bring the bridge down. There's no way of knowing: what's for sure is that no one has ever carried out a control test or experiment on this sort of thing. Suspension bridges come expensive. If the cables were severed here the towers, as far as weight is concerned, would still be in a fair state of equilibrium. Bridge might sag a little or a lot, it might break but it wouldn't drop the whole span clear into the water. My way, success is guaranteed. You wouldn't expect me to charge two hundred million for a botched-up job, would you?'

General Cartland didn't say whether he would or he wouldn't.

'Besides, if things go wrong, that is, if you turn out to be stingy with the money, I intend to trigger off the explosives immediately we take off. I don't want to be within half a mile of six hundred pounds of high explosives when it goes up.'

The President said carefully: 'You mean the triggering device is aboard one of those helicopters?'

Branson gave a patient sigh. 'I've always maintained that all Presidential candidates should undergo an IQ test. Of course it is. In the nearest one. What did you expect me to do? Press a button inside a coach and then go down with the coach and bridge to the bottom of the Golden Gate?'

Branson removed his disbelieving gaze from the President and returned it to the TV screen before him. Bartlett, with Boyard steadying him, had the canvas strip wrapped round the cable, hard up against the saddle and was buckling tight the second of the two straps that held the strap securely in position. That done, he moved back along with Boyard to admire their handiwork. The camera then left them and zeroed in on the section of cable wrapped in the lethal embrace of the high explosive.

Branson smiled broadly. 'Well, now, isn't that a perfectly splendid sight?'

Cartland remained poker-faced. 'It all depends upon your point of view.'

SEVEN

Vice-President Richards switched off the TV set. He looked thoughtful, shocked and concerned all at one and the same time. When he spoke, those emotions were reflected in his voice.

'That was a remarkably effective performance. One has to confess that our villainous friend appears to know exactly what he is about and has the total ability to carry out his numerous threats. At least, that is how I see it, but I'm just a newcomer to the scene. Do you gentlemen see it any differently?'

The Vice-President was a tall, genial, loquacious southerner, much given to slapping – one could not call it clapping – the unwary rather painfully on the back and was an internationally-known gourmet, a fact amply testified to by his ample figure. He was far from being the nincompoop Hagenbach had alleged – Hagenbach's opinion stemmed from the fact that theirs were two totally differing personalities: he was forceful, shrewd, intelligent and was remarkably well informed on a very wide range of topics: if he had one fault it was that he had, unlike Hagenbach, a consuming desire for power. Branson had hardly been exaggerating when he had suggested that a yearning look came into Richards's eyes whenever he entered the Oval Office in the White House.

Richards looked, without much hope, around the company assembled in the office of the hospital supervisor. Hagenbach, Hendrix and the two Secretaries sat around a small table. Newson and Carter, as if to demonstrate the exclusivity of the highest echelons of the military, sat at a second and smaller table. O'Hare, arms folded and leaning against a radiator, wore the wry, slightly amused, slightly condescending expression that most doctors reserve for all those who are not also doctors. April Wednesday sat, quietly and alone, in a corner chair.

From the silence that followed it was clear that none of the gentlemen present saw it any differently.

Richards's geniality yielded to a certain amount of testiness. 'You, Hagenbach, what do you propose to do?'

Hagenbach restrained himself. Even though he was the head of the FBI he had to pay his due respect, albeit lip-service respect, to the Vice-President.

'I suggest we await the transcription of Revson's message, sir.'

'Transcription! Transcription! Was it necessary for this man of yours to complicate things by sending in code?'

'On the face of it, no. Revson has a near-mania for secrecy, that must be admitted, and is extraordinarily security-conscious. The same might be said about myself. Agreed, the message came through with safety and ease. On the other hand, as Miss Wednesday here has testified, Branson did contemplate searching the ambulance. With the proverbial toothcomb, he might have come up with something. But not with this microfilm.' He looked up as a young man, dressed in the immaculate conservative grey of a Wall Street broker, came through the doorway and handed him two typed sheets of paper.

'Sorry it took so long, sir. It was a bit difficult.'

'So is Revson.' Hagenbach read quickly through the papers, totally oblivious of the impatience of the others. He looked up at the young man. 'You like and you value your position in our organization, Jacobs?'

'You don't have to say that, sir.'

Hagenbach tried to smile but, as ever, failed to crack the ice barrier. 'I apologize.' It was a measure of Hagenbach's concern over the matter in hand that he had never previously been heard to say sorry to anyone.

'You don't have to say that either, sir.' Jacobs left the room.

Hagenbach said: 'This is what Revson says. "To give you the maximum time to obtain what I require for my immediate needs, I will state those first of all." '

Admiral Newson coughed. 'Do your subordinates usually address you in such a peremptory tone?'

'Not usually. He goes on: "I want four hundred yards of blue or green thin cord, cylindrical waterfront containers for written messages and a variably hooded morse-flashlight. Then I would like an aerosol, two pens – one white, one red, – and a CAP air pistol. Please order those immediately. Without them, I cannot hope to operate." '

General Carter said: 'Goobledook. What are those terms supposed to mean?'

Hagenbach said: 'I am not sure if I should tell you. That does not refer to you personally, General. Senior officers, cabinet ministers and, of course, senior police officers, are entitled to be privy to such information. But there are – ah – civilians present.'

O'Hare said mildly: 'Doctors don't talk. What's more, they don't leak secret information to the press either.'

Hagenbach favoured him with a very old-fashioned look then said to April: 'And you, Miss Wednesday?'

She said: 'I'd talk my head off if you as much as showed me a pair of thumb-screws. You wouldn't have to put them on, showing would be quite enough. Otherwise, no.'

Hagenbach said to Hendrix: 'How's Branson with thumb-screws and young ladies?'

'No way. Master criminal though he is he has a remarkable reputation for gallantry towards women. He has never carried out a robbery where a woman might be involved, far less hurt.'

'But Mr Revson told me – '

'I rather fancy,' Hagenbach said, 'that Revson wanted you to act scared. So he threw a scare into you.'

April Wednesday was indignant: 'Has he no scruples?'

'In private life, a model of integrity. On business – well, if he has scruples he has so far hidden the fact very well. As to those objects he asked for, the aerosol contains exactly the same knock-out nerve gas that Branson used with such effect on the bridge. No permanent damage whatsoever – the presence of Miss Wednesday testifies to that. The pens – they look like ordinary felt pens – fire tiny tipped needles that also knock out people.'

Admiral Newson said: 'Why two colours?'

'The red knocks you out a bit more permanently.'

'One assumes that a "bit more permanently" means permanently.'

'Could happen. The air pistol – well, it has the advantage of almost complete silence.'

'And the CAP bit?'

Hagenbach's hesitation betrayed a degree of reluctance. 'It means the bullets are tipped.'

'Tipped with what?'

Hagenbach's reluctance turned into something close to embarrassment.

'Cyanide.'

After a brief and understandable silence Richards said heavily: 'This Revson of yours. Is he a direct descendant of Attila the Hun?'

'He is an extremely effective operative, sir.'

'Loaded down with a lethal armoury like that, I don't for a moment doubt it. He has killed?'

'So have thousands of police officers.'

'And what's his score to date?'

'I really couldn't say, sir. In his reports, Revson lists only the essentials.'

'Only the essentials.' Richards's echo had a hollow ring to it. He shook his head and said no more.

'If you will excuse me for a moment.' Hagenbach wrote quickly on a notepad, opened the door and handed the note to a man outside. 'Have those items here within the hour.' He returned and picked up the transcript again.

'To continue. "In what little time I've had I've tried to make an assessment of Branson's character. In original concept, planning, organization and execution, the man is quite brilliant. He would have made an excellent general, for his appreciation of both strategy and tactics is masterly. But nobody can be that good. He has his failings, which I hope can be used to bring him down. He has a divine belief in his own infallibility. This belief carries with it the seeds of his own destruction. No one is infallible. Second, he is possessed of a colossal vanity. He could just as easily have held those TV interviews—I've only seen one of Branson's love affairs with the public but there are bound to be more—at, say, the south tower—but, no, he had to have it smack in the middle, surrounded by his own private press corps. In his place I would have had the whole press corps off the bridge in five minutes. It seems it just has not occurred to him that the ranks of the press corps may have been infiltrated. Third, he should have searched the doctor and Miss Wednesday and then the ambulance, if necessary throwing every single item of medical equipment into the Golden Gate, before allowing it to leave the bridge: in other words, he is not security-conscious enough.

' "How to deal with them? I have no idea yet. I would like

109

some guidance. I have suggestions but I don't think any of them is practical.

' "No one can cope with seventeen heavily armed men. But of those seventeen only two matter. Some of the other fifteen are bright but only Branson and Van Effen are natural leaders. Those two I could kill." '

'Kill!' April Wednesday's shocked green eyes stared out of her pale face. 'The man's a monster.'

Hagenbach was dry. 'At least, he's a realistic monster.' He read on. ' "It's feasible, but unwise. The others would then almost certainly over-react and I wouldn't care to be responsible for the health of the President and his friends. This is a second last resort.

' "Would it be possible to have a submarine standing by under the bridge during the hours of darkness, with only the top of the conning tower showing? I could certainly pass messages and pick up anything I wanted that way. What else, I don't know. I can't for instance, visualize the President descending two hundred feet of rope ladder. He'd fall off after ten feet.

' "When Branson's men are fixing the charges would it be possible to send a two thousand volt jolt through the cables? I know this would electrify the entire bridge but those standing on the roadway or inside the coaches should be safe enough." '

Richards said: 'Why two thousand volts?'

Hagenbach sounded almost apologetic. 'Electric chair voltage.'

'I owe an apology to the shade of Attila.'

'Yes. "One drawback to this is that someone, say the President, might be leaning his elbows on the side of the bridge or sitting on a crash barrier. That would mean a new Presidential election. I need expert advice. Or could we aim a laser beam at the charges when in position? The beam would certainly cut through the canvas. If the charge were to fall on to the bridge it would certainly detonate on impact but as most of the explosive force would be dissipated in thin air, damage to the roadway would not be severe. It is sure that it wouldn't bring the bridge down. Trouble is, the laser beam might detonate the charge instead. Please advise.

' "Under suitable cover would it be possible to introduce men into the tower? Natural fog would be fine. Phoney oil fire depending on the direction of the wind? I don't know.

110

But the thing is to get men to the top, return the lift and then cut off the power to the elevators. Any person who gets to the top after five hundred odd feet of ladders isn't going to be in much shape to do anything.

'"Is it possible to introduce some form of knock-out drugs in the food? Something that would lay them out for half an hour, maybe an hour and not too fast-acting? If anyone were to keel over with the first bite you can imagine Branson's reaction. The individual food trays would have to be marked so that seventeen of them would go to the seventeen for whom they were intended."'

Hagenbach looked at O'Hare. 'There are such drugs?'

'I'm sure of it. The concoction of Mickey Finns is not my speciality, but Dr Isaacs – he's the chief of the Drugs and Narcotics Section – knows as much about those brews as anyone in the country. Catherine de Medici could never have coped with him.'

'That's useful.' Hagenbach returned his attention to the final brief section of the transcript. ' "Please let me have your suggestions. All I myself can really do at the moment is to try to deactivate the radio trigger that sets off the charges without leaving any signs that it has been tampered with. That in itself should be simple. It's getting at the damned thing that's difficult. It has, of course, to be in one of the helicopters and those are bathed in light both night and day and are heavily guarded. I'll try." That's all.'

Newson said: 'You mentioned a second last resort. What's the last resort?'

'Your guess is as good as mine. If he has a last resort, he's keeping it to himself. Now, sooner than pass those notes around I'll have them Xeroxed. Minutes only and you'll each have a copy.' He left the room, approached Jacobs, the man who had handed him the typescript, and said quietly: 'Have this Xeroxed. Ten copies.' He pointed to the last paragraph. 'Blank this off. And for God's sake make sure that this original gets back to me and not anyone else.'

Jacobs was back in the promised few moments. He distributed six and handed the remaining copies and the original to Hagenbach, who folded the original and stuck it in an inside pocket. Then all seven carefully studied the report. And again. And again.

General Carter said, almost complainingly: 'Revson certainly doesn't leave me very much for my imagination to work on. Candidly, he doesn't leave anything. Maybe it's just not one of my days.'

'Then it's not one of mine either,' Newson said. 'Your man seems to have covered the ground pretty comprehensively, Hagenbach. Sounds like a very useful man to have on our side.'

'He is. But even Revson requires room to manoeuvre. He has none.'

Quarry said, tentatively: 'I know this is not my field but it occurs to me that the key lies in the helicopters. We have the means to destroy those?'

Carter said: 'That's no problem. Planes, guns, rockets, wire-guided anti-tank missiles. Why?'

'That's the only way Branson and his men can leave. And as long as he remains on the bridge he can't detonate his charges. So what happens then?'

Carter looked at the Secretary of the Treasury without admiration.

'I can think of three things. First, Branson would call for a mobile crane, have it dump the choppers into the Golden Gate and demand two replacements within the hour or he'd send us a neat little parcel containing the President's ears. Second, whether it's a shell, rocket or missile, it's impossible to localize or contain the blast effect and some innocent bystanders might end up in the same condition as the choppers. Third, has it occurred to you that though the blast might well destroy the radio-activating device for the explosive charge, it might equally well trigger it off? Even with only one end of one cable gone that bridge is going to sag and assume a crazy angle in nothing flat, and nothing that is not nailed down would have a hope of remaining on that bridge. If that were to happen, Mr Secretary, and the President and his guests knew you were the man responsible, I don't think that their last thoughts of you, as they sat there in their coach at the bottom of the Golden Gate, would be very charitable ones.'

Quarry sighed. 'I'd better stick to counting my pennies. I told you this wasn't my field.'

Richards said: 'I suggest we all have twenty minutes' silent meditation and see what we come up with.'

They did just that and when the twenty minutes were up Hagenbach said: 'Well?'

All, apparently, was not well. The silence was profound.

'In that case, I suggest we start considering which are the less awful of Revson's options.'

The return of the ambulance to the centre of the bridge at about six o'clock in the evening was greeted with warmth and interest. Even being in the spotlight of the eyes of the world loses its dramatic effect if one has nothing to do. Branson's TV broadcasts apart, the middle of the bridge offered little in the way of entertainment.

When April, pale-faced and still apparently shaken, stepped from the ambulance, Branson was the first to greet her.

'How do you feel?'

'I feel such a fool.' She rolled up a sleeve to exhibit the punctures O'Hare had inflicted upon her earlier in the day. 'Two little pricks and I'm as right as rain.'

She walked away and sat down rather heavily on one of the many chairs scattered around her. Her colleagues gathered round.

Branson said to O'Hare: 'She doesn't look as right as rain to me.'

'If you mean she's still not back to normal, I agree. Same appearance, different causes. Last time you saw her she was on a high: now it's a low. My guess was right, it seems — just an emotional trauma. She's been sound asleep for the past two hours under heavy sedation. Dopey, that's all. Dr Huron, the psychiatrist, didn't want her to return, but she made such a damned noise about not getting back and this being her last chance or whatever that he decided that it might be better for her to return. No worry. I've brought back enough of the same sedative to last us for a week out here.'

'For the sake of all of us, let's hope you won't need a quarter of it.'

Revson waited until the last of April's welcomers had left her for the TV, a show of peculiar interest to all as the programme was devoted exclusively to a re-run of Branson's early afternoon broadcast. Nobody, Revson was unsurprised to observe, was more interested than Branson himself. But then Branson had no more to occupy his time than anyone else. The only person who seemed remotely active was Chrysler, who visited the rear coach at regular intervals. He wondered why.

Revson sat beside the girl. She looked at him coldly.

He said: 'What's the matter with you?' She remained silent. 'Don't tell me. Somebody's been turning you against me.'

'Yes. You. I don't like killers. Especially I don't like killers who plan their next murders cold-bloodedly in advance.'

'Come, come. That's putting it a bit strongly.'

'Is it? Cyanide guns? Lethal pens? Shot through the back, I should imagine.'

'My, my, we are bitter. Three things. First, those weapons are used only in acute emergency and then only to save lives, to stop bad people killing good people, although perhaps you would rather have it the other way round. Second, it doesn't matter to a dead man where he has been shot. Third, you have been eavesdropping.'

'I was invited to listen.'

'People make mistakes. Clearly, they invited the wrong person. I could be flippant and say I owe a duty to the tax-payer, but I'm not in the mood.' April looked at the hard face, listened to the voice from which all trace of the normal bantering warmth had vanished and realized with apprehension that indeed he was not in the mood. 'I have a job to do, you don't know what you're talking about, so we'll dispense with your moral strictures. I assume you brought the equipment I asked for. Where is it?'

'I don't know. Dr O'Hare does. For some reason he didn't want me to know in case we were questioned and the ambulance searched.'

'For some reason! For an obvious and excellent reason. O'Hare is no fool.' A flush touched the pale cheeks but he ignored it. 'All of it?'

'So I believe.' She tried to speak stiffly.

'Never mind your wounded pride. And don't forget you're in this up to your lovely neck. Hagenbach have any instructions for me?'

'Yes. But he didn't tell me. He told Dr O'Hare.' Her voice was acid or bitter or both. 'I suppose that makes Mr Hagenbach no fool either.'

'Don't take those things so much to heart.' He patted her hand and smiled warmly. 'You've done an excellent job. Thank you.'

She tried a tentative smile. 'Maybe you are a little bit human after all, Mr Revson.'

'Paul. One never knows.' He smiled again, rose and left. At least, he thought, he was semi-human enough not to inflict further damage upon her *amour propre* by telling her that the last little bit of by-play had been purely for the benefit of Branson who had momentarily lost interest in the screen – he was not then on camera – and was casting a speculative look at them. Not that that necessarily meant anything suspicious or sinister. Branson was much given to casting speculative looks at everybody. April was beautiful and he may well have thought that she was wasting this beauty on the wrong company.

Revson sat on a seat not far from Branson and watched the last twenty minutes of the broadcast. The inter-cutting between the Presidential group and the top of the south tower had been most skilfully done and the overall impact was all that Branson could ever have wished. Branson watched it intently. His face betrayed no particular sign of satisfaction, but then Branson's face registered precisely what he wanted it to and was no mirror of his inner thoughts and feelings. When the broadcast finished Branson rose and stopped briefly by Revson's chair.

'Revson, isn't it?' Revson nodded. 'And how does all this strike you?'

'Just the same as it strikes a million other people, I guess.' This was it, Revson thought, this is one part of his Achilles' heel. Branson knew he was a genius but he had no objection to people saying so. 'A feeling of total unreality. This just can't be happening.'

'But it is, isn't it? A very satisfactory beginning, don't you think?'

'I can quote?'

'Certainly. Call it an exclusive if you want. How do you see the scenario developing?'

'Just as you have programmed it. I can't see anything to stop you. You have them, most unfortunately, at your total mercy.'

'Most unfortunately?'

'What else? I don't want to overdo the American citizen bit and although you may be a master criminal, a genius in your own immoral fashion, to me you're still a crook, a crook so bent as to make a spiral staircase look like a fireman's ladder.'

'I rather like that. I may quote you in turn?' Branson seemed genuinely gratified. One could hardly have called him thinskinned.

'There's no verbal copyright.'

'Alas, universal disapproval, not to say disapprobation, would seem to be my lot.' Branson didn't sound too unhappy about it. 'That's a most unusual camera you have there.'

'Almost, but not quite unique.'

'May I have a look at it?'

'If you wish. But if you want to examine it for the reasons I imagine you want to examine it then you're about four hours too late.'

'What is that supposed to mean?'

'It means that your very able lieutenant, Van Effen, has the same nasty suspicious mind as you have. He has already taken my camera apart.'

'No radios? No offensive weapons?'

'Look for yourself.'

'That won't be necessary now.'

'A question. I don't want to inflate your already superexpanded ego –'

'Don't you think you might be taking chances, Revson?'

'No. You have the reputation of being a non-violent criminal.' Revson waved his arm. 'Why all this? You could have made a fortune in any business you cared to enter.'

Branson sighed. 'I tried it. Business is so dull, don't you think? This at least gives me the opportunity to exercise most of my capacities.' He paused. 'You're a bit odd, yourself. A cameraman. You don't look, act or speak like one.'

'How's a cameraman supposed to look, act and speak? You look in the mirror when you shave. Do you see a criminal? I see a Wall Street Vice-President.'

'*Touché*. What's your paper or magazine?'

'Free-lance, but I'm accredited to the London *Times*.'

'But you're American?'

'News has no boundaries. Not any longer. I prefer to work the foreign beat, where the action is.' Revson smiled faintly. 'At least, until today. That used to mean South-East Asia. Not any more. Europe and the Middle East.'

'So what are you doing here?'

'Pure happenstance. Just passing through, you might say, from New York to a special assignment in China.'

'When are you due to leave for there?'

'Tomorrow.'

'Tomorrow? You'll want to get off the bridge tonight. As I've said, members of the media are free to leave whenever they choose.'

'You, Branson, must be out of your mind.'

'China can wait?'

'China can wait. Unless, of course, you're planning to kidnap Chairman Mao.'

Branson smiled the smile that never touched his eyes and walked away.

Revson, camera poised, stood outside the open front right door of the rear coach. He said: 'Do you mind?'

Chrysler turned round. He looked at Revson in some surprise, then smiled. 'Why me for this honour?'

'Because my camera is tired of taking photographs of Branson and the assorted big-wigs. Mind? I'm now compiling a rogues' gallery of Branson's henchmen.' Revson smiled to remove offence. 'You're Chrysler, aren't you? The telecommunications expert?'

'If that's what they call me, yes.'

Revson took two or three shots, thanked Chrysler, and moved away. For good measure and local colour, he took some more pictures of Branson's men. They all seemed to have been infected by Branson's massive self-confidence and cheerfully, in some cases almost eagerly, acceded to Revson's requests. After the last of those shots he crossed to the west side of the bridge, sat on the crash barrier and lit a ruminative cigarette.

After a few minutes O'Hare, hands thrust deep in his white coat, came strolling by. Hundreds of pictures and thousands of words of reports had already been dispatched by the south tower and there were at least twenty of the media men – and women – who now had nothing better to do who were strolling aimlessly up and down the centre of the bridge. Revson took a couple of routine shots of O'Hare, who came and sat beside him.

He said: 'I saw you talking to Miss Wednesday. Suffering from a degree of pique, is she?'

'Our April could be happier. You have it all?'

'Both weapons and instructions.'

'Everything I asked for is camouflaged?'

'I would say so. The two pens are clipped to my medical clipboard, there for anyone to see. We doctors are models of efficiency. The gun with the tipped bullets is in the cardiac arrest unit. This is wax-sealed and the seal has to be broken before the unit can be opened. The unit is sealed. Not that it would matter very much if it were opened. The gun lies in a false bottom and you have to know how to open it. I mean, it can't be done by accident. You have to know. I know.'

'You seem to be positively enjoying yourself, Doctor.'

'Well, yes. It makes a change from treating ingrowing toe-nails.'

'I hope you'll enjoy coming under the heading of "Classified" for the rest of your life. How come you carry those peculiar units in your hospital?'

'We don't. But your director appears to be on very close terms with his counterpart in the CIA. I tell you, we were completely taken over by experts.'

'That means you're double classified for life. My cord and containers?' O'Hare seemed a mile away.

'My cord and containers?' O'Hare returned to the world.

'Modesty compels me to admit that I came up with this one. Four containers. Empty. Lab. samples printed on the outside. Who's going to question that? The cord is wrapped round a square wooden framework with two hooks and two lures attached to one end.'

'You're going fishing over the side of the bridge?'

'I'm going fishing. It can get quite boring out here, you know.'

'Something tells me it's not going to be that way long. I suppose it's unnecessary to ask you about the nerve gas?'

O'Hare smiled broadly. 'I'd rather you did, actually.'

'Must you speak English English?'

'I told you. London educated. It's an aerosol can, clamped just above my note-desk. Anyone can see it. Product, ostensibly, of a nationally-known aerosol company. People called Prestige Fragrance of New York. Rather charming, really. The colour, I mean. Forest brown, I believe. A scaled-down version of their seven-ounce can. Freon pressure three times normal.

Effective range ten feet.'

'Do the Prestige people know about this?'

'Heavens, no. The CIA are not overly concerned with patent rights.' O'Hare smiled, almost dreamily. 'On the back of the can it says "fragrant and piquant" and "keep away from children". On the front it says "Sandalwood". Can't you just see Branson or any of his minions who don't know what sandalwood smells like giving themselves an exploratory whiff?'

'No, I can't. I'll pick up the pens later tonight. Now, what were Hagenbach's instructions?'

'Hagenbach and company. A committee meeting and an agreed decision. The Vice-President was there, along with Admiral Newson, General Carter, Hendrix, Quarry and Milton.'

'And yourself and April Wednesday.'

'We plebs know our place. Total silence on our part. First off, there's no possibility of electrifying the bridge. Nothing to do with the possibility of a President or king sitting where we are now and having their pants roasted. The voltage could be produced, but not the wattage. Not for umpteen thousand tons of steel. Besides, the potential victims would have to be earthed. A bird can perch in perfect safety on a high-tension wire.

'Second piece of expert advice was about laser beams. You wondered if they would slice through the canvas wrapping of the explosive belts. Certainly, say the boys in Berkeley. But the tremendous heat generated when a laser beam strikes a solid object would turn the bridge wire – I think that's what they called it – in the detonator white-hot immediately.'

'Poof?'

'As you so rightly observe, "poof". Four things they did agree on, however.

'A submarine they can provide. Apparently, it will call for some critical underwater navigation to get there and a fair bit of fancy juggling to keep the boat in position once it gets there. Apart from the tides there are lots of very nasty currents in the Golden Gate. But the Admiral reckons he has just the man for the job. And in the absence of any instructions to the contrary they propose to park this boat under the front coach, your press coach, that is.'

'My omission. They're right, of course.' Revson glanced idly round but no one was paying any undue attention to them except General Cartland, a physical fitness fanatic who was counter-marching briskly to and fro along the central section of the bridge. Hè gave them a keen glance in passing but that signified nothing. General Cartland invariably gave everyone a keen glance in passing. Hansen, the energy czar, with the excess nervous energy to burn, was also engaged in the same exercise, but his attention was devoted exclusively to the toes of his shoes. He did not walk with Cartland. There was no antipathy between the two men: they simply had nothing in common.

O'Hare continued. 'They agreed with your suggestion that the south tower be occupied. As you didn't specify whether it was the east or west section which should be occupied, they're a bit in the dark. The meteorological forecast is rather good. Heavy fog is expected before dawn and to remain until about ten in the morning. They'd better be right. The wind tomorrow will be westerly so that any cover from the smoke of burning oil will be out of the question. But they still don't know which section of the tower to occupy.'

'One item I forgot to ask you about. It was about this hooded flashlight with the variable shutter that – '

'I have it.'

'If Branson and company come across it?'

'Medical requisite, my dear fellow. Eye examination, dilation of pupils and so forth. You know morse?'

Revson was patient. 'I just want to read books at night in the coach.'

'Sorry. One of my off-moments. From the east side of the bridge aim approximately forty-five degrees right. They'll have two men on watch in relays, all night. They can't signal you back, of course, so for "message acknowledged and understood" they'll send up a firework rocket from China-town. Followed by lots of others so as not to arouse any suspicions. The setting off of fireworks, bangers, crackers or whatever you call them is illegal in this city, but in China-town the police bend a tolerant and indulgent eye towards it. Chinese national pastime, you know. You should see the Chinese New Year. Shortly after I arrived – just a few months ago – '

Revson was even more patient. 'I am a San Franciscan.'

'Ah, well. But you still don't know which section of the south tower – '

'I'll find out.'

'You seem very sure of yourself?'

'Not at all. But I'm sure of our April Wednesday. Branson has given her more than a passing glance. I shall have her employ her feminine wiles to discover which cable is next for the explosive treatment. And when.'

'You're still very sure of yourself. Now. Your suggestion about drugged food. Unanimous approval. This evening meal. Dr Isaacs – he's our narcotics wizard in the hospital – has been busy stirring up his witch's cauldron. Seventeen unpleasant surprises.'

'Very quick work.' Revson was uneasy. 'How are the surprises to be identified?'

'No problem. The usual airline plastic food in the usual airline plastic trays. Those trays have carrying lugs. The bad trays, if I may put it that way, will have indentations on the underside of the lugs. Tiny, but enough to be detected by normally sensitive finger-tips.'

'Well, Doctor, you haven't been wasting your time, that I have to say. Obviously we'll have to be very careful. If anything can go wrong it will go wrong – one of Parkinson's laws or something like that. I shall appoint myself head waiter with Branson's prior approval. Second, you will have April Wednesday in for a routine check as the meal wagon arrives and will remain there until the meals have been distributed. In the ambulance, I mean.'

'Why?'

'Parkinson's Law. If something goes wrong, you two would be the first under suspicion – you've left the bridge and returned. Third, I can get word to the Presidential coach.'

'How?'

'I'll figure a way.'

'And the press coach?'

'No guarantee. I'm no master-mind. If one or two of them get the wrong trays – well, I can take care of the one or two villains who get the right trays.'

O'Hare looked at Revson with a certain lack of admiration. 'You don't care how you use people, do you?'

'I have things to do and I do what I can. I weigh the odds

but I don't know what the odds are.' Revson paused. 'I'm fighting in the dark. I'm a blind man, if you like, and my hands are tied behind me. Perhaps you'd care to think again about your last remark.'

O'Hare thought. 'I apologize. Your pens and the flashlight will be waiting whenever you care to step by. And one last thing. They approve your intention to neutralize the triggering device.'

'I appreciate that. You don't have any magic potion that will make me invisible?'

'Alas, no.' O'Hare turned and walked away.

Revson lit and smoked another cigarette, tossed the butt over the side, rose and sauntered across to the rows of chairs. April was still sitting where he had left her. He took the seat beside her.

He said: 'When the evening meal wagon comes I want you to go to the ambulance. For a check-up.'

She didn't look at him. 'Yes, sir. Whatever you say, sir.

Revson breathed deeply. 'I shall try to conceal my slow burn, what the Victorians would call my mounting exasperation. I thought we had parted friends.'

'I don't much care for being a mindless puppet.'

'We're all puppets. I, too, do what I'm told. I don't always like it, but I have a job to do. Please don't make my job more difficult than it already is. The doctor will tell you why you're there. He'll also tell you when to leave.'

'Yes, Mr Revson. As a forcibly co-opted member of your secret service, I do what I'm told.'

Revson decided against any more deep breathing. 'Before that, I'd like you to have a word with our Mr Branson. I fancy he has one, if not two, of his cold codfish eyes upon you.'

She turned her head slowly and gave him the full treatment of her luminous green eyes. 'And you, of course, don't?'

Revson held her gaze for some seconds, then considered the tarmac of the Golden Gate Bridge. 'I try to look the other way. Besides, my eyes are not those of a cod. Find out from him on which cable he intends to affix his next explosive charge – and when. Wait a few moments after I've left and then make a casual encounter.'

He looked at her again. The eyes were bigger and greener than ever and held an almost mischievous glint. She was smiling. It wasn't much of a smile, but it was there. She said: 'You'll end up by making me as devious and cunning as yourself.'

'Heaven forfend.' Revson rose and made his way back to his previous seat on the crash barrier, which was less than twenty yards from the demarcation painted line where a man in the middle of the bridge, with a Schmeisser machine-pistol, kept constant vigil. General Cartland, military stride *in excelsis*, was approaching. Revson stood, lifted his camera and snapped off three quick shots.

He said: 'May I have a word with you, sir?'

Cartland stopped. 'You may not. No interview, exclusive or otherwise. I may be a spectator in this damned circus, but I'm no performer.' He walked on.

Revson was deliberately brusque. 'You'd better speak to me, General.'

Cartland stopped again. His glacial stare drilled through Revson's eyes into the wide blue yonder.

'What did you say?' Each word was spaced out slowly and carefully. Revson was on the parade ground, a court-martialled officer about to be stripped of insignia and buttons and have his sword broken over a knee.

'Don't ignore me, sir.' Deference now replaced brusqueness. 'Hagenbach wouldn't like it.'

'Hagenbach?' Cartland and Hagenbach, men possessed of almost identical casts of mind, were as intimate as two loners could ever be. 'What's Hagenbach to you?'

'I suggest you come and sit beside me, General. Please relax and act casual.'

It was entirely alien to Cartland's nature to relax and 'act casual', but he did his best. He sat and said: 'I repeat, what's Hagenbach to you?'

'Mr Hagenbach is very important to me. He pays my salary when he remembers.'

Cartland looked at him for a long moment then, as if to demonstrate that he was not totally like Hagenbach, he smiled. His smile was nowhere near as frosty as his face. 'Well, well. A friend in need is a friend indeed. Your name?'

'Paul Revson.'

'Revson? Revson! James has talked to me about you. And not only once.'

'Sir, you must be the only person in the United States who

knows his first name.'

Cartland nodded his agreement. 'There aren't many around. You know he has you slated for the hot seat in five years' time?'

'I should live that long.'

'Well, well.' Cartland seemed to be very fond of 'well, well'. 'A very neat job of infiltration, if I may say so.'

'The Chief's idea, not mine.' Revson stood up and snapped off some more photographs. He said, apologetically: 'Local colour. You will please not tell any of your colleagues on the Presidential coach –'

'Colleagues? Clowns!'

'You will please not tell any of the clowns that you have met me.'

'I retract my remark. The President is a personal friend.'

'That is known, sir. The President and the clowns. I would not include the Mayor among the latter. If you want to talk to them privately, take a walk. Your coach is bugged.'

'If you say so, Revson.'

'I know so, sir. There's a tape recorder whirling away busily in the rear coach. You heard it. I didn't.'

'I heard it. I've never heard of you.'

'General Cartland, you should join our organization.'

'You think?'

'I retract in turn. A Chief of Staff can go nowhere except down.'

Cartland smiled again. 'To mint a new phrase, tell me all.'

Revson stood, walked away some paces, took more pictures, returned, sat down and told all. When he had finished, General Cartland said: 'What do you want me to do?'

'I don't want. One does not give instructions to the Chief of Staff.'

The Chief of Staff became the Chief of Staff. 'The point, Revson.'

'Take your sedentary friends for a walk. Tell them about the coach being bugged. Tell them how to identify their own safe food trays.'

'No problem. That all?'

'One last thing, General Cartland. I'm a bit hesitant about this, but as you would say, to the point. It is known – at least I know – that you habitually carry a gun.'

'Past tense. I have been relieved of it.'

124

'You still have your holster?'

'I have.'

'I'll give you a replacement that will fit very snugly into your .22.'

'You do your homework, Revson. It will be a pleasure.'

'The bullets are cyanide-tipped, sir.'

Cartland didn't hesitate. 'Still a pleasure.'

EIGHT

The evening meal wagon arrived at seven-thirty. The occupants of the Presidential coach were close to the north painted barrier, huddled in what appeared to be deep conversation. April Wednesday, under the watchful eye of a guard, made her quiet way towards the ambulance. Revson sat, apparently half-dozing, in a chair. He started as a hand touched his shoulder.

'Food, my China-bound friend.' Branson, with his smile.

Revson sat upright. 'Wine, one trusts?'

'The best vintages that money can buy.'

'Whose money?'

'Irrelevancies bore me.' Branson was regarding him with an appraising eye.

Revson stood and looked around him. 'Your honoured guests along there – '

'They are being informed.'

'You might have at least given them time to have their pre-dinner cocktail. Well, not the President's Arab friends – '

'Time for that. The food is in hot cupboards.' Branson did some more appraisal. 'You know, Revson, you interest me. You might even say you intrigue me. There's a certain – what shall I call it – intransigence about you. I still don't see you as a man behind a camera.'

'And I don't see you as the man behind the most massive hold-up of all time. Too late for you to go back to Wall Street?'

Branson clapped Revson on the shoulder. 'On behalf of the President, let's go and sample some of the superior vintages.'

'Explain yourself.'

'Who knows what our Medici friends in the Presidio might be up to?'

'I hadn't thought of that. You trust nobody?'

'No.'

'Me? A guinea-pig?'

'Yes. You and Cartland make me uneasy.'

'A weakness. You should never confess to them. Lead on, MacDuff.'

Arrived at the meal wagon Branson said to the white and blue striped attendant: 'Your name?'

The attendant gave an odd sort of sketchy salute. 'Tony, Mr Branson.'

'What wines do you have?'

'Three reds, three white, Mr Branson.'

'Array them before us, Tony. Mr Revson here is an internationally-known *sommelier*. A judge of wine, in other words.'

'Sir.'

Six bottles and six glasses appeared on the counter. Revson said: 'Just a quarter in each glass. I don't want to fall off the bridge during the night. Have you bread and salt?'

'Yes, Mr Revson.' Tony clearly regarded himself as being in the presence of lunatics.

Interspersed with the bread and salt Revson sampled all six vintages. At the end he said: 'All uniformly excellent. I must tell the French vintners about this. The best Californian matches up with the best French.'

Branson said: 'It would appear that I owe you an apology, Revson.'

'No way. Let's do it again. Or will you join me in one of the – ah – approved wines?'

'It would seem safe to do so.' Tony clearly considered himself in the presence of a couple of head cases.

'I suggest one of your own. A Gamay Beaujolais from your Almaden vineyards.'

'Ah.' Branson pondered. 'Tony?'

'Mr Revson has excellent taste, sir.'

They consumed their wines in a leisurely fashion. Branson said: 'I agree with both of your assessments. You are ready to serve dinner, Tony?'

'Yes, sir.' He smiled. 'I have already served one. About twenty minutes ago, I'd say. Mr Hansen. He snatched a plate and said that as the energy czar he needed energy.'

'It figures.' Branson turned a lazy head. 'In the coach, I presume?'

'No, sir. He took his tray across to the east crash barrier. There.' He followed his pointing finger then softly said: 'Jesus!'

'Jesus what?'

127

'Look.'

They looked. Hansen, slowly toppling off the barrier, fell to the roadway and lay there, his body jerking. Branson and Revson crossed the six road lanes and reached him in as many seconds.

Hansen was vomiting violently. They spoke to him, but he seemed incapable of answering. His body went into strange and frightening convulsions.

Revson said: 'Stay here. I'll get O'Hare.'

O'Hare and April were together in the ambulance when he arrived. Understandably enough, he was welcomed with lifted eyebrows.

Revson said: 'Quickly. I think that Mr Hansen – hungry, it seems – picked up the wrong dinner tray. He looks in pretty bad shape to me.'

O'Hare was on his feet. Revson barred his way.

'I think your Dr Isaacs has stirred up a more powerful brew than he imagined. If this is the effect it has – well, I want you to go across there and diagnose some form of food poisoning. Call in some chemical analyst or whatever you call them. Nobody, but nobody, must touch that food again. I don't want wholesale murder on my hands.'

'I understand.' O'Hare picked up his emergency bag and left at speed.

April said: 'What's gone wrong, Paul?'

'I don't know. Some foul-up. Maybe I'm to blame. Stay here.'

When he arrived across the bridge Branson was standing upright and O'Hare slowly straightening. Revson looked at them both then addressed himself to O'Hare. 'Well?'

O'Hare let go the limp wrist he was holding. 'I'm afraid that Mr Hansen is dead.'

'Dead?' For once, Branson was clearly shocked. 'How can he be dead?'

'Please. For the moment, I'm in charge. This plastic centre plate is almost empty. I assume that Hansen ate it all.'

O'Hare bent over the dead man and breathed deeply. His nose wrinkled. Very slowly, he straightened again.

'Can't be salmonella. That takes time. Not even botulinus. It's quick, but not this quick.' O'Hare looked at Branson. 'I want to talk to the hospital.'

'I don't understand. Perhaps you'd like to talk to me first?'

O'Hare sounded weary. 'I suppose. The smell – it comes from the pancreas – is unmistakable. Some form of food poisoning. I don't know. Doctors have their specialities and this is not one of mine. The hospital, please.'

'You don't mind if I listen in?'

'Listen in all you want.'

O'Hare was on the phone in the rear end of the Presidential coach. Branson held the President's side-phone. Revson sat in the next deeply upholstered chair.

O'Hare said: 'How long will it take you to contact Hansen's private physician?'

'We're in contact now.'

'I'll wait.'

They all waited. They all looked at one another, while carefully not looking at one another. The phone became activated again.

'O'Hare?'

'Sir?'

'Hansen is – was – just recovering from his second – and almost fatal – heart attack.'

'Thank you, sir. That explains everything.'

'Not quite.' Branson was his old balanced self again. 'I want two analytical chemists out here to determine the source of this infection, if that's what you would call it. The food tray, I mean. Separate examinations. If they disagree, one of them is going to go over the side.'

O'Hare sounded even more weary. 'Such specialists we have in San Francisco. I know two of the top people. The only thing they have in common is their total disagreement with each other.'

'In which case they will both be thrown over the side. You will accompany them. Make contact now.'

O'Hare made contact. Revson said to Branson: 'Only an American would have this gift for making friends and influencing people.'

'I'll talk to you later. O'Hare?'

'They'll come. Only if you promise immunity. Damn it all and to hell, Branson, why should their lives be put at risk?'

Branson considered. 'Their lives will not be put at risk. Leave that phone. I want it.' He made a signal through the window. After a few seconds, Van Effen entered. He was carrying his Schmeisser in a rather unsympathetic manner. Branson moved to the rear.

He said: 'Let me talk to Hendrix.'

Not more than two seconds elapsed before Hendrix was on the phone.

'Hendrix?' Branson was his usual unemotional self. 'I have promised immunity to the doctors coming out here. I want you and the Vice-President to accompany them.' There was a brief delay, then Hendrix came through again on the intercom.

'Mr Richards agrees. But you are not to hold the Vice-President as a hostage.'

'I agree in turn.'

'Your word?'

'For what it's worth. You have to believe me, don't you? You're in no position to bargain.'

'No position. I have a dream, Branson.'

'I know. But I think handcuffs are so inelegant. I will see you in a very few minutes. Send out the TV truck. Alert the networks.'

'Again?'

'I think it very important that the nation should be made aware of the establishment's *modus operandi*.' Branson rested the phone.

In the communications wagon just off the Presidio, Hendrix in turn, rested his phone and looked at the six men clustered around him. He addressed himself to Hagenbach.

'Well, you have it. Hansen dead. Nobody's fault, really. How was anybody to know that he had a critical heart condition? And how – and why – did nobody know about it?'

Hagenbach said heavily: 'I knew. Like nearly all senior Government officials Hansen was intensely secretive about his physical health. He was in Bethseda twice in the last nine months and the second time was touch and go. It was reported that he was receiving treatment for overwork, exhaustion. So I think if anyone is to blame it's me.'

Quarry said: 'You're talking nonsense and you know it. Who could possibly have foreseen this? It's not your fault and it's certainly not Dr Isaacs's fault. He told us the drug was perfectly safe for any normal healthy adult. You cannot question the judgement of a man of his reputation. He wasn't

130

to know that Hansen wasn't a normal healthy adult far less anticipating that Hansen would misguidedly pick up the wrong plate. And what's going to happen now?'

Hendrix said: 'It's obvious what's going to happen now. We seven are going to be publicly indicted as murderers.'

The TV crew had arrived on the centre of the bridge but were, momentarily, inactive. The two specialist doctors were analysing the food and, despite O'Hare's predictions, for once seemed to be agreeing with each other. The President was talking quietly to the Vice-President. From the expressions on their faces it seemed they didn't have very much to talk about.

Branson was alone with Hendrix in the Presidential coach. Branson said: 'Do you honestly expect me to believe that you and Hagenbach know nothing about this?'

Hendrix said wearily: 'Nothing. There's been a botulinus outbreak down-town in the past few days.' He pointed towards the TV set in the middle of the roadway. 'If you watch that at all, you must have heard of it.' He pointed again towards the evening meal wagon where the two doctors were busily at work. 'They were convinced before arrival what the trouble was.' He refrained from adding that he'd told the doctors to find not more than a dozen cases of poisoning. 'You have lives on your hands, Branson.'

'Don't we all. Get on that phone there. Some more hot meals. The first three, taken by random sample, will be by the President, the King and the Prince. You do understand, don't you?'

Revson was in the ambulance with O'Hare and April Wednesday. She was lying blanket-covered on the hinged-down bed.

She said, drowsily: 'Did you have to do this to me?'

'Yes. You don't like thumb-screws.'

'No. Maybe you're not the monster I thought you were. But Dr O'Hare —'

'Dr O'Hare, as he would say in his own native tongue, is a different kettle of fish. What did Branson say?'

She said sleepily: 'Same cable. Bay side.'

Her eyelids closed. O'Hare took Revson by the arm. His voice was quiet. 'Enough.'

'How long?'

'Two hours. Not less.'

'The pens.'

O'Hare withdrew the pens from his clip-board. 'You do know what you're doing?'

'I hope.' He thought briefly, then said:

'You're going to be questioned.'

'I know. You want your torch?'

'Later.'

Kylenski was the senior of the two doctors examining the food trays. He said to Branson: 'My colleague and I have found twelve infected food trays.'

Branson looked at Van Effen then back at Kylenski. 'That all? Twelve? Not seventeen?'

Kylenski had a grey beard, grey moustache and aquiline aristocratic stare. 'Twelve. Spoiled meat. Some form of botulinus. You don't even have to taste it. You can smell it. Well, I can. Apparently Hansen didn't.'

'Lethal?'

'In this concentration, normally, no. This infected food didn't kill Hansen. Well, not directly. But it was almost certainly responsible for reactivating this long-standing and severe heart ailment which did kill him.'

'What would the effect of this be on the average healthy adult?'

'Incapacitating. Violent vomiting, possibility of stomach haemorrhaging, unconsciousness or something pretty close to it.'

'So a man would be pretty helpless?'

'He'd be incapable of action. Most likely of thought, too.'

'What a perfectly splendid prospect. For some.' Branson looked again at Van Effen. 'What do you think?'

'I think I want to know what you want to know.' Van Effen turned to Kylenski. 'This poison or whatever it is – could it have been deliberately introduced?'

'Who on earth would want to do a thing like that?'

Branson said: 'Answer the question.'

'Any doctor specializing in this field, any research fellow, even a reasonably competent laboratory assistant could produce the necessary toxin culture.'

'But he would have to be a doctor or in some way associated with the medical profession? I mean, this would call for trained knowledge and laboratory facilities?'

'Normally, yes.'

Branson said to the meal wagon attendant: 'Come out from behind that counter, Tony.'

Tony came. His apprehension was unmistakable.

Branson said: 'It's not all that hot, Tony. It's turning quite cool, in fact. Why are you sweating?'

'I don't like all this violence and guns.'

'No one has offered you any violence or even pointed a gun at you, although I'm not saying that both of them aren't going to happen to you in the very near future. I suggest, Tony, that you are suffering from a guilty conscience.'

'Me? Conscience?' Tony actually mopped his brow; if his conscience wasn't troubling him something else clearly was. 'God's sake, Mr Branson –'

'Fairy stories are fairy stories but they don't run to a dozen coincidences at a time. Only a fool would accept that. But there had to be some way of identifying the poisoned plates. What way, Tony?'

'Why don't you leave him alone, Branson?' Vice-President Richards's voice was at once harsh and contemptuous. 'He's only a van driver.'

Branson ignored him. 'How were the plates to be identified?'

'I don't know! I don't! I don't even know what you are talking about!'

Branson turned to Kowalski and Peters. 'Throw him into the Golden Gate.' His voice was as level and conversational as ever.

Tony made an animal-like noise but offered no resistance as Kowalski and Peters took an arm apiece and began to march him away. His face was ashen and rivulets of sweat were now pouring down his face. When he did speak his voice was a harsh unbelieving croak.

'Throw me off the bridge! That's murder! Murder! In the name of God I don't know –'

Branson said: 'You'll be telling me next that you have a wife and three kids.'

'I've got nobody.' His eyes turned up in his head and his legs sagged under him until he had to be dragged across the roadway. Both the Vice-President and Hendrix moved in to intercept the trio. They stopped as Van Effen lifted his Schmeisser.

Van Effen said to Branson: 'If there was a way of identifying those plates, that would be important and dangerous information. Would you entrust Tony with anything like that?'

'Not for a second. Enough?'

'He'll tell anything he knows. I suspect it won't be much.' He raised his voice. 'Bring him back.'

Tony was brought back and released. He sagged wearily to the roadway, struggled with difficulty to his feet and clung tremblingly to the luncheon wagonette. His voice shook as much as his frame.

'I know nothing about the plates. I swear it!'

'Tell us what you do know.'

'I thought something was far wrong when they loaded the food into my van.'

'At the hospital?'

'The hospital? I don't work at the hospital. I work for Selznick's.'

'I know them. The caterers for open-air functions. Well?'

'I was told the food was ready when I got there. I'm usually loaded and away in five minutes. This time it took three-quarters of an hour.'

'Did you see anybody from the hospital when you were waiting at Selznick's?'

'Nobody.'

'You'll live a little longer, Tony. Provided you don't eat that damned food of yours.' He turned to O'Hare. 'Well, that leaves only you and the fragile Miss Wednesday.'

'You insinuating that either of us might have been carrying secret instructions from your alleged poisoners?' There was more contempt than incredulity in O'Hare's tone.

'Yes. Let's have Miss Wednesday here.'

O'Hare said: 'Leave her alone.'

'You said – who do you think is in charge here?'

'Where a patient of mine is concerned, I am. If you want her here, you'll have to carry her. She's asleep in the ambulance, under heavy sedation. Can't you take my word?'

'No. Kowalski, go check. You know, a couple of stiff fingers in the abdomen.'

Kowalski returned within ten seconds. 'Out like a light.'

Branson looked at O'Hare. 'How very convenient. Maybe you didn't want her subjected to interrogation?'

'You're a lousy psychologist, Branson. Miss Wednesday is

not, as you know, cast in the heroic mould. Can you imagine anyone entrusting her with any vital information?' Branson made no reply. 'Apart from that, the only good thing that's ever been said about you is that you never molest women.'

'How do you know that?'

'Chief of Police Hendrix told me. He seems to know a lot about you.'

'You confirm that, Hendrix?'

Hendrix was curt. 'Why shouldn't I?'

Branson said: 'So that leaves only you, Doctor.'

'As a prime suspect? You're losing your grip.' He nodded at Hansen's sheet-covered form on a stretcher. 'I don't want to sound sanctimonious but as a doctor my job is to save lives, not take them away. I have no wish to be struck off the Medical Register. Besides, I haven't left the ambulance since before the food wagon arrived. I couldn't very well be there identifying your damned food trays and be in the ambulance at the same time.'

Branson said: 'Kowalski?'

'I can vouch for that, Mr Branson.'

'But you were talking to people after you returned and before the food wagon arrived.'

Kowalski said: 'He did. To quite a few people. So did Miss Wednesday.'

'We can forget her. The good doctor here.'

'A fair number of people.'

'Anyone in particular? I mean long earnest chats, that sort of thing?'

'Yes.' Kowalski appeared to be extremely observant or have an uncomfortably good memory or both. 'Three. Two with Miss Wednesday –'

'Forget the lady. She'd plenty of time to talk to him in the ambulance to and from hospital. Who else?'

'Revson. A long talk.'

'Overhear anything?'

'No. Thirty yards away and downwind.'

'Anything pass between them?'

'No.' Kowalski was definite.

Branson said to O'Hare: 'What did you talk about?'

'Medical privilege.'

'You mean mind my own damned business?'

O'Hare said nothing. Branson looked at Revson.

135

'No medical privileges,' Revson said. 'Cabbages and kings. I've talked to at least thirty people, including your own men, since we arrived. Why single this out as a special case?'

'I was hoping you could tell me.'

'There's nothing to tell.'

'You're pretty cool, aren't you?'

'A clear conscience. You should try it some time.'

'And, Mr Branson.' Kowalski again. 'Revson also had a long talk with General Cartland.'

'Oh. More cabbages and kings, General?'

'No. We were discussing the possibilities of ridding this bridge of some of its more undesirable elements.'

'Coming from you, I can well believe it. A fruitful talk?'

Cartland looked at him in icy silence.

Branson looked thoughtfully at Van Effen. 'I have a feeling, just a feeling, mind you, that we have an infiltrator in our midst.'

Van Effen gazed at him with his impassive moonface and said nothing.

Branson went on: 'I think that would rule out the doctor. Apart from the fact that we've checked out on his credentials, I have the odd instinct that there is a trained agent loose on this bridge. That again would rule out O'Hare, who's just here by happenstance anyway. You share my instinct?'

'Yes.'

'Who?'

Van Effen didn't hesitate. 'Revson.'

Branson beckoned Chrysler. 'Revson here claims to be an accredited correspondent of *The Times* of London. How long would it take you to check that out?'.

'Using the Presidential tele-communications?'

'Yes.'

'Minutes.'

Revson said: 'I suppose I'm supposed to show a degree of high indignation, but I won't bother. Why me? Why assume it's any of the news media members? Why not one of your own men?'

'Because I hand-picked them personally.'

'Just the same way that Napoleon did his marshals. And look how many of them turned against him in the end. How you can expect devoted loyalty from a bunch of cut-throats like this, however hand-picked, is beyond me.'

136

'You'll do for the moment,' Van Effen said comfortably. He touched Branson's arm and pointed to the west. 'We may not have all that much time.'

'You're right.' Dark, heavy, ominous clouds were rolling in from the Pacific, although still some miles distant. 'The audiences wouldn't like it at all if they were to see their President and Vice-President, not to mention their oil friends, sitting here getting soaked in a thunderstorm. Ask Johnson to organize the cameras and the seating.' He waited thoughtfully until Van Effen had done this then took him across to where Revson was standing alone. He said to Van Effen: 'Revson tells me that you have already searched his camera.'

'Yes. But I didn't take it to pieces.'

'Maybe we should.'

'And maybe you shouldn't.' For once, Revson let anger show. 'Do you know that it takes a man five years' training to learn just how to assemble one of those cameras? I'd rather you kept the damned thing for the duration of our stay here than have it ruined.'

'Call his bluff and have it stripped,' Branson said.

'I agree.' Van Effen said to Revson, almost soothingly, 'We'll have Chrysler do it. He's as close to a mechanical genius as anyone I know. It will be intact.' To Branson he said: 'I've also searched his carry-all, the upholstery of his seat, below the seat and the rack above. Clean.'

'Search him.'

'Search me?' More than a trace of truculence remained in Revson's face. 'I've already been searched.'

'For weapons only.'

If there had been a grain of rice on Revson's person, including inside the coat lining, Van Effen wouldn't have missed it. Apart from keys, coins and an inoffensive little knife, all he came up with were papers.

'The usual,' Van Effen said. 'Driving licence, social security, credit cards, press cards – '

'Press cards,' Branson said. 'Any of them identify him with the London *Times*?'

'There's this.' Van Effen handed the card across to Branson. 'Looks pretty kosher to me.'

'If he is who or what we think he might be, he wouldn't be likely to hire the worst forger in town.' He handed the card back, a slight frown on his face. 'Anything else?'

'Yes.' Van Effen opened a long envelope. 'Airline ticket. For Hong Kong.'

'It wouldn't be dated for tomorrow?'

'It is. How did you know?'

'He told me so himself. What do you think?'

'I don't know.' For a moment, as Van Effen idly fingered Revson's felt pens both he and Branson were only a heart's beat from death. But Van Effen, his mind on something else, reclipped them and opened Revson's passport. He flipped rapidly through the pages. 'Certainly gets around. Lots of South-East Asia passports, last about two years ago. Near East immigration stamps galore. Not many European or London stamps, but that signifies nothing. They are an idle bunch across there and British and most European – Western European – passport officers only stamp your passports if they feel in need of the exercise. How does it all sound to you?'

'Ties in with his own claims, what he told me himself. You?'

'If he's a bad one, I would call this an excessive cover-up. Why not Milwaukee? Or even San Francisco?'

Branson said: 'You a San Franciscan?'

'By adoption.'

Van Effen said: 'Who'd spend a dozen years travelling the world just to establish a background, an alibi like this?'

Chrysler came up. Branson looked at him in slight surprise. 'Through already?'

'The President has a hot line to London. I hope you don't mind. Revson's clean. He's a fully accredited correspondent of the London *Times*.'

Revson said to Chrysler: 'Branson wants you to take my camera to pieces. There's a time-bomb or a radio inside it. Watch you don't blow yourself up. After that, you'd better make damn sure you put it all together again.'

Chrysler received Branson's nod, smiled, took the camera and left. Revson said: 'Will that be all? Or do you want to unscrew my false heels?'

Branson wasn't amused. 'I'm still not satisfied. How am I to know that Kylenski here is not in cahoots with the poisoners? How am I to know that he was not instructed to find only a dozen poisoned plates so as to kill our suspicions? There should have been seventeen tampered trays. There should – there must be someone on the bridge capable of identifying them. I want you, Revson, to sample one of the trays that

138

Kylenski has declared safe.'

'You want me – you want to kill me off with botulinus on the off-chance that Kylenski has made a mistake? I'm damned if I will. I'm no human guinea-pig.'

'Then we'll try some of them out on the President and his oil friends here. Royal guinea-pigs, if you will. This should make medical history. If they resist, we'll force-feed them.'

Revson was about to make the obvious point that they could force-feed him equally well but immediately changed his mind. Cartland had not yet had the opportunity to inform those in the Presidential coach as to how the infected trays could be identified: O'Hare apart, he was the only one who could. Revson turned his palms upwards. 'God knows what you're after but I trust the two doctors here. If they say there are so many uncontaminated trays, then I believe them. So you can have your plebeian guinea-pig.'

Branson looked at him closely. 'Why have you changed your mind?'

Revson said conversationally: 'You know, Branson, you're endlessly over-suspicious. From the expression of your lieutenant, Van Effen there, I would say that he agrees with me.' No harm could come, Revson thought, from sowing the odd seed of dissension. 'Some people might even interpret it as a sign of weakness, of uncertainty. I'm agreeing because I don't care so much for you. A chink in everybody's armour. I'm beginning to believe that your belief in your own infallibility may rest on rather shaky ground. Besides, plebs are expendable: Presidents and kings are not.'

Branson smiled his confident smile and turned to Tony. 'Lay out ten of the uncontaminated plates on the counter.' Tony did so. 'Now, Revson, which one would you care to sample?'

'You're slipping, Branson. You've still the lingering suspicion that I might be able to identify the poisoned trays. Suppose you choose for me?' Branson nodded and pointed at one of the trays. Revson moved forward, lifted the indicated tray and sniffed it slowly and cautiously. The surreptitious movements of his finger-tips found no traces of tiny indentations on the underside of the plastic lugs. This tray was clean. He took a spoon, dug into the centre of what looked like a browned-over cottage pie, and sampled the meat. He grimaced, chewed, swallowed, then repeated the process. He laid down the tray in disgust.

Branson said: 'Not to your liking?'

'If I were in a restaurant I'd send this back to the kitchen. Better, I'd take it there and empty it over the chef's head – not that the person who made this could ever be called a chef.'

'Contaminated, you'd think?'

'No. Just plain bloody lousy.'

'Perhaps you'd care to sample another one?'

'No, I would not. Besides, you said, just one sample.'

Branson said persuasively: 'Come on. Be co-operative.'

Revson scowled but co-operated. This tray, too, was clean. He went through the same performance and had no sooner done so when Branson handed him a third tray.

This one had indentations on the underside of the lugs.

Revson broke the skin, sniffed suspiciously, tasted a little and at once spat it out. 'I don't know whether this is contaminated or not, but it tastes and smells even lousier than the other two. If that's possible.' He pushed the tray under Kylenski's nose, who sniffed it and passed it across to his colleague.

Branson said: 'Well?'

Kylenski was hesitant. 'Could be. A marginal, a border-line case. It would require lab. testing.' He looked thoughtfully at Revson. 'Do you smoke?'

'No.'

'Drink?'

'Birthdays and funerals only.'

Kylenski said: 'That could account for it. Some non-smokers and non-drinkers can have an extraordinarily acute sense of taste and smell. Revson is obviously one of those.'

Without consulting anyone, Revson examined another six trays. He pushed them all away and turned to Branson. 'My opinion, for what it's worth?' Branson nodded. 'Most – not all, but most – of those trays are off. With some, you've almost got to imagine it. Others stink. I think the whole damn lot is contaminated. In varying degrees.'

Branson looked at Kylenski. 'Possible?'

Kylenski looked uncomfortable. 'It happens. Botulinus can vary widely in its degree of concentration. Only last year there was a double family outing in New England. Ten in all. Among other things, they had sandwiches. Again the botulinus bug.

Five died, two were slightly ill, three unaffected. But the sandwiches were all spread with the same meat paste.'

Branson and Van Effen walked apart. Van Effen said: 'Enough?'

'You mean you see no point in going ahead with this?'

'You stand to lose credibility, Mr Branson.'

'I agree. I'm not happy about it, but I agree. Trouble is, we've really, basically, only got Revson's word for it.'

'But he's identified twenty – in all – contaminated trays: three more than was necessary.'

'Who says so? Revson?'

'After all the proofs, you still don't trust him?'

'He's too cool, too relaxed. He's obviously highly trained, highly competent – and I'm damned sure that it's not in photography.'

'He could be in that, too.'

'I wouldn't doubt it.'

'So you're still going to treat this as a case of deliberate poisoning?'

'Where our vast viewing public is concerned? Who's to gainsay me? There's only one mike and it's in my hand.'

Van Effen looked towards the south tower. 'Food wagon number two on its way.'

Branson had the TV cameras, the honoured guests, the newspapermen and still cameramen in position in very short order indeed. The black thunderous clouds from the west were steadily marching in on them. Among those seated, the only difference in composition was that Hansen's seat had been taken over by the Vice-President. The cameras were turning and Branson, seated next to the President, was talking into the microphone.

He said: 'I am calling upon all viewers in America and throughout the world to be witnesses to a particularly heinous crime that has been committed upon this bridge just over an hour ago, a crime that I trust will persuade you that not all criminals are those who stand without the law. I would ask you to look at this food wagon which, as you can see, has its counter covered with food trays. Harmless, if not particularly appetizing food trays, you would think, such as any major airline would serve up to its passengers. But are they really harmless?' He turned to the man on his other side and

141

the camera was now back on them. 'This is Dr Kylenski, a leading forensic expert on the West Coast. A specialist in poisons. Are those trays really harmless, Dr Kylenski?'

'No.'

'You'll have to speak up, Doctor.'

'No. They are not harmless. Some are contaminated.'

'How many?'

'Half. Maybe more. I have no laboratory resources to hand.'

'Contaminated. That means infected. What are they infected with, Doctor?'

'A virus. Botulinus. A major source of severe food poisoning.'

'How severe? Can it be deadly?'

'Yes.'

'Frequently?'

'Yes.'

'Normally it occurs naturally – spoiled food, things like that?'

'Yes.'

'But a culture of it can be manufactured synthetically or artificially in a laboratory.'

'That's putting it very loosely.'

'We're talking primarily to laymen.'

'Yes.'

'And it could be injected synthetically into already prepared but otherwise harmless food?'

'I suppose so.'

'Yes or no?'

'Yes.'

'Thank you, Dr Kylenski. That will be all.'

Revson, still without his camera, was standing by the ambulance with O'Hare. 'For a person who's never been inside a court-room, Branson seems to have mastered the prosecuting counsel bit pretty well.'

'It's all this TV.'

Branson said: 'I put it to all of you who are watching that the authorities – military, police, FBI, Government or whoever – have made a deliberate attempt to murder or at least incapacitate those of us who have taken over the Presidential entourage and this bridge. There must be someone on this bridge who knew how to identify poisoned trays and see that they fell into the right hands – that is, the hands of my colleagues and myself. The attempt, fortunately, failed, but there has been one casualty whom I shall mention later.

'Meantime, I would draw your attention to the fact that a second food wagon has arrived.' A camera obligingly drew the viewers' attention to this fact. 'It seems incredible that the authorities would be so obtuse as to try the same gambit again but, on the other hand, they have already shown that they are incredibly obtuse. So we are going to select three trays at random and offer them to the President, King and Prince. If they survive, we may reasonably assume that the food is uncontaminated. If, on the other hand, they become seriously ill – or worse – the world will know that the guilt cannot be laid at our door. We are in permanent radio-telephone contact with the police and military authorities ashore. They have one minute to tell us whether this food is contaminated or not.'

Mayor Morrison was on his feet. Van Effen lifted his Schmeisser fractionally but Morrison ignored him. He said to Branson: 'Apart from the personal indignity and affront you are heaping on the President and his royal guests couldn't you pick someone a bit lower down the scale for your experiment?'

'Such as yourself?'

'Such as myself.'

'My dear Mayor, your personal courage is beyond dispute. That is well known. Your intelligence, however, isn't. If anyone is to be put to the test it will be the three men who are probably the most important in the United States today. Their untimely disappearance from the scene would have the maximum inhibiting effect on would-be poisoners. In the olden days, the serfs tasted the food of their rulers: I find it rather amusing that the roles should be reversed. Please sit.'

'Megalomaniac bastard,' Revson said.

O'Hare nodded. 'He's all of that but a lot more. He knows damn well there isn't a chance in the world of the food being spiked but he's going through the charade all the same. He's not only enjoying his own showmanship, he's getting a positively sadistic kick out of it all, particularly in humiliating the President.'

'You think he's sick? In the head? Certifiably, I mean?'

'I'm no psychiatrist. He could get all he wants without those histrionics and TV spectaculars. What's for sure, he's got a grudge against society in general and the President in particular. Certainly, he's in it for the money, but he's in it for something else: as if he wanted to become a nationally – or internationally – recognized figure.'

'In that case, he's made a fair start. In fact, he's gone as far as he can go. Now it seems as if he's overcompensating for something. Lord knows what.'

They watched three trays of food being brought towards the rows of chairs. O'Hare said: 'Reckon they'll sample that stuff?'

'They'll eat it. In the first place, they couldn't bear the indignity of being force-fed in front of hundreds of millions of viewers. The President's courage is known well enough – you will remember his record during World War Two in the Pacific. Again, as President, he has to give a lead to the nation – if he refused to eat while his oil friends did, he'd be a dead duck at the next election. Conversely, his oil friends would lose face if the President ate and they didn't.'

They ate. After Chrysler had given a negative signal from the Presidential coach, Branson nodded towards the trays. The President – inevitably, he was not a man to be upstaged by anyone – was the first to get busy with knife and fork. It could hardly be said that he ate with unrestrained gusto but he plodded along stolidly enough and had finished more than half his meal before he laid down his eating tools.

Branson said: 'Well?'

'I wouldn't offer it to my guests in the White House but it's palatable enough.' In spite of the deep humiliation he must have been experiencing, the President was maintaining a remarkable degree of *sang-froid*. 'A little wine would have helped, though.'

'You shall have as much as you want in a few moments. I imagine a great number of people are also going to feel like a restorative pretty soon, too. Incidentally, if you people are still interested, we shall be fixing our second strap of explosives at nine o'clock tomorrow morning. Our time, of course. And now, could we have the cameras on that stretcher there.'

Two men stood at the head of the canvas-shrouded stretcher. At a word from Branson they pulled back the top section of the canvas. The cameras zoomed in on the pallid, haggard face of the dead man, held it for all of ten interminable and hushed seconds, then returned to Branson.

He said: 'John Hansen, your energy czar. Death certified as due to botulinus poisoning. For what may be the first time in history a wanted criminal accuses the legal authorities of murder. Second degree murder it may be, but I nevertheless indict them on a charge of murder.'

Hagenbach was in full vitriolic flow. Some phrases like 'evil, twisted, macabre, vicious bastard' were just identifiable, but the rest was wholly unprintable. Newson, Carter, Milton and Quarry were momentarily silent but their faces showed clearly enough that they totally identified themselves with Hagenbach's expressed convictions. Hagenbach, being only human, finally ran out of breath.

'He's made us look very very bad indeed.' In the circumstances, Milton's restraint was remarkable.

'Bad?' Quarry looked around for another word then gave up. 'If he pulls another one like this – if we pull another one like this – Branson will have half the nation on his side. What's to do next?'

Hagenbach said: 'Wait till we hear from Revson.'

'Revson?' Admiral Newson seemed unenthusiastic. 'He's hardly distinguished himself so far.'

'A hundred to one it wasn't Revson's fault,' Hagenbach said. 'And don't forget the final decision was ours. We bear a collective responsibility, gentlemen.'

They sat around the table bearing this intolerable responsibility, each one an Atlas bearing his own private world on his shoulders.

NINE

On the Golden Gate Bridge that evening events happened in fairly quick but ordered fashion. A special ambulance appeared and took away the stretcher bearing the remains of Hansen. An autopsy was to be performed, which seemed to be a singular waste of time but was apparently mandatory under State law when a person had died under unusual circumstances. Dr Kylenski and his colleague, with a marked absence of reluctance, accompanied the ambulance. Newsmen, captives and captors had their evening meal, the first two with a notable but understandable lack of appetite but with a thirst, equally notable and understandable, so marked that further liquid supplies had to be commandeered. The two TV trucks left and, shortly afterwards, the two food wagons. Last to go were Vice-President Richards and Hendrix. The Vice-President had spent a long time in a long and earnest private discussion with the President, just as had General Cartland with Hendrix. Both Branson had watched with a certain amused tolerance but had paid little attention. From their grim and depressed expressions it was clear that their discussions had been totally fruitless. No other result could have been expected. It may well have been that Branson was suffering from a certain degree of euphoria after the dramatic effect of his last broadcast: from his expression it was impossible to tell.

Branson approached Kowalski, just as Richards and Hendrix turned towards their waiting police car. 'Well?'

'My life on it, Mr Branson. I had my eye on Hendrix and the Vice-President every second. At no time did Revson approach within twenty yards of either man.'

Branson was aware that Kowalski, a very bright youngster indeed, was looking at him with an expression of barely restrained curiosity. Branson gave his usual faint and empty smile.

'You wondering what's bugging me about Revson?'

'Not wondering, sir. Interested. I've known you for three years now, sir. I shouldn't imagine you see many fairies at the bottom of your garden.'

'Don't you, now?' Branson turned and called to Richards. 'Wait.' To Kowalski: 'What's that supposed to mean?'

'Well. Revson. He's been searched to pieces. He's passed every test. Maybe if the boys and I knew what you are –'

'Every test. With flying colours. Perhaps his flag flies too high. Would you have sampled those charming botulinus dinners?'

'My oath and I wouldn't.' He hesitated. 'Well, if it was a direct order from you –'

'And with a gun in your back?'

Kowalski said nothing.

Branson said: 'Revson doesn't take orders from me. And he had no gun in his back.'

'Maybe he takes orders from someone else.'

'Maybe he does at that. Just a very close eye, Kowalski.'

'If I have to stay awake all night.'

'You know, I think I'd rather appreciate that.' Branson walked away towards the police car. Kowalski looked after him very thoughtfully indeed.

The Vice-President and Hendrix were standing impatiently by the opened doors of the police car. Branson came up and said: 'You will not have forgotten the deadline, gentlemen?'

'Deadline?'

Branson smiled. 'Do not be so deliberately obtuse, Mr Vice President. The transfer of certain monies to Europe. Half a billion dollars – plus, of course, my quarter million expenses. Noon. Tomorrow.'

Richards's chilling glare should have petrified Branson on the spot. Branson remained unaffected.

'And don't forget the escalation clause. Two million dollars for every hour's delay. And, of course, the free pardon. I expect that will take some time, I suppose your Congress will be a little stuffy about that. But we – your friends and I – can rest comfortably in the Caribbean till that comes through. I bid you good evening, gentlemen.'

He walked away and stopped at the opened door of the rear coach. Revson was there, slinging over his shoulder the strap of the camera which Chrysler had just handed back to him. Chrysler smiled at Branson.

'Clean as a whistle, Mr Branson. My word, I wish I had one of those.'

'You can have a dozen very soon. You had another camera, Revson.'

'Yes.' Revson sighed. 'Do you want me to fetch it for you?'

'I'd rather not. Will you get it, Chrysler?'

'Five back, inside seat,' Revson said helpfully. 'It's on the seat.'

Chrysler returned with the camera, showed it to Branson. 'An Asahi-Pentax. I have one myself. Those things are so jammed with miniaturized electronic equipment that you couldn't hide a pea inside it.'

'Assuming, of course, that it is not just an empty shell.'

'Ah.' Chrysler looked at Revson. 'Loaded?' Revson shook his head. Chrysler opened the back just as Van Effen joined them and displayed the rear of the camera. 'The genuine article.' He snapped the back closed.

Revson took his camera back. He spoke to Branson, his tone as cold as his face. 'Maybe you'd like to look at my watch. Could be a transistorized two-way radio. All the best investigators in the comic strips wear one.'

Branson said nothing. Chrysler took Revson's wrist, pressed a knob on either side of the watch. Illuminated red figures appeared, one set giving the date, the other the time. Chrysler dropped the wrist.

'Pulsar digital. You couldn't hide a grain of sand inside one of those things.'

Revson turned with deliberate contempt on his heel and walked away. Chrysler went inside the coach. Van Effen said: 'Still bugged, Mr Branson? So he's annoyed. Wouldn't you be if you'd been put through the hoop the way you've put him through the hoop? Besides, if he'd anything to hide he wouldn't let his animosity show so plain, he'd keep a very low profile indeed.'

'Maybe that's the way he expects us to react. Or maybe he's clear.' Branson looked thoughtful almost to the extent of being worried. 'But I can't shake off the feeling that there's something wrong, and it's a feeling that's never let me down before. I'm convinced, don't ask me how, that someone on the bridge has some means of communicating with someone on land. I want every inch of every person – and that includes our illustrious guests – searched, and to hell with the ladies' feelings. Every inch of their personal belongings, every inch of every coach.'

'Immediately, Mr Branson.' There was acquiescence in the tone but no great enthusiasm. 'And the rest rooms?'

'Those too.'

'And the ambulance?'

'Yes. I think I'll attend to that myself.'

O'Hare looked up in mild surprise as Branson entered the ambulance. 'Don't tell me that the botulinus has struck again?'

'No. I'm here to search this ambulance.'

O'Hare rose from his stool, his face tight. 'I don't allow civilians to touch my medical supplies.'

'You're going to allow this one. If necessary, I'll call one of my men and have you held either at pistol-point or tied up while I conduct my search.'

'And just what in the hell do you think you're looking for?'

'That's my concern.'

'So I can't stop you. I just warn you that we carry quite a lot of dangerous drugs and surgical equipment here. If you poison yourself or slice an artery, here's one doctor who's not going to help you.'

Branson nodded to April Wednesday who was sleeping peacefully on the side bunk. 'Lift her off.'

'Lift her – what do you think – '

'Do it immediately or I call a guard.'

O'Hare lifted the slight form in his arms. Branson pummelled every inch of the thin mattress, lifted it, looked under it and said: 'Put her back.'

Branson carried out a thorough search of all the medical equipment in the ambulance. He knew exactly what he was looking for and nothing he examined looked even remotely like what he hoped to find. He looked around, picked up a torch suspended from one side of the ambulance, switched it on and twisted the top, opening and then narrowing the hooded shutter. 'A peculiar flashlight, O'Hare.'

O'Hare said wearily: 'It's an ophthalmic torch. Every physician carries one. You can diagnose a dozen different diseases by the dilation of the pupils of the eyes.'

'This can be useful. Come with me.' He went down the rear steps of the ambulance, went round to the front and jerked open the driver's door. The driver, peering at a lurid magazine in the now fading light, looked round in surprise.

Branson said: 'Out!' The man descended and Branson, offering no explanation, searched him comprehensively from head to foot. He then climbed inside the driving compartment, examined the upholstery, opened various lockers and shone the torch inside. He descended and said to the driver: 'Open the engine hood.'

This was done. Again with the aid of the torch he carried out a thorough inspection of the compartment and found nothing worthy of his attention. He went round to the rear of the ambulance and re-entered. O'Hare followed, politely removed the torch from Branson's hand and replaced it. Branson indicated a metal canister held in place by a spring clip. He said: 'What's that?'

O'Hare gave a creditable impression of a man whose patience was wearing very very thin. 'An aerosol air-freshener.' It was the fake Prestige can that contained the knock-out gas.

Branson freed the can. 'Sandalwood,' he said. 'You have an exotic taste in perfumes.' He shook the can, listened to the gurgling inside, then replaced the canister in its clip. O'Hare hoped that the dampness on his brow didn't show.

Branson finally directed his attention to the big oiled-wood box on the floor. 'And what's this?'

O'Hare didn't answer. Branson looked at him. O'Hare was leaning with a negligent elbow on top of a locker, his expression a mixture of barely concealed impatience and bored indifference.

Branson said sharply: 'You heard me.'

'I heard you. I've had just about enough of you, Branson. If you expect me to show any obedience or respect for you, then you're way out of your mind. I'm beginning to think you are illiterate. Can't you see those big red letters? They spell out "Cardiac Arrest Unit". Emergency equipment for patients who have, or may shortly be expected to have, a heart attack.'

'Why the big red seal in front?'

'There's more to it than just that red seal. The whole unit is hermetically sealed. The entire interior of that box and all the equipment it contains is completely sterilized before the box is sealed. One does not inject an unsterilized needle in or near the heart of a cardiac patient.'

'What would happen if I broke that seal?'

'To you, nothing. You'd just be committing the most cardinal sin in any hospital. You'd render the contents useless.

150

And the way you're carrying on the President is a prime candidate for a heart attack at any moment.' O'Hare was acutely conscious that the aerosol can was only inches from his hand. If Branson broke the seal and started delving deeper he intended to use the aerosol without a second thought: Branson could hardly be expected to be the person who would fail to recognize a cyanide air pistol when he saw it.

Branson's face was without expression. 'The President –'

'I'd sooner turn in my licence than insure the President for anything. I am a doctor. Twice your needling and public humiliation have driven him into a state of near-apoplexy. You never know, third time you may be lucky. Go on and break the bloody seal. What's another death on your conscience?'

'I've never been responsible for anybody's death in my life.' Without as much as looking at O'Hare, Branson abruptly left the ambulance. O'Hare went to the rear door and looked after him thoughtfully. Revson was ambling across the roadway and Branson spared him neither a word nor a glance, behaviour uncharacteristic of Branson who was much given to directing penetrating glances at everyone, usually for no reason whatsoever. Revson looked after him in some puzzlement, then strolled off towards the ambulance.

Revson said: 'You just been put through the grinder, too?'

'That you can say again.' O'Hare spoke with some feeling. 'You, too?'

'Not me. I've been searched so often that nobody would bother. Everybody else was, though. It must have been pretty thorough. I heard more than one ladylike scream of protest.' He looked after the departing Branson. 'Our mastermind seems unusually preoccupied.'

'He was acting a bit oddly when he left.'

'He drew a blank, obviously.'

'Yes.'

'Didn't even investigate your one sealed container – the cardiac unit?'

'That's when he started behaving oddly. I'm pretty sure that he was about to break the seal when I pointed out that that would de-sterilize the equipment and render it useless. I also pointed out that I considered the President a prime candidate for a heart attack and that I regarded him as being the prime cause for this. That was when he backed off.'

'Understandable, I would have thought. He doesn't want to lose his principal hostage.'

'That wasn't the impression he gave me. He also said another funny thing when he left, that he'd never been responsible for anyone's death in his life.'

'To the best of my knowledge that's true. Maybe he just didn't want to spoil his good record.'

'Could have been, could have been.' But the puzzled expression was still on O'Hare's face.

Van Effen regarded Branson with a curiosity that his face didn't register. Branson, he thought, was a shade less than his old ebullient self. Van Effen said: 'Well, how did you find the ambulance and the good doctor? Clean?'

'The ambulance is. God damn it all, I quite forgot to go over O'Hare.'

Van Effen smiled. 'One tends to. Pillars of moral rectitude. I'll go look at him.'

'How did it go with you?'

'There were ten of us and we were pretty thorough – and pretty thoroughly unpopular. If there was a silver dollar on the Golden Gate Bridge we'd have found it. We didn't find any silver dollars.'

But then Branson and his men had been searching the wrong places and the wrong people. They should have searched Chief of Police Hendrix before he'd been allowed to leave the bridge.

Hagenbach, Milton, Quarry, Newson and Carter were seated round the long oblong table in the communications wagon. There were bottles of liquor on a wall-mounted sideboard and, judging from the levels of the liquids in the bottles and the glasses in front of the five men, they weren't there for purely decorative purposes. The five appeared to be concentrating on two things only: not speaking to one another and not looking at one another. The bottoms of their glasses appeared to hold a singular fascination for them: comparatively, the average funeral parlour could have qualified as an amusement arcade.

A bell rang softly at the inner end of the wagon. A shirt-sleeved policeman, seated before a battery of telephones, lifted one and spoke softly into it. He turned and said: 'Mr

Quarry, sir. Washington.'

Quarry rose to his feet with the alacrity of a French aristocrat going to the guillotine and made his way to the communications desk. His end of the conversation appeared to consist of a series of dispirited grunts. Finally he said, 'Yes, as planned,' returned to the table and slumped into his chair. 'The money has been arranged just in case it's needed.'

Milton said heavily: 'Can you see it not being needed?'

'The Treasury also agrees that we should stall them for up to twenty-four hours from noon tomorrow.'

Milton's lugubriousness didn't alter. 'By Branson's escalation demands that means close on another fifty million dollars.'

'Peanuts to what he's asking.' Milton made a still born attempt to smile 'Might give one of our brilliant minds time to come up with a brilliant idea.' He relapsed into a silence which no one seemed inclined to break. Hagenbach reached for a bottle of scotch, helped himself and passed the bottle around. They resumed their mournful inspection of the depth of their glasses.

The bottle was not long left undisturbed. Richards and Hendrix entered and, without speaking, sat down heavily in two vacant chairs. The Vice-President's hand reached the bottle just fractionally before that of Hendrix.

Richards said: 'How did we look on TV tonight?'

'God-damned awful. But no more awful than the seven of us sitting around here without a single idea in our heads.' Milton sighed. 'Seven of the allegedly best governmental and law enforcement minds in the business. The best we can do is drink scotch. Not a single idea among us.'

Hendrix said: 'I think perhaps Revson has.' He fished a piece of paper from the inside of a sock and handed it to Hagenbach. 'For you.'

Hagenbach unfolded the note, cursed and shouted to the operator.

'My decoder. Quick.' Hagenbach was back in business and, predictably, he turned to Hendrix: he wouldn't have asked Richards for the time of day. 'How are things out there? Anything we don't know? How come Hansen died?'

'To put it brutally, hunger, greed. Seemingly he snitched one of the food trays before he could be warned which were the dangerous ones and how they could be identified.'

Milton sighed. 'He always was a voracious eater. Compulsive, you might say. Something wrong with his metabolic system, I suppose. Speak no ill of the dead but I often told him that he was digging his grave with his own teeth. Looks like that's what happened.'

'No fault of Revson's?'

'None in the world. But there's worse. Your man Revson is under heavy suspicion. Branson, as we all have cause to know, is a very very clever man and he's convinced there's an infiltrator in their midst. He's also almost equally convinced that it's Revson. I think the man is working on sheer instinct. He can't pin a thing on Revson.'

'Who's also a very very clever man.' Hagenbach paused then looked sharply at Hendrix. 'If Branson is so suspicious of Revson would he let him get within a mile of you, knowing that you were going ashore?'

'Revson didn't come anywhere near me. General Cartland gave me the message. Revson gave the message to Cartland.'

'So Cartland is in on this?'

'He knows as much about it as we do. Revson is going to give him the cyanide pistol. Never thought our Chief of Staff was so positively blood-thirsty. He seems actually to be looking forward to using it.'

Carter said: 'You know Cartland's reputation as a tank commander in the Second World War. After all the comparatively decent Italians and Germans he disposed of then, do you think he's going to worry about doing away with a few really bad hats?'

'You should know. Anyway, I went into one of their awful rest rooms and shoved the note down my sock. I suspected that the Vice-President here and I might be searched before we left the bridge. We weren't. Your Revson is right. Branson is both over-confident and under-conscious of security precautions.'

Revson and O'Hare watched Van Effen walk away. Revson himself walked away a few steps, indicating that O'Hare should follow him. Revson said: 'Well, that was a pretty thorough going-over our friend gave you. I don't think he much appreciated your remark about your hoping that he would be a patient of yours some day.'

O'Hare looked up at the darkly threatening sky, now almost directly overhead. The wind was freshening and, two hundred feet below, the white horses were showing in the Golden Gate.

O'Hare said: 'Looks like a rough night coming up. We'd be more comfortable inside the ambulance, I think, and I've some excellent whisky and brandy in there. Used, you understand, solely for the resuscitation of the sick and ailing.'

'You're going to go far in your profession. Sick and ailing describes my symptoms precisely. But I'd rather be succoured out here.'

'Whatever for?'

Revson gave him a pitying look. 'If it weren't for your good fortune in having me here, you'd very probably be the main object of Branson's suspicions. Has it not occurred to you that, during his intensive search of your ambulance, he might have planted a tiny electronic bug which you wouldn't discover in a week of searching?'

'It occurs to me now. There's a dearth of devious minds in the medical profession.'

'Do you have any gin?'

'It's odd you should ask that. I do.'

'That's for me. I told Branson that I didn't drink and that's why I have a nose like a bloodhound. I shouldn't care for him to see me with a glass of something amber in my hand.'

'Devious, devious minds.' O'Hare disappeared inside the ambulance and reappeared shortly with two glasses, the clear one for Revson. 'Health.'

'Indeed. I shouldn't wonder if that's going to be in short supply inside the next twenty-four hours.'

'Cryptic, aren't we?'

'Psychic.' Revson looked speculatively at the nearest helicopter. 'I wonder if the pilot – Johnson, I think – intends to sleep in his machine tonight.'

O'Hare gave a mock shiver. 'You ever been in a helicopter?'

'Oddly, perhaps, no.'

'I have several times. Strictly, I assure you, in the line of medical duty. These army jobs are fitted with steel-framed canvas chairs, if that's the word for them. For me, it would be a toss-up between that and a bed of nails.'

'So much I suspected. So he'll probably bed down with his fellow-villains in the rear coach.'

'The chopper appears to interest you strangely.'

155

Revson glanced casually around. There was no one within possible earshot.

'The detonating mechanism for the explosives is inside there. I intend – note that I only say intend – to deactivate it tonight.'

O'Hare was silent for a long moment, then said kindly: 'I think I should give you a medical. For that space between the ears. There'll be at least one armed guard on all night patrol. You know the bridge is a blaze of light all night long. So you just dematerialize yourself –'

'The sentry I can take care of. The lights will be switched off when I want them.'

'Abracadabra!'

'I've already sent a message ashore.'

'I didn't know that secret agents doubled as magicians. You produce a carrier pigeon from your hat –'

'Hendrix took it ashore for me.'

O'Hare stared at him then said: 'Another drink?'

'No befuddled wits tonight, thank you.'

'Then I'll have one.' He took both glasses and reappeared with his own. 'Look, that guy Kowalski has the general appearance and the eyes of a hawk. I'm not exactly short-sighted myself. He never took his eyes off you all the time the Vice-President and Hendrix were out here. Branson's orders, I'm certain.'

'Me, too. Who else? I never went near Hendrix. I gave the message to Cartland who passed it on to Hendrix. Kowalski was too busy watching me to bother about Cartland and Hendrix.'

'What time will the lights go off?'

'I don't know yet. I'll send a signal.'

'This means Cartland is in on this?'

'What else? By the way, I promised the General the cyanide gun. Can you get it to him?'

'One way or another.'

'No way, I suppose, of replacing that seal on the cardiac unit once it has been broken?'

'You mean in case our suspicious Mr Branson visits the ambulance again. No.' He smiled. 'It just so happens that I am carrying *two* spare seals inside the box.'

Revson smiled in turn. 'Just goes to show. A man can't think of everything. Still on the side of law and order? Still like to see Branson wearing a nice shiny pair of bracelets?'

'It's becoming a distinct yearning.'

'It might involve bending your code of ethics a little.'

'The hell with the medical ethics.'

Hagenbach positively snatched the sheet of typewritten paper from his decoder. He glanced rapidly through it, his brow corrugating by the second. He said to Hendrix: 'Revson appeared to be perfectly normal when you left him?'

'Who can tell what Revson appears to be?'

'True. I don't seem to be able to make head or tail of this.'

Richards said acidly: 'You might share your little secrets with us, Hagenbach.'

'He says: "It looks as if it's going to be a lousy night, which should help. I want two fake oil fires set now. Or a mixture of oil and rubber tyres. One to my south-west, say Lincoln Park, the other to the east, say Fort Mason – a much bigger fire there. Ignite the Lincoln Park one at twenty-two hundred hours. At two-two-oh-three, infra-red sights if necessary, use a laser beam to destroy the radio scanner on top of the rear coach. Wait my flashlight signal – SOS – then ignite the other. After fifteen minutes blacken out bridge and northern part of San Francisco. It would help if you could at same time arrange a massive fireworks display in Chinatown – as if a firework factory had gone up

' "Submarine at midnight. Please provide transistorized transceiver small enough to fit base camera. Pre-set your frequency and mine and have submarine patch in on same frequency." '

There was a lengthy silence during which Hagenbach, perhaps very understandably, again reached for the scotch. The bottle was rapidly emptied. Richards finally passed his judgement.

'The man's mad, of course. Quite, quite, mad.'

Nobody, for some time, appeared inclined to disagree with him. Richards, *pro tem.* the Chief Executive of the nation, was the man to make the decision, but, apart from his observations on mental instability, he was clearly in no mood to make any kind of decision. Hagenbach took the decision out of his hands.

'Revson is probably a good deal saner than any of us here. He's brilliant, we've had proof of that. Almost certainly, he lacked the time to go into detail. Finally, anyone here got any better idea – let me amend that, anybody here got *any* idea?'

If anyone had, he was keeping it to himself.

'Hendrix, get hold of the deputy Mayor and the Fire Chief. Have those fires set. How about the fireworks?'

Hendrix smiled. 'Fireworks are illegal in San Francisco. Nineteen hundred and six and all that. It so happens we know an illegal underground factory in Chinatown. The owner will be anxious to co-operate.'

Richards shook his head. 'Mad,' he said. 'Quite, quite mad.'

TEN

From far out at sea came the first faint flickers of lightning and the distant rumble of approaching thunder. A now-recovered if somewhat wan April Wednesday, standing with Revson by the centre of the bridge, looked up at the indigo sky and said: 'It looks like being quite a night.'

'I've a feeling that way myself.' He took her arm. 'Are you afraid of thunderstorms as you appear to be of everything else?'

'I don't much fancy being stuck out on this bridge in the middle of one.'

'It's been here for almost forty years. It's not likely to fall down tonight.' He looked upwards as the first drops of rain began to fall. 'But getting wet I object to. Come on.'

They took their seats inside the lead coach, she by the window, he by the aisle. Within minutes the coach was full and within half an hour most of the occupants were dozing if not asleep. Each seat had its own individual reading light, but without exception those were either dimmed or completely out. There was nothing to see, nothing to do. It had been a long, tiring, exciting and in many ways a nerve-racking day. Sleep was not only the sensible but inevitable recourse. And the sound of drumming rain, whether on canvas or on a metal roof, has a peculiarly soporific effect.

And that the rain was now drumming was beyond dispute. It had been increasing steadily ever since the passengers had entered the coach and could now fairly be described as torrential. The approaching thunderstorm, though still some miles distant, was steadily increasing in violence. But neither rain, thunder nor lightning were any deterrent to the prowling Kowalski: he had promised Branson that he would keep his eye on Revson all night long if he had to, and that he clearly intended to do. Regularly, every fifteen minutes, he entered the coach, peered pointedly at Revson, spoke a few brief words to Bartlett, who sat sideways on guard, in the seat next the driver's, then left. Bartlett, Revson apart, was the only alert person in the coach and this, Revson suspected,

159

was due more to Kowalski's recurrent visits than to anything else. On one occasion Revson had overheard Bartlett ask when he was to be relieved and been curtly told that he would have to remain where he was until one o'clock, which suited Revson well enough.

At nine o'clock, when the rain was at its heaviest, Kowalski made another of his routine checks. Revson took out and armed his white pen. Kowalski turned to go. His heel was just descending the riser of the first step when he appeared to stumble. Then he fell, heavily, face-first out of the coach on to the roadway.

Bartlett was the first to reach him, Revson the second. Revson said: 'What the hell happened to him?'

'Lost his footing, far as I could see. Coach door has been open all evening and the steps are slippery as all hell.' Both men stooped to examine the unconscious Kowalski. He was bleeding quite heavily from the forehead which had obviously taken the main brunt of his fall. Revson felt his head gently with his fingers. The needle protruded almost a quarter of an inch behind Kowalski's left ear. Revson removed and palmed it.

Revson said: 'Shall I fetch the doctor?'

'Yes. Sure looks as if he needs one.'

Revson ran to the ambulance. As he approached, the light came on inside the ambulance. Revson took the aerosol can from O'Hare and thrust it into his pocket. The two men, O'Hare carrying his medical bag, ran back to the lead coach. By this time quite a number of curious journalists from the coach – activated, almost certainly, by the inbuilt curiosity that motivates all good journalists, were crowded round the unconscious Kowalski.

'Stand back,' O'Hare ordered. The journalists made way respectfully but didn't stand all that far back. O'Hare opened his bag and began to wipe Kowalski's forehead with a piece of gauze. His opened bag was quite some distance from him, and in the dim light, the driving rain and aided by the total concentration of all on the injured man, it was no great feat for Revson to extract an oil-skinned packet from the bag and send it spinning under the coach. He, but only he, heard the gentle thump as it struck the kerb on the far side. He then pressed in among the curious onlookers.

O'Hare straightened. 'A couple of volunteers to help me get him across to the ambulance.' There was no lack of volunteers. They were about to lift him when Branson came running up.

'Your man's had a pretty nasty fall. I want him in the ambulance for a proper examination.'

'Did he fall or was he pushed?'

'How the hell should I know? You're wasting what could be valuable time, Branson.'

Bartlett said: 'He fell all right, Mr Branson. He slipped on the top step and hadn't a chance to save himself.'

'Certain?'

'Of course I'm bloody certain.' Bartlett was justifiably indignant. He spoke again, but a crashing peal of thunder drowned out his next words. He repeated himself. 'I was within two feet of him at the time – and I hadn't a chance to save him.'

O'Hare paid no more attention to him. With the help of two others he carried Kowalski across to the ambulance. Branson looked at the group of journalists still there, caught sight of Revson.

'Where was Revson at the time?'

'Revson was nowhere near him. He was in his seat, five back there. Everyone was in their seats. Christ, Mr Branson, I'm telling you. It was a pure bloody accident.'

'Must have been.' Clad only in already totally sodden shirt-sleeves and trousers, Branson shivered. 'Jesus, what a night!' He hurried across to the ambulance and as he arrived the two men who had helped O'Hare to carry Kowalski came down the ambulance steps. Branson went inside. O'Hare had already had Kowalski's leather jacket removed and his right sleeve rolled beyond the elbow, and was preparing a hypodermic injection.

Branson said: 'What's that for?'

O'Hare turned in irritation. 'What the hell are you doing here? This is doctor's work. Get out!'

The invitation passed unheeded. Branson picked up the tube from which O'Hare had filled his hypodermic. 'Anti-tetanus? The man's got a head wound.'

O'Hare withdrew the needle, covered the pin-prick, with antiseptic gauze. 'I thought even the most ignorant layman knew that when a man has been injured in the open the first thing he gets is an anti-tetanus injection. You've obviously never seen tetanus.' He sounded Kowalski with his stethoscope, took his pulse and then his temperature.

'Get an ambulance from the hospital.' O'Hare pushed Kowalski's sleeve further up and started to wind the blood-pressure-band round it.

Branson said: 'No.'

O'Hare didn't answer until after he'd taken the pressure. He then repeated: 'Get the ambulance.'

'I don't trust you and your damned ambulances.'

O'Hare didn't answer. He jumped down the steps and strode off through rain that was now rebounding six inches high off the roadway. He was back shortly with the two men who had helped him carry Kowalski across. O'Hare said: 'Mr Grafton. Mr Ferrers. Two highly respected, even eminent journalists. Their words carry a great deal of weight. So will their word.'

'What's that meant to mean?' For the first time since his arrival on the bridge Branson wore just the slightest trace of apprehension.

O'Hare ignored him, addressed himself to the two journalists. 'Kowalski here has severe concussion, possibly even a skull fracture. The latter is impossible to tell without an X-ray. He also has shallow, rapid breathing, a weak and feathery pulse, a temperature and abnormally low blood pressure. This could indicate a few things. One of them cerebral haemorrhaging. I want you gentlemen to bear witness to the fact that Branson refuses to allow an ambulance to come for him. I want you to bear witness to the fact that if Kowalski dies Branson and Branson alone will be wholly responsible for his death. I want you to bear witness to the fact that Branson is fully aware that if Kowalski dies he will be guilty of the same charge as he recently levelled against persons unknown – murder. Only, in his case, I think it would have to be an indictment of the first degree.'

Grafton said: 'I shall so solemnly bear witness.'

Ferrers said: 'And I.'

O'Hare looked at Branson with contempt. 'And you were the person who said to me that you'd never in your life been responsible for the death of a single person.'

Branson said: 'How am I to know that once they get him ashore they won't keep him there?'

'You're losing your grip, Branson.' The contempt was still

in O'Hare's voice: he and Revson had deliberated long enough on how best to wear down Branson psychologically. 'As long as you have a President, a king and a prince, who the hell is going to hold a common criminal like this as a counter-ransom?'

Branson made up his mind. It was difficult to tell whether he was motivated by threats or a genuine concern for Kowalski's life. 'One of those two will have to go tell Chrysler to call the ambulance. I'm not keeping my eyes off you until I see Kowalski safely transferred to the other ambulance.'

'Suit yourself,' O'Hare said indifferently. 'Gentlemen?'

'It will be a pleasure.' The two journalists left. O'Hare began to cover Kowalski in blankets.

Branson said with suspicion: 'What are you doing that for?'

'Heaven preserve me from ignorant laymen. Your friend here is in a state of shock. Rule number one for shock victims – keep them warm.'

Just as he finished speaking there was a massive thunder-clap directly above, so close, so loud, that it was positively hurtful to the ear-drums. The reverberations took many long seconds to die away. O'Hare looked speculatively at Branson then said: 'Know something, Branson? That sounded to me just like the crack of doom.' He poured some whisky into a glass and added a little distilled water.

Branson said: 'I'll have some of that.'

'Help yourself,' O'Hare said agreeably.

From the comparative comfort of the lead coach – comparative, for his clothes were as soaked as if he had fallen into the Golden Gate – Revson watched another ambulance bear away Kowalski's stretchered form. For the moment Revson felt as reasonably content as was possible for a man in his slowly chilling condition. The main object of the exercise had been to get his hands on the cord, canister, torch and aerosol. All of those he had achieved. The first three were still under the bus by the kerb-side: the fourth nestled snugly in his pocket. That all this should have been done at the expense of Kowalski, the most relentlessly vigilant of all Branson's guards and by a long way the most suspicious, was just an added bonus. He bethought himself of the aerosol. He gave April Wednesday a gentle nudge and, because people were still talking in varying degrees of animation about the latest incident, he did not find it necessary to keep his voice especially low.

'Listen carefully, and don't repeat my words, no matter how stupid my question may appear. Tell me, would a young lady of – ah – delicate sensibilities – carry a miniature aerosol air-freshener around with her?'

Beyond a blink of the green eyes she showed no reaction. 'In certain circumstances I suppose so, yes.'

He placed the can between them. 'Then please put this in your carry-all. Sandalwood, but I wouldn't try sniffing it.'

'I know very well what's in it.' The can disappeared. 'I suppose it doesn't matter very much if I'm caught with it? If they bring out those old thumb-screws – '

'They won't. They already searched your carry-all, and the person who made the search almost certainly wouldn't remember the contents of one of a dozen bags he's searched. No one's keeping an eye on you: I'm way out on my own as Suspect Number One.'

By ten o'clock silence and sleep had returned to the coach. The rain had eased, until it could be called no more than heavy, but still the lightning crackled and the thunder boomed with unabated enthusiasm. Revson glanced over his shoulder to the south-west. There were no signs of any unusual activities in the direction of Lincoln Park. He wondered if those ashore had misinterpreted his message or deliberately ignored it. Both possibilities he thought unlikely: more likely, because of the heavy rain, they were having difficulty in igniting a fire.

At seven minutes past ten a red glow appeared to the south-west. Revson was almost certainly the first person on the bridge to notice it but he thought it impolitic to draw attention to the fact. Within half a minute the dark oily flames were at least fifty feet high.

It was Bartlett who first called attention to this phenomenon and he did so in a very emphatic fashion. He stood in the open doorway behind the driver's seat and shouted: 'Jesus, would you look at that!'

Almost everyone immediately started awake and looked. They couldn't see much. Rain still lashed the outside of the windows and the insides were pretty well steamed up. Like a bunch of lemmings hell-bent on a watery suicide they poured out through the door. The view was certainly very much better from there and well worth the seeing. The flames, already a hundred feet high and topped by billowing clouds of oily smoke, were increasing by the second. Still of the same lemming-like mind and totally oblivious of the rain, they began to run across the bridge to obtain a better view. The occupants of the Presidential and rear coaches were doing exactly the same. Nothing attracts people more than the prospects of a good-going disaster.

Revson, though among the first out of the lead coach, made no attempt to join them. He walked unhurriedly round the front of the coach, walked back a few feet, stooped and recovered the oil-skin package. No one paid any attention to him, even had he been visible beyond the bulk of the coach, because they were all running in and looking towards the opposite direction. He removed the torch from the package, angled it forty-five degrees to his right and made his SOS signal, just once: he then pocketed the torch and made his more leisurely way across to the other side of the bridge, glancing occasionally over his left shoulder. Half-way across he saw a rocket, a not very spectacular one, curving up to the south-east.

He reached the far crash barrier and joined O'Hare who was standing some little way apart from the others. O'Hare said: 'You'd make quite an arsonist.'

'That's just by the way of introduction. Wait till you see the next one. Not to mention the fireworks. Sheer pyromania, that's what it is. Let's look at the front end of the rear coach.'

They looked. A full minute passed and nothing happened. O'Hare said: 'Hm. Worrisome?'

'No. Just running a little bit behind schedule, I should think. Don't even blink.'

O'Hare didn't and so he saw it – a tiny intense spark of bluish-white that could have lasted only milli-seconds. O'Hare said: 'You saw it too?'

'Yes. Far less than I thought it would be.'

'End of radio-wave scanner?'

'No question.'

'Would anyone inside the coach have heard it?'

'That's academic. There's no one inside the rear coach.

They're all across here. But there is some sign of activity at the rear of the Presidential coach. A dollar gets a cent that Branson's asking some questions.'

Branson was indeed asking some questions. Chrysler by his side, he was talking forcefully into a telephone.

'Then find out and find out now.'

'I'm trying to.' It was Hendrix and he sounded weary. 'I can be held responsible for a lot of things but I can't be held responsible for the forces of nature. Don't you realize this is the worst lightning storm the city has had in years? There are dozens of outbreaks of small fires and the Firemaster tells me his force is fully extended.'

'I'm waiting, Hendrix.'

'So am I. And God only knows how you imagine this fire in Lincoln Park can affect you. Sure, it's giving off clouds of oil smoke, but the wind's from the west and the smoke won't come anywhere near you. You're jumping at shadows, Branson. Wait. A report.' There was a brief silence then Hendrix went on: 'Three parked road oil tankers. One had its loading hose partly on the ground so it was earthed. Witnesses saw this tanker being struck by lightning. Two fire engines are there and the fire is under control. Satisfied?'

Branson hung up without replying.

The fire was indeed under control. Firemen, taking their convincing time, were now smothering the barrels of blazing oil with foam extinguishers. Fifteen minutes after the fire had first begun – or been noticed – it was extinguished. Reluctantly, almost – they were now so wet that they couldn't possibly get any wetter – the watchers by the west barrier turned and made their way back to the coaches. But their evening's entertainment had only just begun.

Another fire bloomed to the north. It spread and grew with even greater rapidity than the previous one, becoming so bright and intense that even the lights in the concrete towers of down-town San Francisco seemed pale by comparison. Branson, who had made his way back to his own coach, now ran back to the Presidential coach. A bell was ringing in the communications section in the rear. Branson snatched the phone. It was Hendrix.

Hendrix said: 'Nice to forestall you for once. No, we are

not responsible for this one either. Why in the hell should we set off a fire where all the smoke is being carried away from you east over the bay? The meteorological officer says that there's a lightning strike once every three or four seconds. And it's not cloud to cloud stuff, it's mainly cloud to earth. On the law of averages, he says, something combustible has to go in one in twenty. I'll keep you posted.'

For the first time, Hendrix hung the phone up on him. Branson slowly replaced his own. For the first time, lines of strain were beginning to etch themselves round the corners of his mouth.

The blue-veined flames were towering now to a height of six or seven hundred feet, as high as the highest building in the city. The smoke given off was dense and bitingly acrid, which is generally the case when several hundred used tyres are added to an oil-based fire. But half a dozen giant fire engines and as many again mobile foam wagons were in very close attendance indeed. On the bridge the more nervous of the newspapermen and cameramen were speculating as to whether the fire would spread to the city itself, a rather profitless speculation as the wind was entirely in the wrong direction. Mayor Morrison stood by the eastern crash barrier, fists clenched, tears streaming down his face, cursing with a non-stop fluid monotony.

O'Hare said to Revson: 'I wonder if the King and the Prince see the irony in all this. After all, it's probably their own oil that they're seeing going up.' Revson made no reply and O'Hare touched his arm. 'Sure you haven't overdone things a bit this time, old boy?' In moments of stress, his English education background tended to show through.

'I wasn't the one with the matches.' Revson smiled. 'No worry, they know what they're about. What I am looking forward to seeing now is the firework display.'

In the Presidential communications centre the phone rang again. Branson had it in a second.

'Hendrix. It's an oil storage tank in Fort Mason.' There was no oil storage tank in Fort Mason, but Branson was not a Californian far less a San Franciscan and it was highly unlikely that he was aware of that. 'I've just been on the radio to the Fire Commissioner. He says its bark is worse than its bite and that there's no danger.'

'And what the hell is that, then?' Branson's voice was a shout, his normal monolithic calm in at least temporary abeyance.

'What's what?'

Hendrix's calm served only to deepen Branson's apprehension. 'Fireworks! Dozens of them! Fireworks! Can't you see them?'

'Not from where I sit I can't. Wait.' Hendrix went to the rear door of the communications wagon. Branson hadn't been exaggerating. The sky was indeed full of fireworks, of every conceivable colour and design, at least half of them exploding in glittering falling stars. If Branson had been his usual calm and observant self, Hendrix reflected, he might have noticed that the fireworks, nearly all of a medium trajectory, were firing to the north-east which was the shortest distance between where they were coming from and the nearest stretch of water. All of them, without exception, would fizzle out in the waters of San Francisco Bay. Hendrix returned to the phone.

'They appear to be coming from the Chinatown area and sure as hell they aren't celebrating the Chinese New Year. I'll call back.'

Revson said to O'Hare: 'Take your white coat off. It's too conspicuous or will be when it gets dark.' He gave O'Hare his white felt pen. 'You know how to use this?'

'Depress the clip and press the button on top.'

'Yes. If anyone comes too near – well, aim for the face. You'll have to extract the needle.'

'Me and my medical ethics.'

Branson picked up the phone. 'Yes?'

'It was Chinatown. A firework factory there was struck. That damned thunder and lightning doesn't just seem to want to go away. God knows how many more outbreaks of fire we'll have tonight.'

Branson left the coach and joined Van Effen by the east barrier. Van Effen turned.

'Not often you see a sight like this, Mr Branson.'

'I'm afraid I'm not in the mood to enjoy it.'

'Why?'

'I've a feeling that this is being staged for our benefit.'

'How could this possibly affect us? Nothing's changed as far as we're concerned. Don't let's forget our presidential and royal hostages.'

'Even so – '

'Even so your antennae are tingling?'

'Tingling! They're jumping. I don't know what's going to happen next but I've the feeling that I'm not going to enjoy it.'

It was at that moment that the bridge and the whole of northern San Francisco blacked out.

For some few seconds the silence on the bridge was total. The darkness wasn't total but it came fairly close to being that way. The only illumination came from the faint lighting from the coaches – to conserve the batteries most of the individual reading lights were out, the others dimmed – and the orange-red glow from the distant oil fire. Van Effen said softly: 'Your antennae, Mr Branson. You know you could make a fortune hiring them out.'

'Start up the generator. We'll have the searchlights on the north and south towers. See that the self-propelled guns are ready, loaded, crews standing by. Three men with submachine-guns to be by each gun. I'll go south, you north and alert them. After that, you're in charge of both. I'll try to find out from that bastard Hendrix what this is all about.'

'You don't seriously expect a frontal assault, Mr Branson.'

'I frankly don't know what the hell to expect. What I do know is that we take no chances. Hurry!'

Branson ran south. As he passed the rear coach he shouted: 'Chrysler! The generator. Quick, for God's sake.'

The generator was running before either Branson or Van Effen reached the respective defensive positions. The powerful searchlights came on illuminating both towers: the reverse effect was to plunge the central portion of the bridge into even deeper gloom than before. The guns were readied, machine-gunners in close attendance. Van Effen stayed where he was. Branson ran back towards the central coach. But both Branson and Van Effen were concentrating their efforts on the wrong things and in the wrong directions. They should have been where Revson was.

Revson was crouched in the nose section of the leading helicopter, the variably shuttered flashlight in his hand reduced to scarcely more than a pin-hole of light. He had had no trouble in locating the triggering device: it was between the pilot's seat and the one opposite to it.

With the screwdriver blade of his knife Revson had already removed the four screws that secured the top-plate and the top-plate itself. It was a simple enough device. On the outside of the device was a vertical lever padlocked in position in its top position. When this was depressed it brought a copper arm down between two spring-loaded interior copper arms, so completing the circuit. Twin pieces of flex led from those last two to two crocodile spring-loaded clamps, each secured to the terminals of two nickel-cadmium Nife cells connected up in series. That would produce a total of only three volts, little enough, one would have thought, to activate the radio trigger: but that Branson would have it all expertly calculated out in advance Revson did not for a moment doubt.

He didn't bother to sever or disconnect anything. He merely removed the crocodile clips from the terminals, lifted the Nife cells free, broke the connection between them and stuffed one in each jacket pocket. Had he disconnected or severed anything Branson could have carried out some sort of jury rig: but Revson would have wagered heavily that Branson carried no spare Nife cells. There was no earthly reason why he should have done. He began to replace the cover-plate.

Hendrix sounded angry, a man near the breaking point of exasperation. 'What do you think I am, Branson? A bloody magician? I just sit here and snap my fingers and presto! all the lights in the north half of the city go out? I've told you and I tell you again that two of the main transformers have gone out. How I don't know yet, but you don't have to be a genius to know that our old friend from the skies above has been at work again. What did you expect us to do – throw in a tank regiment against you? We knew you had those heavy guns and searchlights – and your priceless hostages. Think we're morons? I'm beginning to think that you're the moron. I'm beginning to think that you're losing your grip. I'll call back.' Hendrix hung up. Branson did the same, almost smashing the rest in the process. It was the second occasion in a very brief space of time that it had been suggested to him that he was losing his grip. His lips were compressed. It was a suggestion he didn't much care for, far less care to contemplate. He remained seated where he was.

Revson closed the helicopter door softly and dropped lightly to the ground. A few paces away he could see O'Hare silhouetted against the still towering but slowly diminishing flames. He called his name softly and O'Hare approached.

'Let's walk to the west side,' Revson said. 'No shooting practice?'

'Nobody as much as looked at the place, far less came near it. Even if they had looked, I doubt whether they would have seen anything. After staring so long at that fire and the fireworks, looking back to the centre of the bridge would have been like looking into total darkness. You know, no night sight.' He handed Revson the white pen. 'Have your little toy back. I remain ethically unbent.'

'And you can have your flashlight back.' Revson handed it over. 'I suggest you return it to your ambulance. At the same time I suggest we might retrieve that pistol and give it to General Cartland. I also suggest you give it to him. I don't want to be seen being too chummy with the General. Tell him not to use it till he gets the word. Ever seen one of those before?' He took a Nife cell from his pocket and handed it to O'Hare who peered at it in the near darkness.

'Some sort of battery?'

'Yes. There were two of them and I have the other. They were to be used to power the explosives' triggering device.'

'And you left no trace of your coming and going?'

'None.'

'So we walk towards the side of the bridge.'

They lobbed the cells into the Golden Gate and walked to the ambulance. O'Hare ushered Revson in first, then followed, closing the door. He said: 'I think we should use the torch. The sudden appearance of bright lights in the windows might attract suspicious attention. After all, we're supposed to be out there enjoying the sights.

It took O'Hare less than two minutes to break the Cardiac Arrest Unit seal, lift out some equipment, open up, after a series of intricate operations, a secret compartment in the bottom of the box, retrieve the cyanide gun, replace the equipment, close and reseal the lid. O'Hare placed the gun in an inside coat pocket and said complainingly: 'I'm beginning to become ethical all over again.'

Hendrix said over the phone: 'It wasn't the transformers after all. There have been so many breaks and shorts in the city's electrical equipment tonight that the generators' overload coils just packed up.'

'How long?' Branson asked.

'A few minutes. No more.'

As was his habit, General Cartland was standing alone by the east barrier. He turned and saw O'Hare who said quietly: 'A word, sir, if you please.'

The lights of San Francisco and the Golden Gate Bridge came on five minutes later. Branson left the Presidential coach and went to meet Van Effen. He said: 'Still think I could make a fortune hiring out my antennae?' He was smiling.

Van Effen wasn't. He said: 'Do me a favour. Just hang on to them a little while yet.'

'Don't tell me your antennae are at work too?'

'If they're not, they sure have good stand-ins.'

The last of the fireworks fizzled to extinction, the oil fire in Fort Mason sank down into a sullen deep-red glow, the lightning and thunder eased, although not markedly so, but the rain showed no sign of abating: had fire broken out in San Francisco that night, it would surely have been rained to extinction. Now that the night's entertainment was patently over, everyone became very conscious that the rain had become very chilly indeed. There was an almost concerted movement back to the coaches.

Revson was in the window seat by the time April Wednesday came in. She hesitated, then sat down beside him. She said: 'And why do you want my seat? I thought it was customary for the lady to be offered the inside seat.'

'To keep her from falling into the aisle during the night? Don't you know this is the golden age of women's lib? However, that's not my real reason. Is it possible for me to reach the aisle without disturbing you in the process?'

'That's a silly question.'

'Is it? I mean, possible?'

172

'You can see it isn't.'

'Would you be prepared to swear – short of thumb-screws, that is – that I never once disturbed you in the course of the night?'

'You propose to disturb me, then?'

'Yes. Will you?'

She smiled. 'I think I've shown that I can lie with the best of them.'

'You're not only beautiful, but you're good.'

'Thank you. Where were you thinking of going?'

'Do you really want to know? I think you'd better not. Think of the thumb-screws, the rack, being broken on the wheel –'

'But Chief of Police Hendrix said that Branson never offered violence to women.'

'That was the Branson of yore. But he's become jittery now, more than a little rattled. He might find himself driven to a point where he's compelled to abandon his scruples.'

It wasn't the completely sodden thin silk dress she was wearing that made her shiver. 'I think I'd rather not know. When are you –'

'Just before midnight.'

'Then I shan't sleep a wink before then.'

'Excellent. Give me a shake at five minutes to.' Revson closed his eyes and appeared to relax comfortably in his seat.

By five minutes to midnight everyone in the coach appeared to be asleep: despite their cold and discomfort nearly all had been asleep for over an hour. Even April Wednesday was asleep, her head on Revson's shoulder, huddling close to him for warmth. She was quite unaware of this. Even the guard, Bartlett, almost certainly because Kowalski's prowling figure was no longer there to keep him on the qui vive, was much nearer sleep than wakefulness, his head nodding on his chest, only occasionally, and with longer intervals in between, jerking his head upright. Only Revson, his eyes closed, was as awake and alert as a cat on a midnight prowl. He nudged April and whispered in her ear. She started awake and looked at him, her eyes uncomprehending.

'Time to go,' he said softly. It was almost dark inside the coach, the only illumination coming from the dimmed light over the driver's seat and from the lights of the bridge itself. 'Give me the aerosol.'

'The what?' Suddenly she was wide awake, the white of the smudged eyes – the pupils could have been any colour – huge in the gloom. 'Of course.' She reached under her seat and brought up the aerosol can. Revson tucked it in his inside left coat pocket. She said: 'How long will you be?'

'With luck, twenty minutes. Perhaps half an hour. I'll be back.'

She kissed him lightly on the cheek. 'Please take care.'

Revson had no comment on this highly unnecessary advice. 'Move into the aisle. Quietly as you can.'

He passed by her and moved silently forwards, his white pen in his hand. Bartlett's head was on his chest. Revson pressed the button at a distance of less than a foot and the needle lodged behind Bartlett's left ear. Revson eased him back until his head dangled over the back of his seat. The drug, apart from inducing unconsciousness, had a temporarily paralysing effect so there seemed little enough likelihood that Bartlett would slip off his seat. April watched all this without any expression: the only indication of her feelings was the tip of a tongue that sought to moisten dry lips.

There had to be a patrolling guard, Revson knew – he had, in fact, seen him several times – and he had to be taken care of. He peered cautiously through the open driver's doorway. A guard was indeed approaching, coming up from the south, walking a few feet wide of the coaches and carrying a shoulder-slung machine-carbine. Revson thought he recognized him as Johnson, one of the helicopter pilots, but couldn't be sure. Revson switched off Bartlett's dimmed light and remained where he was. He had the aerosol can in his hand but at the last moment changed his mind and brought up the pen instead. A person recovering from the effects of the knock-out needles invariably awoke none the worse for his experience and usually assumed that he had just dropped off to sleep: but as Revson could tell from his own experience of that morning, a person awakening from a gas knock-out felt nauseated and thoroughly hungover and under no illusion at all that he had been anaesthetized in one way or another. It didn't seem a good idea to have Johnson report this to Branson.

Revson pressed the button and jumped down at the same

instant to catch Johnson before he keeled over on to the roadway, less for humanitarian reasons than to prevent the metallic sound of the carbine striking the roadway. He removed the needle from Johnson's forehead, hauled him as silently as possible inside the coach and jammed him in a very uncomfortable position in front of the driver's seat. Johnson was in no position to feel any discomfort and Revson didn't want to risk the possibility of any passenger awakening – highly unlikely though it seemed – and finding an unconscious stranger lying in the aisle.

April Wednesday had gone back to her lip-licking.

Revson emerged by the nearside front door. In the bright lights of the bridge he might almost as well have stepped out into daylight. He had no doubt that his activities were being carefully watched from both north and south shores through powerful night glasses, but that was of no concern. What mattered was that he was effectively shielded from the other two coaches, though he seriously doubted whether there was anyone keeping watch in either or, indeed, whether anybody at all was awake. In point of fact both Van Effen and Chrysler were talking quietly to each other in the rear coach, but it was impossible for them to see Revson.

Revson crossed the crash barrier, pulled himself to the rail and peered down. Below, all was total blackness. The submarine could or could not have been there: he just had to hope it was.

He descended and pulled the oil-skin container from under the coach. Inside was the fishing line and a weighted lab. sample canister – weighted, because the wind was still gusting and he had to be sure that the line descended reasonably vertically.

He cut off hooks and lures at the end of the fishing line and attached the canister to the line. He eased the canister over the side and started unwinding the line from its square wooden framework. After about thirty seconds of this he stopped, held the line delicately between forefinger and thumb and waited for some sort of acknowledging tug. There was none. He lowered it another ten feet. Still no answering tug. Perhaps the submarine wasn't there, perhaps the captain was finding it impossible to maintain position because of the tides and strong currents. But then Admiral Newson had said that he knew just the very man who could do just that and it was unlikely that a man of Newson's reputation would make any mistake. Revson lowered the line another ten feet then sighed aloud with relief when he felt two sharp tugs on the line.

Twenty seconds later there came another two sharp tugs. Revson overhanded the line in with all possible speed. When he estimated there were only a few feet of line left he leaned far out and pulled in at a much slower speed. He had no wish to bang the radio, however gently, against the steelwork of the bridge. Finally, he had it in his hand, a waterproof bag with the line securely fixed round its neck. He descended to the side of the bus to examine his catch. He cut the securing line with his knife and peered inside. There it was – a tiny gleaming transistorized transceiver.

'Strange hour to go fishing, Revson,' Van Effen said behind him. For a second, no more, Revson remained immobilized. He was holding the bag at chest level and his hand slid stealthily into his left inner pocket. 'I'd like to see just what kind of fish one catches at night in the Golden Gate. Turn round, Revson, slow and easy. I'm a nervous character and you know what that can do to trigger fingers.'

Revson turned round, slow and easy, in the manner of a man who knows all about nervous trigger fingers. He already had the aerosol inside the bag. He said resignedly: 'Well, I suppose it was too good to last.'

'So Branson was right all along.' Van Effen, moon-shaped face as expressionless as ever, was between five and six feet away. He had his machine-pistol in both hands, held loosely, but with his forefinger indubitably on the trigger. Revson would have been a dead man before he'd covered half the distance between them. But Van Effen was clearly expecting no resistance. 'Let's see what you have there. Slow and easy, now. Slow and easy.'

Slowly, easily, Revson withdrew the aerosol. It was so small that it was almost hidden in his hand. He knew that the can was pressurized to three times the normal and that its effective range was ten feet. Or so O'Hare had told him and Revson had a great deal of faith in O'Hare.

Van Effen shifted the gun under his right arm and pointed the barrel straight at Revson. 'Let me see that.'

'Slow and easy?'

'Slow and easy.'

Revson stretched his arm out unhurriedly. Van Effen's face was no more than three feet away when he pressed the button. He dropped the aerosol and snatched Van Effen's machine-pistol: again he wished to obviate any metallic sounds. He looked down at the crumpled figure at his feet. He had come to form a certain regard for Van Effen, both as a man and a professional: but regrets were not in Revson's line of business. He retrieved the aerosol, took the transceiver and pressed a switch.

'Revson here.'

'Hagenbach.' Revson lowered the volume.

'This is a closed VHF line? No possibility of interception?'

'None.'

'Thank you for the radio. I have a problem here. One of disposal. Van Effen caught me but I caught him. Gas. He recognized me, of course, and can't remain on the bridge. I could throw him into the Golden Gate but I don't want to. He's done nothing to deserve anything like that. He might even turn State evidence. May I speak to the submarine captain, please.'

A new voice came through. 'Captain here. Commander Pearson.'

'My congratulations, Captain, and thank you for the radio. You heard what I said to Mr Hagenbach.'

'Yes.'

'Would you be prepared to accept another passenger even although he is unconscious?'

'We aim to please.'

'Would you have a line or rope aboard easy enough for me to haul up but strong enough to take a man's weight? I'd need about five hundred feet.'

'Goodness, no. Wait till I check.' There was a brief silence, then Pearson's voice came through again. 'We have three thirty-fathom coils. Joined together that should be more than enough.'

'Splendid. I'll send my cord down again. Moment, please. I'll have to get a weight for it first.' He strap-hung the radio round his neck to leave his hands free and his eye lighted almost immediately on Van Effen's machine-pistol. He secured the cord to the trigger guard and immediately began to lower away. He spoke into the radio.

'The line's on the way down. It's weighted with Van Effen's

177

machine-pistol and the cord is tied to the trigger-guard. I mean, I wouldn't like anyone to shoot themselves by accident.'

'The Navy is accustomed to the handling of offensive weapons, Mr Revson.'

'No offence, Captain. When I get the rope up I'll pass it over a rail and secure it to Van Effen. Double bowline round the thighs, a turn round his waist and his hands tied behind his back so that the rope can't slip over his shoulders.'

'We have openings in the Service for resourceful young men like you.'

'I'm afraid the age qualification cut-off lies far behind me. When I have him ready can you have two or three of your men lower him down over the rail? Damned if I'm going to try myself. As I said, it's my age.'

'You wouldn't believe how modernized today's Navy is. We'll use a winch.'

Revson said apologetically: 'I'm just a land-lubber.'

'We have your cord and gun and nobody's shot down anybody.' There was a brief pause. 'Haul away.'

Revson brought in the rope. It looked hardly thicker than a clothes-line, but Revson didn't doubt that Pearson knew what he was about. He trussed Van Effen in the manner he'd described then dragged him to the edge. He said into the radio: 'Ready to take the strain?'

'Ready.'

Revson eased him over the edge. For a moment Van Effen dangled there, then disappeared downwards into the darkness. The rope over the rail went slack and Pearson's voice came over the radio.

'We have him.'

'Intact?'

'Intact. All for tonight?'

'Yes. Thank you for your co-operation.' Revson wondered briefly what Van Effen's reaction would be when he found himself in a submarine, then spoke again into the radio. 'Mr Hagenbach?'

'Here.'

'You heard it all?'

'Yes. Not a bad job.' Hagenbach was not much given to showering fulsome congratulations on his subordinates.

'I've been lucky. The triggering mechanism for the explosives has been deactivated. Permanently.'

'Good. Very good.' This, from Hagenbach, was the equivalent to the Roman tribute offered a highly successful general after he'd conquered his second or third country in succession. 'Mayor Morrison *will* be pleased to know this.'

'When he knows it. I suggest that in a couple of hours' time you douse the bridge lights again and effect entry into the east side south tower. You have the men, sir?'

'Hand-picked.'

'Don't forget to tell them to remove the detonators on the explosives. Just precautionary, you know.'

'Ha!' Hagenbach's deflation was like a snowflake in the river. 'Of course.'

'And another thought. Before you cut the lights you might use the laser on their south-facing searchlight.'

'We will, my boy, we will.'

'Please don't contact me at any time. I might be carrying the radio on me and might be in a very awkward position, such as talking to Branson, when the call-up buzzer goes off.'

'We'll keep a permanent listening watch for you.'

Hagenbach looked round his colleagues. His face almost broke into a smile but he just managed to keep his record intact. He looked at each one in turn, trying to conceal his complacency, but not trying too hard, then finally directed his attention towards the Vice-President.

' "Mad" was the word you used, sir. "Quite mad." '

Richards took it very well. 'Well, perhaps a divine sort of madness. Deactivating that triggering device is a major step forward in itself. If only, as you say, Morrison knew.'

'There do appear to be no limits to his resourcefulness,' Quarry said. 'The right man, in the right place, at the right time, if ever there was. But it still doesn't solve the central problem of the plight of our hostages.'

'I wouldn't worry.' Hagenbach leaned back comfortably in his chair. 'Revson will think of something.'

ELEVEN

The only thing Revson was thinking about was how very pleasant it would be to have a few hours' blissful sleep. He'd dragged an already stirring Johnson from his cramped position in front of the driver's seat and propped him on the second step of the coach entrance, head and shoulders resting more or less comfortably against the hand-rail. A minute or two, Revson thought, and he would come to. Even Bartlett was beginning to stir restlessly in his drugged sleep. Different people reacted widely in the length of time it took them to recover from the effect of the knock-out needles. Johnson and Bartlett appeared to have very similar reaction times.

Revson moved silently down the aisle. April Wednesday was wide awake. She swung out to let him pass to the inside seat then sat again. Before removing his soaking coat and dumping it on the floor, he passed her the aerosol. She stooped and thrust it in the bottom of her carry-all. She whispered: 'I didn't think I'd see you again. How did it go?'

'Well enough.'

'What happened?'

'You want to know? Really?'

She thought and shook her head. There were still visions of thumb-screws in her head. Instead, she said softly: 'What's that round your neck?'

'Good God!' From sleepiness Revson was jerked into immediate wide-awakeness. The little transceiver still dangled from his neck. What a sight for a roving Branson. He lifted the transceiver from his neck, unclipped the straps, picked up his camera and inserted the radio in its base.

She said: 'What's that?'

'Just a teeny-weeny hand camera.'

'It's not. It's a radio.'

'Call it what you like.'

'Where did you get it from? I mean, this coach – everything – has been searched from top to bottom.'

'From a passing friend. I have friends everywhere. You may well have saved my life there. I could kiss you for it.'

'Well?'

When it came to kissing she was nowhere near as fragile as she looked. Revson said: 'That was the nicest part of the whole evening. Of the whole day. Of a whole lot of days. Some day, some time, when we get off this damned bridge, we must try that again.'

'Why not now?'

'You're a brazen –' He caught her arm and nodded. Somewhere up front someone was stirring. It was Johnson. He rose to his feet with surprising quickness and looked up and down the bridge. Revson could just picture what was going on in his mind. His last recollection would have been of seeing the steps of the lead coach and his natural assumption would be that he had just sat down for a moment to rest. One thing was for sure, he would never admit to Branson that he'd slept for even a second. He stepped into the bus and prodded Bartlett with the muzzle of his machine-gun. Bartlett started awake and stared at him.

'You asleep?' Johnson demanded.

'Me? Asleep?' Bartlett was amazed, indignant. 'Can't a man rest his eyes for a moment without having accusations like that thrown at him?'

'Just see that you don't rest them for too long.' Johnson's voice was coldly self-righteous. He descended the steps and walked away.

Revson murmured to April: 'I was sleepy but I'm not now. But I not only want to appear to be asleep, I want to *be* asleep if any turmoil breaks out in the very near future, which I strongly suspect might happen. Don't happen to have any sleeping tablets on you, do you?'

'Why on earth should I? This was supposed to be a day trip, remember.'

'I remember.' He sighed. 'Well, there's nothing else for it. Give me the aerosol can.'

'Why?'

'Because I want to take just the tiniest whiff of it. Then take the can from my hand and tuck it away again.'

She hesitated.

'Remember this dinner – those lots of dinners – I'm going to take you to just as soon as we get ashore.'

'I don't remember anything of the kind.'

'Well, remember it now. But I can't very well take you if

181

I'm at the bottom of the Golden Gate, can I?'

She shuddered and reached reluctantly into her carry-all.

In the rear coach Chrysler put his hand on Branson's shoulder and shook him gently. Branson, despite what must have been his exhaustion, was immediately awake, immediately alert.

'Trouble?'

'I don't know. I'm worried, Mr Branson. Van Effen left here just, he said, to make a normal check on things. He hasn't come back.'

'How long ago was that?'

'Half an hour, sir.'

'God, Chrysler, why didn't you wake me before now?'

'Two things. I knew you needed sleep and we all depend on you. And if ever I knew a man who could take care of himself it's Van Effen.'

'He was carrying his machine-pistol?'

'Have you ever seen him without it since we came on this bridge?'

Branson rose from his seat, picked up his own gun and said: 'Come with me. Did you see which way he went?'

'North.'

They walked to the Presidential coach. Peters, the guard, was sitting sideways in the driver's seat, smoking. He turned quickly as a gentle tap came on the door, removed a key from an inner pocket and turned it in the lock. Branson opened the door from the outside and said quietly: 'Have you seen any signs of Van Effen?' He could, in fact, have raised his voice a couple of dozen decibels and it would have made no difference: when it comes to the terms of stertorous snoring, presidents, royalty, generals, mayors and assorted government ministers are no different from the common run of mankind.

'Yes, Mr Branson. Must have been about half an hour ago. I saw him walk towards the nearest rest room there.'

'Did you see him come out again?'

'No. Quite frankly, I wasn't looking outside. I don't bother much. My job is to see that none of those gentlemen makes for the communications desk or rushes me and takes away my gun and key. I don't much fancy having my own gun pointed at my own head. I keep my eyes for what goes on inside this coach not what goes on outside it.'

'And right you are. No reflections on you, Peters.' Branson

closed the door and heard the key turn in the lock. They made for the nearest rest room. A very brief search indicated that it was empty. So was the other rest room. They made their way to the ambulance. Branson opened the rear door, used a small torch to locate a switch and flooded the ambulance with light. A shirt-sleeved O'Hare covered with a single blanket, was sound asleep on the side-hinged cot. Branson shook him awake. It took some shaking.

O'Hare opened the rather bleary eyes, winced at the bright overhead light, looked at the two men then at his watch.

'Quarter to one! What the hell do you want at this time of the morning?'

'Van Effen's missing. Have you seen him?'

'No, I haven't seen him.' O'Hare showed a faint stirring of what could have been professional interest. 'Was he sick or something?'

'No.'

'Then why bother me? Perhaps,' O'Hare said hopefully, 'he's fallen over the side.'

Branson studied the doctor briefly. O'Hare's eyes were slightly puffy, but Branson was experienced enough to realize that it was the puffiness of sleepiness not of sleeplessness. He gestured Chrysler to leave, followed, switched out the light and closed the door behind him.

Johnson, machine-gun slung, was walking towards them. He came up to them, stopped and said: "Evening, Mr Branson. 'Morning rather.'

'Have you seen Van Effen?'

'Van Effen? When?'

'Inside the past half hour.'

Johnson shook his head positively. 'Definitely not.'

'But he was out on the bridge. You were on the bridge. If he was here, then you must have.'

'Sorry. No. It's possible he was and possible that I didn't see him. I walk to and fro all the time – it's the best way of keeping awake. I don't keep glancing over my shoulder all the time.' Johnson thought or appeared to think. 'He may have been on the bridge but he may have left it. By that I mean he may for reasons best known to himself have chosen to walk on the other side of the buses.'

'Why should he do that?'

'How should I know? Maybe he wanted to keep in concealment. Maybe anything. How should I know what goes on in Van Effen's mind?'

'True.' Branson had no particular wish to antagonize Johnson, who, apart from being an ex-naval officer, was a highly experienced helicopter pilot and an essential part of his escape plans. He said mildly: 'I just suggest that you stand in the middle here and look around from time to time. You're hardly likely to go to sleep on your feet – you're due for relief in fifteen minutes.'

He and Chrysler made their way towards the lead coach. There was a half-dimmed light up front and they could see the glow of Bartlett's cigar. Branson said: 'Well, at least all the guards seem to be on the alert – which makes it all the more difficult to understand Van Effen's disappearance.'

Bartlett said briskly. ''Morning, Mr Branson. Making your rounds? All's well here.'

'Have you seen Van Effen? In the past half hour?'

'No. You can't find him?'

'Let's say he's missing.'

Bartlett thought. 'I won't ask stupid questions like "How can he be missing?" Who saw him last?'

'Peters. Not that that helps. Anybody left this coach in the past half hour?'

'Nobody's left this coach since we came in after the fire.'

Branson walked back to Revson's seat. April Wednesday was wide awake. Revson, eyes closed, was breathing deeply, heavily. Branson shone the torch in his eyes. There was no reaction. Branson lifted an eyelid. There was no involuntary twitching or muscular resistance in the eyelid which is invariable when the eyelid of a conscious person is raised. Branson concentrated his beam on one eye. A rather glazed eye looked out unseeingly, unblinkingly. Branson dropped the eyelid.

Branson said: 'Out like a light. That's for sure.' If there was disappointment in his voice he concealed it well. 'How long have you been awake, Miss Wednesday?'

'I haven't been to sleep. Maybe I shouldn't have come back to the bridge.' She smiled tremulously. 'I'm just a cowardy-custard, Mr Branson. I hate thunderstorms.'

'I'm not going to hurt you, Miss Wednesday.' He reached out a hand and ran a finger gently across her lips while she looked at him in perplexity. Her lips were as dry as dust.

184

Branson remembered O'Hare's summing up of her emotional and nervous stability or lack of it.

'You *are* scared.' He smiled and patted her shoulder. 'Not to worry. The storm's almost passed away.' He left.

She was scared, but not for the reasons given. She'd been terrified that Branson would try to shake or even slap Revson awake and find it impossible to arouse him.

Twenty minutes later Branson and Chrysler stood by the doorway of the rear coach. Chrysler said: 'There's no way he can be on the bridge, Mr Branson.'

'I agree. Let me hear you think aloud, Chrysler.'

Chrysler made a deprecating gesture. 'I'm a follower, not a leader.'

'Nevertheless.'

'I'll try. I can speak freely?' Branson nodded. 'First, Van Effen didn't jump. Not only is he the last person I'd ever associate with suicide, but he was also only days away from a seven-figure fortune. He didn't defect. You said I could speak freely. Again he stood to lose a fortune, he was totally loyal and to defect he'd have had to walk two thousand feet towards either tower and Johnson couldn't have missed that. So he's met with an accident. You're sure it couldn't have been the doctor?'

'Positive.'

'And it wasn't Revson. The only other person I could think of is General Cartland. He could be dangerous. But Peters — ' Chrysler broke off and thought. 'You know, Mr Branson, I don't think this would have happened if Kowalski had been on the prowl tonight.' He paused. 'I'm beginning to wonder if Kowalski's accident really *was* an accident.'

'I have wondered. Your conclusions, Chrysler?'

'Somewhere in this barrel there's another rotten apple. It could be one of us.'

'A disquieting thought but one that has to be considered. Although why anyone should throw away a fortune — '

'Maybe the Government, some way, some how, has promised someone to double their cut if — '

'This is just idle speculation.' Branson's creased brow gave the lie to his words. 'Suspecting everyone in sight only leads to hysteria and hysterics is one thing we can't afford. And your final conclusion on Van Effen?'

'The same as yours. He's at the bottom of the Golden Gate.'

Van Effen was, in fact, seated in the communications wagon ashore. Hagenbach and Hendrix were seated across the table from him. Two policemen with drawn guns stood by the doorway. Van Effen wasn't quite his usual expressionless self. He looked slightly dazed, whether from the shock of finding himself in the predicament he was in or because he was still suffering from the after-effects of the gassing was difficult to say.

Van Effen said: 'So I under-estimated Revson?'

'When you get up to San Quentin you'll find quite a few others who will endorse your views.' Hagenbach looked at Van Effen. 'Speaking of San Quentin, you appreciate you can't hope for less than ten years with no hope of remission.'

'There's an occupational hazard in every job.'

'There doesn't have to be.'

'I don't understand you.'

'We can do a deal.'

'No deal.'

'You've nothing to lose and a great deal to gain. Ten years of your life, to be precise.'

'No deal.'

Hagenbach sighed. 'I rather thought that might be your attitude. Admirable but misguided.' He looked at Hendrix. 'You would agree?'

Hendrix said to the policemen: 'Handcuff him and take him to the maximum security wing of the military hospital. Tell the doctors that Mr Hagenbach will be along in a few minutes. Make sure the recorders are working.'

Van Effen said: 'Hospital? Recorders? You mean drugs.'

'If you won't co-operate with us we'll just have to settle for your unwilling co-operation. Unconscious co-operation, if you wish.'

Van Effen cracked his moonface in an almost contemptuous smile. 'You know that no court will accept a confession made under duress.'

'We don't need any confession from you. We already have enough on you to put you away for as long as we wish. We just want a little helpful information from you. A judicious mixture of sodium pentothal and a few other choice herbs will make you sing like a lark.'

'That's as maybe.' The contempt was still in Van Effen's face. 'Even you have to obey the law of the land. Lawmen who extract information by illegal means are subject to automatic prosecution and automatic imprisonment.'

Hagenbach was almost genial. 'Dear me, dear me. I thought even you, Van Effen, would have heard of a Presidential pardon. Or have you forgotten that you kidnapped a President?'

At ten minutes to three that morning an Air Force lieutenant on the south shore twirled two knobs on a highly sophisticated piece of equipment until the cross-hairs on his ultra violet telescopic sights were lined up dead centre on the centre of Branson's southern-facing searchlight. He jabbed a button, just once.

At five minutes to three, three men climbed into a strangely-shaped low-slung vehicle which was concealed from the bridge by the communications truck. A rather nondescript individual in a grey coat climbed behind the wheel while the other two sat in the back seat. They were clad in grey overalls and looked curiously alike. Their names were Carmody and Rogers. They were both in their mid-thirties and looked tough and competent in a rather gentlemanly way. Whether they were gentlemen or not was not known: whether they were tough and competent was beyond dispute. They didn't look like explosives experts but they were that too. Both carried pistols and both carried silencers for those pistols. Carmody carried a canvas bag containing a tool kit, two aerosol gas cans, a ball of heavy cord, adhesive tape and a torch. Rogers had a similar bag with a walkie-talkie, Thermos and sandwiches. They were obviously well-equipped for whatever task they had in mind and prepared for a stay of some duration.

At three o'clock all the lights on the Golden Gate Bridge and the adjacent parts of the city blacked out. The man in the grey coat started up his flat truck and the electric vehicle whirred almost silently towards the south tower.

The duty policeman picked up the phone in the communications wagon. It was Branson and he wasn't in a jovial mood. 'Hendrix?'

'The Chief is not here.'

'Then get him.'

'If you could tell me what the matter – '

'The bridge lights have gone again. Get him.'

The policeman laid down his phone and walked to the rear of the wagon. Hendrix sat on a stool by the open door, a walkie-talkie in his hand, a cup of coffee in the other. The walkie-talkie crackled.

'Carmody here, Chief. We're inside the tower and Hopkins is half-way back with the electric cart already.'

'Thank you.' Hendrix put down the walkie-talkie. 'Branson? A mite anxious?'

Hendrix finished off his coffee in a leisurely fashion, crossed the wagon, picked up the phone and yawned.

'I was asleep. Don't tell me. The lights are out again. We've been having black-outs all over the city tonight. Hold on.'

In the Presidential coach, Branson held on. Chrysler came running down the aisle. The President looked at him blearily. The oil barons snored steadily on. Branson, phone still in hand, looked round. Chrysler said quickly: 'South searchlight is out of action.'

'It's not possible.' Branson's face was beginning to show deeper lines of strain. 'What's wrong?'

'God knows. It's black out there. Generator seems fine.'

'Then run for the north one and turn it round. No. Wait.' Hendrix was on the phone. 'One minute you say?' He turned to Chrysler. 'Forget it. The lights are coming on again.' Branson spoke into the phone again. 'Don't forget. I want Quarry on this phone at seven sharp.'

Branson replaced the phone and walked up the aisle. The President stopped him.

'When is this nightmare going to stop?'

'That's up to your Government.'

'I've no doubt the Government will accede to your requests. You interest me, Branson, you interest all of us here. Why this bitter grudge against society?'

Branson smiled his empty smile. 'Society I can take or leave.'

'Then why the grudge against me? Why the public humiliation? You've been invariably polite to everyone else. Isn't it enough to hold the nation to ransom without making a fool of me at the same time?'

Branson made no answer.

'You don't like my politics, perhaps?'

'Politics bore me.'

'I was speaking to Hendrix today. He tells me your father is an extremely wealthy banker back east. A multi-millionaire. You envy a man who's made it to the very top. You couldn't wait to inherit his bank and his millions so you took the only other course open to you. Crime. And you haven't made it. And you haven't had recognition – except that of a few top policemen. So you're a failure. So you bear a grudge. So you take it out, symbolically, on America's leading citizen.'

Branson said wearily, 'You, Mr President, are a lousy diagnostician and an even lousier psychiatrist. Okay, okay, insults again, but this is private. You may fear no more the lash of my tongue. But to think that your decisions can affect over two hundred million Americans.'

'What do you mean?'

'It's how wrong you can get. Branson, senior, that model of integrity and propriety, is a double-dyed bastard. He was also – and still is a double-dyed crook. A renowned investment banker, you understand, but it didn't do his investors much good. They were mainly people of modest means. I at least rob wealthy institutions. I found this out when I worked in his bank. I wouldn't have taken a lousy dollar from him. I didn't even give him the pleasure of disinheriting me. I just told him what I thought of him and his lousy bank and walked out. As for recognition – who wants it?'

'You certainly achieved more in the past eighteen hours than your father did in a lifetime.' The President was understandably sour.

'That's notoriety. Who wants that either? And for money – I already am a multi-millionaire.'

'And still you want more?'

'My motives are my business. Sorry to have interrupted your sleep, sir.' Branson left.

Muir, in the next armchair, said: 'Now, that was rather peculiar.'

'So you weren't asleep?'

'One hates to interrupt. The Branson in the still watches of the night is not the Branson of the daylight hours. Forthcoming, one might almost say. Polite. Almost as if he was seeking for some kind of self-justification. But obviously bitter as hell about something.'

'If he doesn't want recognition and doesn't need the money then what the hell are we doing stuck out on this damned bridge?'

'Ssh. Mayor Morrison might hear you. I don't know. With your permission, Mr President, I'm going back to sleep.'

When Carmody and Rogers reached the top of the south tower and stepped outside the lift, Carmody reached an arm in, pressed a button and withdrew his arm as the door began to close. Both men stepped outside and gazed down silently at the darkened and barely visible bridge some five hundred feet below them. After a minute Carmody withdrew the walkie-talkie from his canvas bag, extended the aerial and said: 'You can cut the power now. The lift's been down for thirty seconds.'

He replaced the walkie-talkie and removed his overalls. Over his purposely-chosen dark shirt he wore a leather harness with a heavy steel buckle at the back. A nylon rope spliced to the buckle was wound several times round his waist. He was in the process of unwinding this when the bridge lights and the aircraft warning lights on top of the towers came on again. Carmody said: 'A chance of our being spotted, you think?'

'Thinking of the aircraft lights?' Carmody nodded. 'No chance. Not from their angle. And I understand their south searchlight isn't working too well.'

Carmody unwound the rest of the rope and passed the end to Rogers. 'A couple of turns, if you would, Charles, then hang on real good.'

'Depend on it. If you take a dive that means I'll have to disarm the damned thing myself – with no one to hold me.'

'We should get danger money for this.'

'You're a disgrace to the Army bomb disposal squad.'

Carmody sighed, moved out on to the giant cable and began to remove the detonators from the explosives.

It was six-thirty in the morning when Revson stirred and woke. He looked at April and saw that her green eyes were

190

on his. There were heavy shadows under her eyes and her normally pale skin was now even more unnaturally so.

He said: 'You don't look to me as if you've rested any too well.'

'I didn't sleep all night.'

'What? With me here to look after you?'

'It's not me I'm worried about. It's you.'

He said nothing.

'Do you feel hung-over? After your – your sleeping pill?'

'No. Guess I must have slipped into a natural sleep. That all you worried about?'

'No. Branson was here just before one o'clock. He examined your eyes with a torch to see if you were still asleep.'

'No sense of privacy, that man. You'd think – '

'I think he's again cast you in the role of prime suspect.'

'Suspected of what?'

'Van Effen's missing.'

'Is he now?'

'You don't seem much concerned.'

'What's Van Effen to me or me to Van Effen? No more alarms during the night?'

'At three o'clock the bridge lights went off again.'

'Ah!'

'Nothing surprises you much, does it?'

'Why should the lights going out surprise me? Could have been a dozen reasons for it.'

'I think the reason is sitting right by me.'

'I was asleep.'

'You weren't asleep when you were out on the bridge at midnight. I'll bet your new little – ah – camera wasn't all that inactive either.' She leaned towards him, her eyes moving from one of his to the other. 'You didn't by any chance just happen to kill Van Effen last night?'

'What do you think I am? A murderer for hire?'

'I don't know what to think. You will not have forgotten that I heard the contents of the message you sent when I was taken to the hospital. I remember the exact words. "Only Branson and Van Effen are natural leaders. Those two I could kill." '

'I did say that. I didn't kill Van Effen last night. My life on it. Van Effen, in my opinion, is alive and well, if not exactly flourishing.'

'That's not what Branson thinks.'

'How should you know that?'

'After Bartlett left – was relieved – '

'Bartlett didn't mention to Branson that he might just possibly have dozed off for a moment?'

'What do you think?'

'Okay, so he was alert and watchful as all hell. And then?'

'And then this – this gorilla came on.' Revson looked at the new guard. Hirsute, incredibly beetle-browed, with a negligible clearance between brows and hairline: April's description didn't flatter gorillas any.

'Yonnie,' Revson said. 'Branson's mobile think-tank.'

'Chrysler came by, more than once. I heard him saying to that man that he and Branson knew that Van Effen was at the bottom of the Golden Gate.'

'I'm looking forward to seeing his face when he finds out, just possibly for the first time in his life, how wrong he can be.'

'You don't want to tell me?'

'No. Neither do you.'

'You seem very sure of yourself.'

'About that, yes.'

'Can you make an end to all this?'

'That, I'm afraid, is another matter.' He thought and smiled. 'If I try very hard, can I take you out for dinner tonight?'

'Tonight!'

'You heard.'

'You can take me to Timbuctoo if you want.'

'Hussies. You can always tell them.'

The phone call-up in the communications centre in the Presidential coach buzzed at exactly seven o'clock. Branson picked it up. 'Yes.'

'Quarry here. We have acceded to your preposterous demands and made the necessary arrangements. We're waiting to hear from your contact in New York.'

'Waiting to hear – you should have heard two hours ago.'

Quarry said wearily: 'We're waiting to hear from him again.'

'When did he call?'

'As you said, two hours ago. He's making some arrangements with what he calls "European friends".'

'He was to have given you a password.'

'He did. Hardly original, I thought. "Peter Branson."'

Branson smiled broadly and replaced the receiver. He was still smiling when he stepped out into the early morning sunlight. Chrysler was there and he wasn't smiling at all. Chrysler was exhausted, he'd temporarily taken over the roles of both Van Effen and Kowalski. But the reason for his worry lay elsewhere. Branson said: 'Money side is all fixed up.'

'That's splendid, Mr Branson.'

Branson's smile disappeared. 'You seem less than overjoyed.'

'There are a couple of things I'd like to show you.'

Chrysler led them to the south-facing searchlight. 'You probably know that a searchlight is not like an ordinary torch or flashlight, I mean it doesn't use lamps. It comes from an electric arm that jumps between two electrodes. Something like the sparking plug in a car except that there the spark is intermittent. Here the arc is continuous. Look at the electrode on the left.'

Branson looked. 'It looks as if it's been melted or bent or something like that. And one must assume that those electrodes are designed to withstand the tremendous heat generated by the arc.'

'Precisely. And something you haven't seen. This tiny hole here in the glass.'

'What are you trying to tell me, Chrysler?'

'There's something else.' Chrysler, walking slowly back with Branson, pointed to the roof of the rear coach. 'The radio-wave scanner. It's kaput, knocked out. Since we checked and double-checked that there are no transceivers – apart from ours – on the bridge, we haven't bothered using it. I just happened to check by accident this morning. I went up and had a look. There's a scorch mark on the base of the revolving spindle.'

'Could have been caused by lightning? Both cases? After all, God knows there was plenty of it around last night.'

'I would point out, Mr Branson, that neither the radio-wave scanner or the searchlight are earthed: both are mounted on rubber wheels.'

'The scanner –'

Chrysler said patiently: 'The coach's rubber wheels.'

'Then what?'

'I think they're using a laser beam on us.'

Even at that early hour all seven of the decision-makers ashore were gathered round the table in the communications wagon when the phone rang. The duty policeman picked it up.

'Branson here. Get me General Carter.'

'He can't be far away. Hang on, please.' The policeman covered the mouth-piece. 'It's Branson for you, General.'

'Switch on the speaker so that we can all hear what he has to say. Tell him I've just come in.'

'The General has just arrived.'

Carter took the phone. 'Branson?'

'Carter, use that laser beam on us just once again and we'll throw, say, Mr Muir over the side. For starters.'

The other six at the table looked at one another with quick apprehension and, possibly, the relieved thought in their minds that it was Carter who had to field this one.

'Explain yourself.'

'One of our searchlights and radio-wave scanner have been knocked out. All signs point to a laser beam.'

'You're a fool.'

There was a brief silence. Branson, clearly, had been taken momentarily aback. Then he said: 'Muir won't think so when he's on his way down to the Golden Gate.'

'I repeat you're a fool and if you can listen I'll tell you why. In the first place you're not an expert and wouldn't recognize the signs of laser damage if it was on your breakfast plate. In the second place, there are no such units in the Bay area – if there were I'd be the first person to know. In the third place, if we had laser beams we could have picked off every one of your villains as they walked about the bridge – or don't you know how accurate and deadly a laser beam is? With the proper telescopic sights you can puncture a football at ten thousand yards.'

'You seem to know a suspiciously great deal about lasers, General.' It was a negative remark and Branson could have been either thinking or stalling for time.

'I don't deny it. I've been trained in them, I even helped in the development of them. Every general has his own trade or speciality. General Cartland is an explosives expert. I'm an electronics engineer. Where was I? Yes. In the fourth place we could have immobilized your helicopters without your knowing anything about it until you tried to take off. You're putting ideas into my head, Branson. Lastly, the probable cause was an electrical discharge – lightning.'

'Neither the searchlight nor scanner was earthed. They're mounted on rubber wheels.'

Carter let irritation creep into his voice. 'I'd stick to robbing banks if I were you. You don't have to be earthed to be struck by lightning. It happens to planes hundreds of times a year at altitudes up to twenty-five thousand feet. Would you call those earthed? Lightning has also quite an affinity for metal.' He paused. 'Of course, you have a generator for your searchlight, almost certainly a petrol generator and as you wouldn't want to be asphyxiated by carbon monoxide fumes you wouldn't have it inside a coach. Tell me, do you also use the generator to recharge your coach batteries – through a transformer, I mean?'

There was the barest pause then Branson said: 'Yes.'

Carter sighed. 'Must I do all the thinking for you, Branson? There you have a massive great lump of metal solidly earthed to the roadway and directly connected to both searchlight and scanner. What a target for any wandering lightning flash. Would there be anything more?'

'Yes. Pass the word that I want the TV cameras in position and ready at nine a.m.'

Carter hung up. Richards said approvingly: 'Quite a performance for the crack of dawn. Takes more than a few stars to make a general, I suppose. I have a feeling that our Branson must be feeling more than a little harried by this time. And when shall we be giving our own TV performance?'

Hagenbach said: 'Directly after Branson's, I should think. Nine-thirtyish. Moment of maximum psychological impact and all that sort of thing.'

'As our – ah – anchor-man, you have your lines ready?'

Hagenbach didn't deign to reply.

Branson said: 'Well, you go along with that?'

'Carter's no fool, that's sure.' Chrysler was uncertain. 'But if it were lightning transmitted through the generator why didn't it just jump from one electrode to the next instead of making a hole in the searchlight glass? I mean, where was it going?'

'I'm afraid it's not my field.'

'I'm beginning to think it's not mine either. But I'm damned sure there's something fishy afoot.' He hesitated. 'Maybe I wasn't so bright with that one but I've another idea, Mr Branson.'

'Ideas are what I need. Myself, I'm fresh out of them.' Coming from Branson, Chrysler thought, that was quite a remarkable statement.

'I do my best, but I'm no Van Effen. Besides, I feel just about all in. Even you can't keep going twenty-four hours a day. You need a new lieutenant – not to say a fresh one – and with respects to my colleagues, well – '

'Out with it.'

'Now that our men are in possession of the Mount Tamalpais radar stations, I think Parker is quite capable of looking after things himself. I suggest you send a chopper to bring in Giscard. You know him even better than I do. He's tough, he's a leader, he's resourceful, he doesn't panic and in some ways he's very astute: by that I mean, all respects to you, Mr Branson, he's never seen the inside of a court-room. It would take a helluva load off your back.'

'You're quite right, of course. If I didn't need a break I should have thought of that myself. Get hold of either Johnson or Bradley – no, Bradley: Johnson had guard duty. Tell him to move right away. I'll get on the phone and tell Giscard. I'll also warn our friends ashore what's going to happen to them if they try to interfere. Not that they should need telling by now.'

Branson made his calls, winced at the clattering roar as the Sikorsky lifted cleanly off the bridge and headed north. At least Carter had been telling the truth about one thing: the helicopter hadn't been subjected to the attentions of a laser beam.

Revson said to April: 'I don't want to sound indelicate but wouldn't you like to pay a visit to the ladies' – ah – powder room?'

She stared at him. 'What on earth for? Oh, well, you'll have a reason.'

'Yes. Just repeat this after me.' She repeated it four times then said: 'Is that all?'

'Yes.'

'Once would have been enough.'

'Well, you never know what the help's like these days.'

'Why can't you do it yourself?'

'It's urgent and I want it done now. There are four ladies aboard this bridge and at least fifty men. Your chances of privacy and seclusion are all that higher.'

'And what are you going to do? You look pretty scruffy to me.'

'To re-phrase the old song, I've left my razor in San Francisco. Then breakfast. The wagon's due at seven-thirty.'

'I wish I had an appetite.' She rose and spoke briefly to Yonnie who bared his teeth in a fearful grimace that he probably regarded as being a charmingly graceful assent.

The transistor in front of Hagenbach buzzed. He pulled it towards him and raised the volume. The other six men bent forward in eager expectancy. This call could be from only one source. They were wrong.

'Mr Hagenbach?' A feminine voice.

'Speaking.'

'April Wednesday.'

Hagenbach took it with remarkable aplomb. 'Carry on, my dear.'

'Mr Revson wants to know as soon as possible if it's possible to reduce the last resort to a non-lethal level. He wants you to have as much time as possible to try. That's why I'm calling now.'

'I'll try. I can't guarantee.'

'He says to lay down a pattern of smoke bombs one minute before. He says he'll radio you one minute before that.'

'And I want to talk to Revson just as urgently. Why isn't he doing this himself?'

'Because I'm in the ladies' toilets. Somebody's coming.' The voice trailed away in a whisper and the transceiver went dead.

Hagenbach called to the communication desk: 'The armoury. Emergency. General Carter. I'm going to need your help on this one.'

'The ladies' toilet,' Quarry said unbelievingly. 'Are there no depths to which this man of yours won't descend?'

'Be reasonable. You didn't expect him to be there himself. Knowing Revson, I rate that an "A" for gentlemanly conduct.'

Vice-President Richards spoke slowly and distinctly. 'Up in the hospital you told us that you didn't know what "the last resort" was.'

Hagenbach looked at him coldly. 'Vice-Presidents should know better. No one has ever become the head of the FBI without being a master of prevarication.'

Breakfast arrived on mid-bridge at seven-thirty. Branson passed it up which, in view of the shock awaiting his nervous system, was perhaps as well. At seven-forty-five Bradley made a perfect touch-down in his Sikorsky. Giscard, grim-faced and purposeful, stepped down on to the bridge not, oddly enough, looking at all incongruous in his police sergeant's uniform. He probably had more photographs taken of him in the next five minutes than he'd had in the whole of his previous existence – which would not have been difficult: Giscard, as a purely professional safeguard, made it his business never to have his photograph taken. But even the redoubtable Giscard had come too late. At eight o'clock an already troubled Branson – no hint of concern showed in his composed and confident face – received his first and far from faint intimations of mortality.

Branson was deep in conversation with a fresh and confident Giscard when Reston, duty guard on the Presidential coach, came hurrying up. 'Phone, Mr Branson.'

Giscard said: 'I'll take care of things, Mr Branson. You try to get some rest.' He touched him lightly on the shoulder. 'There's nothing to worry about.' Giscard had no means of knowing it but it was the most way-out prophecy he'd ever made or would ever be likely to make again.

It was Hagenbach on the phone. He said: 'I've bad news for you, Branson. Kyronis doesn't want to see you. Not now. Not ever.'

'Who?' Branson saw the marbled knuckles on the hand holding the phone and made a conscious effort to relax.

'K-Y-R-O-N-I-S. The president of that Caribbean island paradise of yours. I'm afraid you're not welcome.'

'I don't know what you're talking about.'

'I'm afraid you do. And I'm afraid your world-wide publicity campaign has scared the poor man out of his wits. We didn't find him, he called us. He's on the international line right now. Shall I patch him in?'

Branson didn't say whether he should patch him in or not. A high-pitched voice with a pronounced Caribbean accent came to his ear.

'You fool, Branson. You madman. You wide-mouthed boaster. You had to tell the world that you were going to the Caribbean. You had to tell the world that it had a prison stockade in one corner. You had to tell the world that it had no extradition treaty with the United States. You damn fool, how long do you think it would take American Intelligence to piece that together? I called them before they came calling on me. Their fleet has already moved out from their Guantanamo base in Cuba. Their C54s are lined up on the runways in Fort Lauderdale with God knows how many paratroopers and marines standing by. They could take our little principality over in ten minutes and your Vice-President has assured me that they would consider it a pleasure.' Kyronis stopped to take what appeared to be his first breath since he started his tirade.

Branson said nothing.

'Megalomania, Branson. Megalomania. I always warned you it was the one thing that could bring you down. Sheer, bloody megalomania.'

Branson hung up the phone.

TWELVE

Giscard took the news with remarkable aplomb. 'So Kyronis has ratted on us. It's not the end of the world and I don't see that it changes a single thing. I think this is just part of a war of nerves, attrition, you know, psychological warfare. Okay; so you've been here – what is it? – twenty-three hours and I don't know what the strains have been like. But I'm sure of this – with no other way of getting at you they're trying to pressurize you into making a mistake. It's kind of like a poker game but with no cards in their hands all they can do is bluff.' Giscard nodded to the Presidential coach. 'What's bluff when you hold all the cards in your hands?'

'There speaks the voice of reason, is that it?' Branson smiled. 'You forget that I *know* Kyronis's voice.'

'Sure you do. I don't doubt it was Kyronis. I also don't doubt that the Government, through some fast checking by the CIA or the FBI, got to him first.'

'What makes you think that?'

'Because Kyronis has your VHF number. He could have radioed you direct instead of causing all this hullabaloo. But that wouldn't have suited our friends' department of psychological warfare.'

'And I've had an idea, Mr Branson.' Chrysler had shed much of his weariness since Giscard's arrival. 'Who needs Kyronis? The Presidential Boeing can reach half a dozen countries anywhere in the world that have no extradition treaty with the USA. A dozen, for all I know. But there's no need to go further than the Caribbean. You've been thinking big all along, Mr Branson. Now's the time to keep on thinking big.'

Branson rubbed his forehead. 'Think big aloud. Someone has to this morning.'

'Havana. There's no extradition treaty with them. Sure, there's an agreement to repatriate hi-jackers, but no one's going to return the hi-jacker of the Presidential Boeing – especially if the President has a pistol to his head. Okay, so the US is prepared to take over Kyronis's tiny islet. Cuba is a vastly different proposition. Castro has a first-class army, air force and navy. Any attempt to get the President out would lead to nothing short of full-scale war. And don't forget that Castro is Moscow's blue-eyed boy. An armed invasion of Cuba would bring a violent reaction and I don't think the US would be prepared to risk an eyeball-to-eyeball nuclear confrontation over a miserable half billion dollars.'

Branson nodded slowly. 'Curiously enough, that was where Van Effen wanted to go. And for much the same reasons.'

'And can't you see how Castro would just love it? He'd go on TV and weep and wail and wring his hands and say how much he'd love to be of help but his hands are hopelessly tied. Then when the cameras are switched off he falls about the place laughing.'

Branson said: 'Gentlemen, you have restored my faith in human nature. At least my own nature. Havana it is. Now. Our next show is at nine. All the tackle and explosives as before. Peters can drive the electric truck as before. Bartlett and Boyard fixed the last lot — let's give Reston and Harrison a go.' Branson smiled. 'They think they're better than Bartlett and Boyard and should have had the privilege of the first attempt. See they carry walkie-talkies. Which reminds me. Chrysler, I want to be in a position where I can lay hands on a telephone wherever I happen to be. I don't want to have to keep running to the President's coach. I just want a direct line to Hagenbach and company. You can fix one up in our coach?'

'I'd have to go through the local exchange.'

'So what? By all means. Tell them to keep the line permanently open. I want a lead to where I'll be sitting when the TV is on. And can you get a radio-telephone link from the lead helicopter?'

'Turn a knob, is all. What's that for, Mr Branson?'

'We're going to need it some time. Better sooner than never.'

It was another glorious morning of blue and gold, a cloudless sky, a fairy-tale setting which achieved the impossible of making even the grim fortress of Alcatraz into an islet of shimmering beauty. As on the previous day a low deep bank of fog was approaching from the west. Out of all three coaches there was only one person who was not savouring the delights of the morning or, in the case of Branson's men, on duty.

Revson sat in his seat, elbow on the window ledge, hand cupped to his cheeks so that no one could see his lips moving.

Hagenbach said: 'Turn the volume down, put the transceiver to your ear.'

'Impossible. My head and shoulders are above window level. I can bend down for a few seconds. But be quick.'

Revson's camera was upside down on his knees, the transceiver nestling in the opened recess. He turned down the volume and put his head low. After about fifteen seconds he straightened and looked carelessly around. Nobody was paying any attention to him. He turned up the volume.

'Well?' Hagenbach's voice was querulous. 'Aren't you surprised?'

'Not all that much. Are you going to tell him?'

'Remember, you don't give any signal to go until I'm all through at this end.'

'I'll remember. How about the CUBs?'

'The experts aren't all that happy about the prospects.'

'Then use a few of them only and make up for the rest in gas bombs. Are you in touch with the two men at the top of the tower?'

'Carmody and Rogers. Yes.'

'Tell them if they nab anyone to take them down to the pier of the tower.'

'Why?'

'Look. I'm exposed. Is the Admiral there?'

Hagenbach refrained from questions though it must have cost him a considerable effort. Newson came through.

Revson said: 'Do you have any small, quiet boats, sir?'

'Electrically powered?'

'Ideally.'

'In abundance.'

'When the fog comes in, do you think you could get one alongside the pier of the south tower?'

'Consider it done.'

'With a breeches buoy pistol and suitable ropes?'

'No problem.'

'Thank you, sir. Mr Hagenbach?'

'Yes. Secretive bastard, aren't you?'

'Yes, sir. The laser unit is ready for action? Ah, good. Would you have it lined up on the drive shaft of the rotor of the lead helicopter – that's to say, the one furthest from you. Have it locked in position so that it can hit its target even through dense smoke.'

'Why on earth – '

'Somebody coming.'

Revson looked around. There was nobody coming, but he'd no desire to bandy words with Hagenbach. He clipped the base of the camera, slung it over his shoulder and left the coach.

'A bit of trouble, sir.' Chrysler handed a walkie-talkie to Branson.

'Reston here, Mr Branson.' Reston and Harrison had set off less than ten minutes earlier for the south pier. 'The lift is out of order.'

'Damn. Wait.' Branson looked at his watch. Eight twenty five. His performance was due to start at nine. He crossed to the rear coach where Chrysler had already obtained a direct line to the communications centre ashore.

'Branson here.'

'Hendrix. Don't tell me what you're after. I know. I was speaking to the bridge commissioners a few moments ago. They tell me that the breaker for the tower lifts was burnt out during the night.'

'Why isn't it repaired?'

'They've been working on it for three hours.'

'And how much longer – '

'Half an hour. Perhaps an hour. They can't be certain.'

'Call me the moment it's fixed.'

He returned to his walkie-talkie. 'Sorry, you'll have to climb. The lift's being repaired.'

There was a silence then Reston said: 'Jesus. All that way?'

'All that way. It's not Everest. Should be straightforward. And you have your manual.' He laid down the walkie-talkie and said to Giscard: 'I don't envy them, myself. Another psychological pin-prick?'

'Could be. But after a night like last night, well – '

Revson joined O'Hare by the west barrier. He said without preamble: 'How hermetic is the rear door of your ambulance?'

O'Hare had ceased to be surprised at anything Revson said. 'Why?'

'Say oxygen were to be abstracted from the inside. How

would you get on?'

'We've oxygen bottles, of course. Not to mention the oxygen in the cardiac unit.'

'You may need it. Ever heard of CUB-55s? Short for Cluster Bomb Units.' O'Hare shook his head. 'Well, there's liable to be a few around in the next hours – this morning, I shouldn't be surprised. They are lethal asphyxiation bombs, one of the more delightful of the recent advances in weaponry. They suck the oxygen from the air and leave not a mark on the victims.'

'You should know. But – well, it's far fetched.'

'A pity you couldn't ask the hundreds who died at Xuan Loc because of them. The Cambodian Government made frequent use of them in South-East Asia. The bombs, I regret to say, were supplied then by the United States Navy.'

'This classified information?'

'No. Hanoi made plenty of noise about it at the time.'

'And you're going to use those bombs?'

'Yes. I'm trying to have them denatured, you know, their lethal potential lessened. At least, the experts are.'

'Can they do it?'

'There's a certain lack of optimism.'

'Who thought this one up? You?' Revson nodded, just once. 'You, Revson, are a cold-blooded bastard. Hasn't it occurred to you that the innocent will suffer, maybe die, as well as the guilty?'

'Not for the first time, I repeat that all doctors should be given an intelligence test before they're allowed to practise. The innocent will not suffer. The innocent will be in their coaches and, because it's going to be hot, they'll have the air-conditioning on. That means closed doors and the recirculation of cleaned used air. When you see the first smoke bomb drop, make for cover.'

Revson walked away and touched Grafton on the arm. 'May I have a word with you?' Grafton hesitated, shook his head in puzzlement, then followed. When he judged they were out of earshot of the nearest person, Revson stopped.

Grafton said: 'Do we have to take a walk to talk?'

'In this case, yes. We haven't been introduced. You're Mr Grafton of UP, doyen of the newsmen on this bridge?'

'If you want to flatter me, yes. And you're Mr Revson, food-taster to Royalty.'

'Just a sideline with me.'

'You have another business. Don't tell me.' Grafton regarded him with cool grey, judicial eyes. 'Federal Bureau of Investigation.'

'Thank you for sparing me the trouble of convincing you. I'm glad your name's not Branson.'

General Cartland said: 'If you can't have those CUB-55s denatured, as you call it, some local funeral parlour is in for a brisk bit of business.'

'You prepared to use that cyanide pistol?'

'*Touché.*'

Several minutes before nine Branson had his usual stage set. He seemed as calm and relaxed as ever, the only change in his normal behaviour being that he had been polite, almost deferential, in his seating of the President. At nine o'clock the cameras began to turn.

At nine o'clock, too, Reston and Harrison, sweating profusely and complaining bitterly of the pain in their legs, reached the top of their last ladder. Rogers, eyeing them over his silenced pistol, said sympathetically: 'You must be *exhausted* after your long climb, gentlemen.'

Giscard whispered in Branson's ear: 'You better get on with it, Mr Branson. Looks as if that fog is coming in just about bridge level.'

Branson nodded, then carried on speaking into the microphone. 'So I'm sure you will be all as delighted as I am to know that the Government has acceded to our very reasonable requests. However, until we receive final confirmation, we feel we might as well pass our time profitably and instruct and entertain you at the same time. In show-business jargon, there will be repeat performances at eleven and one o'clock. I really do urge you to watch those. You will certainly never see other performances like them in your lives.

'As before, you can see the electric truck with its explosives and equipment leaving for the south tower. Now if we can have the zoom camera we shall be seeing two of my colleagues appearing on top of the south tower.' The zoom camera obliged but the top of the tower was bereft of any sign of life. A minute later it was still bereft.

Branson said easily: 'There seems to be a slight hold-up. A temporary delay. Please don't go away.' He was smiling the confident smile of one who knew that not one of his millions of watchers would have dreamed of going away when the phone on the road beside his chair rang. Branson smiled at the unseen millions, said: 'Excuse me', covered the microphone with his hand and picked up the phone.

'Hendrix here. Lift's fixed.'

'Now you tell me. Do you know how long it should take a man to climb up to the top?'

'Don't tell me your men have – rather are trying to climb to the top. They must be mad. You must be mad to have sent them.'

'They have a manual.'

'What manual?'

'A copy of the original.'

'Then they can be lost for days. Because of internal changes that manual was scrapped twenty years ago. They can be lost all day in there.'

Branson replaced the phone. Still covering the microphone he said to Giscard: 'Lift's working. Get Bartlett and Boyard here at the double. Tell them not to forget the weight.' He spoke into the microphone again. 'Sorry, viewers. A slight hitch.'

The viewers spent the next ten minutes being rewarded with a variety of panoramic shots of the Golden Gate and the marvellous surrounding scenery, with Branson giving an occasional commentary. After ten minutes he said: 'Right. South tower again.'

Bartlett and Boyard were there, hands held high in salute. Then, along with Peters, they repeated their previous day's performance and had the second strap of explosives alongside the first in a remarkably short space of time. Bartlett and Boyard waved again and disappeared inside the tower. Rogers eyed them over his silenced pistol. 'You really are experts. What a pity. Now you've put us to the trouble of having to remove a second set of detonators.'

The phone by Branson rang as he was delivering a farewell speech to the camera. He picked it up.

'Hagenbach here. Sorry to have to cut in and cut you off but we have our own little show to watch. You're off the air now and your viewers are now seeing and watching us. Same channel. We've just watched your splendid production. Now, perhaps, you'd like to watch our little show.'

The screen's picture changed to a close-up of Hagenbach. To San Franciscans, at least, his background was unquestionably that of the Presidio.

Hagenbach said: 'There seems little we can do to prevent this criminal Branson from achieving his criminal ends. But from all this, some good might yet come. I give you Mr Richards, the Vice-President of the United States.'

Richards made an imposing figure at the microphone. A convivial and highly articulate man at the best of times, years of dominating conferences and campaigning across the nation had honed his natural abilities as a speaker until he had reached a stage where he could have recited the alphabet backwards and still held his audience spell-bound. But he put his gifts into cold storage that morning: this was a moment that was neither for conviviality nor rhetoric. As became a man at the very heart of a national crisis, he was stern, quiet and, exceptionally for him, brief and to the point.

'Unfortunately, what you have just heard is correct. No matter how distasteful and humiliating this present situation may be, there is no possibility in the world of endangering the President, his royal guests and the good name of America. We submit to blackmail. This criminal Branson would appear to have got away with the blackmailing equivalent of murder but I wish him to listen to me very carefully. On information I have received this morning, information, as I shall shortly prove, of the most reliable kind, I believe that Branson is very near the end of his road. I believe he will very soon be alone and friendless. I believe he will have no one left in the world to turn to. I believe every man's hand will be against him. And I believe that those hands that will be reaching out most eagerly to strike him down, as they most surely will, are the hands of his devoted criminal followers who misguidedly imagine their leader to be a man of honour and integrity.' Richards lapsed into momentary rhetoric. 'Those are hands that will literally cut him down just as he, figuratively, intends to stab them all in the back.'

Some of Branson's men were looking at him in a vague and baffled incomprehension. Revson and O'Hare exchanged enquiring glances. Only Branson seemed entirely at his ease, lounging back in his chair, a faintly contemptuous smile on his lips.

'I said that I had information of the most reliable kind. As your Vice-President, I have been accused more than once of not exactly being given to understatement. In this case I was. What I have is impeccable proof. Ladies and gentlemen and, indeed, viewers, throughout the world, may I present to you the man who, until the early hours of this morning, was Branson's most devoted lieutenant. Mr Johann Van Effen.'

The camera changed to a picture of five men in medium shot sitting in adjoining chairs. The man in the centre was unquestionably Van Effen, who appeared to be his normal relaxed self and to be chatting with seeming amiability to his companions. The picture wasn't close enough to show the glazed eyes, the fact that he was still under the influence of drugs, the drugs which had made him talk his head off during three long hours of probing by a skilled police psychiatrist who, in turn, had received continual prompting from Hagenbach.

Richards went on: 'From left to right: Admiral Newson, naval commander, west coast: San Francisco Chief of Police Hendrix: Mr Van Effen: Mr Hagenbach, head of the FBI: and General Carter, officer commanding, west coast. If I may be permitted a feeble joke, I doubt whether Van Effen has ever found himself in such law-abiding company in his life.'

Branson had very definitely stopped both lounging and relaxing. He was sitting far forward in his chair and for once his feelings were showing: the expression on his face could be described as nothing else other than stunned disbelief.

'Van Effen,' Richards said, 'defected in the very early hours of this morning. He defected for what he, and indeed I, believed to have been very compelling reasons. He departed for the excellent reason that he is still a comparatively young man and would like to live a little longer. Incidentally, as the acting Head of State, I have already guaranteed Van Effen immunity from the due processes of the law. His information has been invaluable, as has been his information of eight major robberies in the past three years in each of which – as we now know – Branson was the leader.

'But I digress. He defected because he feared for his life. He defected because Branson had suggested to him that he and Van Effen share the ransom money equally. The rest could go to hell and, presumably, prison. Apart from the fact that Van Effen does appear to be possessed of a belief in honesty between thieves, he was only too well aware that if he went along with this the next back to feel the blade of a knife – literally – would be his own. Van Effen feels strongly that his ex-comrades should be made aware of what lies in store for them. He has, he tells me, already persuaded four of Branson's men to defect along with him and we expect them shortly. When they arrive we shall show them on the screen. If you can at all, I suggest you don't stray too far from your television sets.'

O'Hare said. 'Jesus! Talk about sowing seeds of dissension. How's Branson going to cope with this, recover from this? Brilliant. As the Veep says, who's going to trust him now among his own men. This your idea, Revson?'

'I wish it were. But even I am not as crafty, evil and devious as that. The unmistakable hand of Hagenbach.'

'I never thought that Van Effen –'

'Whatever you're about to say, he didn't. Hagenbach made sure that there were no close-ups of Van Effen. Had there been, even a layman would have seen that Van Effen was doped to the eyes.'

'Doped? If he defected –'

'An involuntary defection. I gassed him and lowered him down to an – ah – passing submarine.'

'Of course. What else? An – ah – passing submarine.' O'Hare favoured him with the look of a psychiatrist who finds himself with an intractable case on his hands.

'Dear, dear. You don't believe me.'

'But of course, old boy.'

'You're under stress again,' Revson said kindly. 'Talking English English.' He patted the base of his camera. 'How do you think I got hold of a brand-new radio transceiver in the middle of the night?'

O'Hare stared at him. He said with an effort: 'And the four other promised defectors. Submariners all?'

'Hell, no. Forcible abduction, all within the past half hour.'
O'Hare got back to his staring.

In the Mount Tamalpais radar station, Parker, until lately Giscard's number two, looked away from the TV set and at the four men gathered around him. He said: 'Sold down the river.'

From the silence that met this observation, it was clear that the others agreed with him. But it could hardly have been called an agreeable silence.

Richards was trying hard to show that he was not actively enjoying himself. He said into his microphone: 'I can see that the fog is going to pass over the bridge so you won't be able to see me in a couple of minutes. Don't suppose it will last long, though. When it clears, we'll show you your four other faithful henchmen who have defected from you. I will leave you with one last observation. Your money's guaranteed, but watch how you go: I understand it takes exactly six minutes to block the major runways at Havana Airport.'

Branson, his face quite without expression, rose and walked to the rear coach, Giscard following. It was noticeable that his own men either looked at him with puzzlement or thoughtfulness or just averted their eyes. After entering the coach, Giscard went to the back and returned with scotch and two glasses. He poured two large drinks and said: 'I'm against drinking in the morning, too.'

Branson, most uncharacteristically, drained half his glass in one gulp. He said: 'How does your back feel, Giscard?'

'With eleven years working for you and a seven figure bank balance, my back feels okay. I suggest we cut the comedy, Mr Branson. This could be damned serious. With the exception of Van Effen, Yonnie and myself, none of your men has known you for even as long as a year. I forgot Chrysler. But the rest – did you watch their faces as we came here?'

Branson shook his head slowly. 'They just didn't know what to think. Blame them?'

'No. Blame Van Effen?'

'If I believed the sun wasn't going to set tonight, I'd believe he defected. He didn't. Notice that the camera showed no close-up, and that he wasn't invited to speak?' He broke off as Chrysler appeared at the doorway.

Branson said: 'It's all right. Come in. You look unhappy.'

'I am unhappy. I heard what Giscard just said. They let Van Effen stay in the background because he was drugged. I'll bet he told them his life story without realizing one word of what he was saying. Van Effen defect? Never. And there's another thing I'm unhappy about. Bartlett and Boyard should have been back by this time. They haven't even appeared at the south tower. What's more, they're not going to. I know who the next four so-called defectors are going to be.'

Branson said: 'Drugs. No defection. Coercion. We're all agreed on that. But – *how did Van Effen leave the bridge?*'

Giscard said: 'God knows. I wasn't here. Could it have been during one of the two black-outs you had that night?'

Branson said: 'He was with me on both occasions. Any ideas, Chrysler?'

'None. It's as I said, Mr Branson. There's a rotten apple in the barrel somewhere.' He looked out moodily at the fog drifting over the bridge. 'It's getting so that I don't like this bridge much any more.'

Carmody removed the last of the detonators from the second strap of explosives and gingerly rejoined Rogers on the top of the south tower. He picked up the walkie-talkie. 'General Carter please.' There was a few seconds' delay then Carter came through Carmody said: 'We've got them, sir. Shall Rogers and I take a stroll across to the other side? Branson, I believe, has promised another show at eleven. It'll be the west cable, this time, and we quite like our job of being a reception committee.'

'It's a sensible precaution although I somehow don't think that Branson is going to risk any more of his men in the south tower.'

'Ah! Our four friends made it to *terra firma*, sir?'

'With me now. Pity you haven't a TV up there, you and Rogers. Some splendid shows on today.'

'There'll be repeats. We must leave, sir. Fog's thinning quickly down below.'

The fog, in fact, moved into the bay in less than five minutes leaving the bridge brilliant in the bright sunshine. Branson, pacing up and down a short section of the bridge, stopped as Chrysler approached.

'Hagenbach on the phone, Mr Branson. He says to switch on the television in two minutes' time.'

Branson nodded. 'We all know what this is going to be.'

This time Hagenbach was the master of ceremonies. He hadn't prepared his lines as well as the Vice-President but he made his point with considerable impact.

'It does look as if Branson's criminal empire, if not at least crumbling, is showing signs of coming apart at the seams. The Vice-President promised you that more defectors would appear. That Van Effen had talked four more into deserting the sinking ship. Well, they have just so done as you can see for yourselves.'

Another camera picked up a table with four men sitting around it, each with a glass in his hand. A bottle stood on the middle of the table. They could hardly be described as a gay and happy group but then they had no reason to be.

Hagenbach moved into camera range. 'There they are then, ladies and gentlemen. Left to right, Messrs Reston, Harrison, Bartlett and Boyard. Incidentally, one of Branson's top men is in hospital with a fractured skull. One does wonder what will happen next. Thank you for your kind attention.'

The cameras had just stopped turning when a policeman came running up to Hagenbach. 'Telephone for you, sir. It's Mount Tamalpais.'

Ten seconds later Hagenbach was inside the communications wagon, listening intently. He replaced the receiver and looked at Hendrix, Newson and Carter. 'How long would it take to provide two helicopters, one with a TV camera and crew, the other with armed police?'

Carter said: 'Ten minutes. Twelve at the most.'

Giscard said bitterly. 'Attrition, attrition, attrition. Pin-pricks and more pin-pricks. A steady undermining of confidence in those of us who are left. And not a thing in the world you can do about it, nothing to justify any violent retaliatory action against the hostages. They're just using the TV to play you at your own game, Mr Branson.'

'Yes, they are.' Branson didn't seem unduly disturbed:

what he'd seen had come neither as shock nor surprise to him. 'One has to admit that they're quite good at it.' He looked at Giscard and Chrysler. 'Well, gentlemen, I've made up my mind. Your thoughts?'

Giscard and Chrysler looked briefly at each other. It was not in character with Branson that he should ask anyone's opinion. 'We've got our hostages trapped here,' Chrysler said. 'Now I'm the one who's beginning to feel trapped on this damned bridge. We've no freedom of movement.'

Giscard said: 'But we would have in the Presidential Boeing. And it has the finest communications system in the world.'

'So we make orderly preparations for, if need be, an emergency take-off. I am in agreement. They shall pay for this. Just to show them I mean what I say, I'm still going to bring down their damned bridge. Now, I hardly think it would be wise to wrap the remaining two explosive devices round the west cable at the top of the north tower.'

'Not,' Giscard said, 'unless you want to have another couple of involuntary defectors.'

'So we wrap them round the cable just where we are here. At the lowest point, between the two helicopters. That should do satisfactorily enough, I think.'

Some half hour later, shortly after the last two of the explosive straps had been secured to the west cable, Chrysler came up to Branson. 'Hagenbach. He says there'll be an interesting programme coming on in just two minutes. Five minutes after the programme he's going to call you. He says two very important messages are coming through from the east.'

'I wonder what that conniving old devil is up to now?' Branson went and took his accustomed viewing place. Automatically, the seats beside and behind him filled up. The screen came to life.

It portrayed something that looked like an enormous white golf ball – one of the Mount Tamalpais radar scanners. Then the camera zoomed in on a group of about ten men, policemen in their shirt sleeves, all armed with submachine-guns. Slightly in front of them stood Hendrix, a microphone in his hand. The camera followed as Hendrix moved forwards towards an opening door. Five men emerged, all with their hands high. The leading man of the five stopped when he was within three feet of Hendrix.

Hendrix said: 'You're Parker?'

'Yes.'

'I'm Hendrix. Chief of Police, San Francisco. Do you men surrender voluntarily?'

'Yes.'

'Why?'

'Better than being hunted and gunned down by you – or stabbed in the back by that bastard Branson.'

'You're under arrest. Get into the van.' Hendrix watched them go then spoke again into the microphone. 'When it comes to making speeches, I'm afraid I'm not in the same league as the Vice-President or Mr Hagenbach, so I won't even try. All I can say, with due modesty on the part of all of us, is that ten defectors is not a bad morning's bag. And the morning is not over yet. Incidentally, there will be no more broadcasts from us for at least an hour.'

Revson stood up and glanced round casually. In the space of only two seconds he caught the eye of both General Cartland and Grafton. Slowly, casually, the newsmen and the hostages began to drift off to their separate coaches, the former presumably to write up their dispatches or refill cameras, the later, almost certainly, in the pursuit of refreshments – the President looked particularly thirsty. Besides, the comfort of an air-conditioned coach was vastly to be preferred to the already uncomfortable heat out on the bridge.

Giscard said in anger: 'The fool, the fool, the bloody fool! Why did he have to let himself be duped so easily?'

There was just a trace of weary acceptance in Branson's voice. 'Because he had no Giscard there beside him, that's why.'

'He could have phoned you. He could have phoned me.'

'What might have been. No older phrase in any language. I don't really blame him.'

Chrysler said: 'Has it occurred to you, Mr Branson, that when you've received your ransom money and returned the hostages, they might want most if not all of it back if you want their prisoners freed? They're no fools and they know damned well that you wouldn't let your men down.'

'There'll be no deal. I admit it's going to make things a bit more tricky, but there'll be no deal. Well, I suppose I'd better go and see what friend Hagenbach wants.' Branson rose and walked towards the rear coach, his head bent in thought.

Mack, the guard, waited until the last of his illustrious hostages had entered the Presidential coach, locked the door and pocketed the key. His machine-pistol was dangling from one hand. He turned round to see Cartland's little pistol not three feet from him.

Cartland said: 'Don't try anything, I beg you. Try to lift and fire that gun and it is the last thing you ever do.' Cartland's calm impersonal voice carried immense conviction. 'Gentlemen, I ask you to bear witness to – '

'That funny little pop-gun?' Mack was openly contemptuous. 'You couldn't even hurt me with that thing, but I'd still cut you to pieces.'

'Bear witness to the fact that I warned this man that this "pop-gun" is loaded with cyanide-tipped bullets. Just has to break the skin and you won't even feel it. You'll be a dead man before you hit the floor.'

'In my country,' the King observed, 'he'd already be dead.'

With the possible exception of Yonnie, none of Branson's men was a fool. Mack was no fool. He handed over his gun. Cartland marched him to the rear of the coach, pushed him into the washroom, extracted the inside key and locked the door from the outside.

The President said: 'Well?'

Cartland said: 'There's going to be some rather violent unpleasantness outside in a minute or two. I don't want to risk any of you at this late date. I want this door kept sealed and locked because our friends ashore are going to use a special and very lethal bomb which sucks oxygen from the atmosphere and leaves you very dead. Thirdly, Branson is going to come around very quickly with the intention of shooting up one or two of you if the nastiness doesn't stop. But if the door's locked and he can't get in he can fire all day at this bullet-proof glass and make no impression. Fourthly, although we now have two guns, we're not going to use them when we do leave here as we must eventually. I don't want a gunfight at the OK corral. We'll be loaded into a helicopter but the helicopter isn't going any place.'

The President said: 'Where did you get all this information from?'

'A well-informed source. Fellow who gave me this gun. Revson.'

'Revson. How does he tie in? Don't know the chap.'

'You will. He's stated as Hagenbach's successor in the FBI.'

The President was plaintive. 'It's like I always say: no one ever tells me anything.'

Revson was much less verbose and not at all forthcoming with explanations. Ensuring that he was the last man in, he turned and chopped the unsuspecting Peters below the right ear just as Peters turned the key in the lock. Revson relieved him of both key and machine-pistol, dragged him in and propped him in the driver's seat, then brought out his radio.

'Revson here.'

'Hendrix.'

'Ready yet?'

'Hagenbach's still on the phone to Branson.'

'Let me know immediately he's through.'

'So the money's in Europe,' Branson said into the phone. 'Excellent. But there had to be a code-word.'

'There was. Very appropriate this time.' Hagenbach's voice was dry. ' "Off-shore." '

Branson permitted himself a slight smile.

Hendrix's voice came through on Revson's receiver. He said: 'They're through.'

'Clear with Hagenbach.'

'Clear.'

'Now.'

Revson didn't replace the transistor in his camera case. He put it in his pocket, unslung his camera and laid it on the floor. He unlocked the door, leaving the key in the lock, opened the door a judicious crack and peered back. The first smoke bomb burst about two hundred yards away just as Branson descended from the rear coach. A second, twenty yards nearer, burst about two seconds later. Branson still remained as he was, as if momentarily paralysed. Not so O'Hare, Revson observed, who moved very swiftly into the back of his ambulance, closing the door hard behind him: the driver, Revson assumed, was already inside.

Branson broke from his thrall. He leapt inside the rear coach, lifted a phone and shouted: 'Hagenbach! Hendrix!' He had apparently overlooked the fact that if Hendrix had been at Mount Tamalpais some five minutes previously, he could hardly have returned by that time.

'Hagenbach speaking.'

'What the hell do you think you're up to?'

'I'm not up to anything.' Hagenbach's voice was infuriatingly unconcerned.

The dense clouds of smoke were now no more than a hundred yards away.

'I'm going inside the Presidential coach.' He was still shouting. 'You know what that means.' He thrust the phone back and pulled out his pistol. 'Giscard, tell the men to prepare for an attack on the south. They must be mad.' Johnson and Bradley had advanced from the rear of the coach but he thrust them back. 'You two I can't afford to lose. Not now. Stay here. That goes for you, too, Giscard. Tell the men, get back here, and tell Hagenbach what I'm doing.' Giscard eyed him with understandable concern. An erratic, repetitive and slightly incoherent Branson he had not encountered before: but then Giscard had not spent the previous twenty-four hours on the Golden Gate Bridge.

Two more smoke bombs had fallen by the time Branson jumped down to the roadway. The pall of smoke, thick and dense now totally obscuring the south tower was no more than fifty yards away. He rushed to the door of the Presidential coach, grabbed the handle and tried to wrench the door open: but the door remained immovable.

Another smoke bomb exploded. This one was just short of the rear coach. Branson battered at the window of the door with the butt of his pistol and peered inside. The driver's seat, the seat which Mack, the guard, should have been occupying, was empty. General Cartland appeared at the doorway as the next smoke bomb burst not ten yards away.

Branson shouted at him, quite forgetting that he was only mouthing words – for the coach was totally sound-proof – and pointed at the driver's seat. Cartland shrugged his shoulders. Branson loosed off four quick shots at the lock and wrenched the handle again but the Presidential coach had been specifically designed to withstand assaults of this nature, which was as well for Branson: Cartland's right hand, held behind his back, had the forefinger on the trigger of the cyanide gun.

The next bomb burst directly opposite Branson and the dense, acrid evil-smelling fumes were on him in seconds. Branson fired two more shots at the lock and tried again.

Revson withdrew the key from the door of the lead coach, dropped down to the roadway, shut the door, locked it and left the key in position. A smoke bomb burst immediately opposite him.

Vile though the fumes were to both nostrils and throat, they were not incapacitating. Running his fingers along the side of the Presidential coach, Branson made his way back to the rear coach, opened the now closed door and went inside, closing the door behind him. The air in the coach was clear, the lights were on, the air-conditioning unit was functioning and Giscard was on the phone.

Branson managed to control his coughing. 'I couldn't get in. Door's locked and no sign of Mack. Get anything?'

'I got Hagenbach. He says he knows nothing about this. I don't know whether to believe him or not. He's sent for the Vice-President.'

Branson snatched the phone from him and as he did Richards's voice came through. 'You this fellow Giscard?'

'Branson.'

'There is no attack. There will be no attack. Do you think we're mad – you there with guns at the heads of seven hostages? It's the Army, in the shape of Carter, who's gone mad. Heaven alone knows what he intended to achieve. He refuses to answer the phone. I've sent Admiral Newson to stop him. It's that or his career.'

In the communications wagon, Richards turned to look at Hagenbach. 'How did I sound?'

For the first time in his years of contact with Richards, Hagenbach permitted an expression of approval to appear on his face. 'You're keeping the wrong kind of company, Mr Vice-President. You're as devious as I am.'

Giscard said: 'Do you believe him?'

'God only knows. It's sense. It's logical. Stay here. And keep that door closed.'

Branson dropped down to the roadway. The smoke was thinning now but there was still enough of it to make his eyes water and start him coughing again. On his third step he bumped into a vaguely-seen shape in the opacity. 'Who's that?'

'Chrysler.' Chrysler was almost convulsed in his paroxysms of coughing. 'What the hell's going on, Mr Branson?'

'God knows. Nothing, according to Richards. Any signs of an attack?'

'Any signs of an – I can't see a bloody yard. No sounds, anyway.'

Just as he spoke, there came half a dozen cracks in rapid succession. Chrysler said: 'Those weren't smoke bombs.'

In a few seconds it was clear that they were indeed not smoke bombs. Both men started to gasp, searching for oxygen and unable to find it. Branson was the first to guess at what might be happening. He held his breath, grabbed Chrysler by the arm and dragging him towards the rear coach. Seconds later they were inside, the door closed behind them, Chrysler lying unconscious on the floor, Branson barely conscious on his feet.

Giscard said: 'What in God's name –'

'Air-conditioning maximum.' Branson's voice came in short painful gasps. 'They're using CUBs.'

Unlike O'Hare, Giscard knew what CUBs were. 'Asphyxiation bombs?'

'They're not playing any more.'

Neither was General Cartland. Mack's machine-pistol in hand, he unlocked the washroom door. Mack gave him a baleful glare but with the machine-pistol's muzzle six inches from his stomach was unable to give any more direct expression of his feelings.

Cartland said: 'I'm the Army Chief of Staff. In an emergency such as this I am responsible to no one, including the President, for my actions. Give me the door key or I'll shoot you dead.'

Two seconds later the door key was in Cartland's hand. Cartland said: 'Turn round.'

Mack turned and almost immediately collapsed to the floor. The impact from the butt of Cartland's machine-pistol may have been too heavy, but from the indifferent expression on Cartland's face it was clear that he didn't particularly care one way or another. He locked the washroom door behind him, pocketed the key, walked forward, thrust the machine-pistol out of sight beneath the chair of a rather dazed President, and made his way to the control panel in front of the driver's seat. He touched a few buttons without effect, pulled and pushed some switches then turned sharply as the entrance window slid down. He took two paces, sniffed the air, wrinkled his nose and quickly moved back to push the last switch he'd touched in the other direction. The window closed. Again, very briefly, Cartland touched the switch. The window slid down an inch. Cartland moved across and dropped the door key outside, returned and closed the window.

Two minutes later the gentle western breeze from the Pacific had blown the now dispersing fumes into the bay. The bridge was clear. Branson opened the door of the rear coach: the air was sweet and fresh and clean. He stepped down, looked at the figures lying on the ground and started running. Giscard, Johnson and Bradley followed him. A slowly recovering Chrysler sat up but remained where he was, shaking his head from side to side.

They checked the men lying on the bridge. Giscard said: 'They're all alive. Unconscious, totally knocked out, but they're still breathing.'

Branson said: 'After CUBs? I don't understand. Load them aboard your chopper, Bradley, and take off when you're ready.'

Branson ran towards the Presidential coach and immediately saw the key on the ground. He picked it up and opened the bullet-scarred door. Cartland was standing by the driver's seat. Branson said: 'What happened here?'

'You tell me. All I know is that your guard locked the door from the outside and ran. He ran when the smoke reached here. I assume that the smoke wasn't really smoke, just a smoke-screen, to allow another defector to escape.'

Branson stared at him, first shook his head, then nodded. 'Stay here.'

He ran towards the lead coach. He at once saw the key in the lock, twisted it and opened the door. He looked at the slumped and clearly unconscious Peters, mounted the steps and looked down the coach. He said: 'Where's Revson?'

'Gone.' A well-rehearsed and apparently uncomprehending Grafton spoke in a weary voice. 'I can tell you only three things. He chopped your guard. He spoke on what looked like a miniature radio. Then, when the smoke came, he left, locked the door from the outside and ran. Look, Branson, we're only bystanders, civilians from your point of view. You promised us safety. What's happening out there?'

'Which way did he run?'

'Towards the north tower. He'll have reached there long ago.'

Branson remained silent for quite some time. When he spoke, it was in his accustomed measured tones. 'I am going to destroy this bridge. I do not kill innocent people. Can anybody here drive a coach?'

A young journalist stood up. 'I can.'

'Get this coach off the bridge. Immediately. Through the south barrier.'

He closed the door and ran towards the ambulance. The rear door opened as he approached. O'Hare appeared and said: 'Well, you certainly know how to lay on entertainment for your guests.'

'Get off this bridge. This moment.'

'Whatever for?'

'Stay if you like. I'm going to blow up this damned bridge.'

Branson left, not running now, just walking quickly. He saw a dazed Chrysler emerging from the rear coach. He said: 'Go stay by the President's coach.'

Giscard and Johnson were standing by the rear helicopter. Bradley was leaning through an opened window. Branson said: 'Go now. Meet you at the airport.'

Bradley lifted his helicopter cleanly off the bridge even before Branson had reached the President's coach.

Revson lifted himself from his cramped position on the floor of the rear seat of the lead helicopter and glanced briefly through a window. The seven hostages, escorted by Branson, Giscard and Chrysler, were approaching the helicopter. Revson sank back into hiding and pulled the transceiver from his pocket. He said: 'Mr Hagenbach?'

'Speaking.'

'Can you see the rotor on this helicopter?'

'I can. We all can. We all have glasses on you.'

'First turn the rotor takes, the laser beam.'

The seven hostages were ushered in first. The President and the King sat in the two front seats on the left, the Prince and Cartland on the right. Behind them, the Mayor, Muir and the oil sheikh took up position. Giscard and Chrysler took up separate positions in the third row. Each had a gun in his hand.

The ambulance was approaching the south tower when O'Hare tapped on the driver's window. The window slid back.

O'Hare said: 'Turn back to the middle of the bridge.'

'Turn back! Jesus, Doc, he's about to blow up the damn bridge.'

'There's going to be some sort of an accident but not the kind you think. Turn back.'

Johnson was the last to enter the helicopter. When he was seated Branson said: 'Right. Lift off.'

There came the usual ear-numbing clattering roar, a roar which rapidly developed into a screaming sound, the sound of an engine running far above its rated revolutions, but even so not loud enough to drown a fearsomely clattering sound outside. Johnson leaned forward and all the noise suddenly ceased.

Branson said: 'What's wrong? What happened?'

Johnson stared ahead, then said quietly: 'I'm afraid you were right about the laser beam, Mr Branson. The rotor's just fallen into the Golden Gate.'

Branson reacted very quickly. He lifted a phone and pressed a button. 'Bradley?'

'Mr Branson?'

'We've had some trouble. Come back to the bridge and pick us up.'

'I'm afraid I can't do that. I've had some trouble myself – a couple of Phantom jets riding herd on me. I'm to land at the International Airport. I'm told there will be a welcoming committee.'

Revson was silently on his feet, white pen in hand. He pressed the button twice and, almost in unison, both men slumped forward then, quite unexpectedly and to Revson's shocked dismay, toppled far from silently into the aisle, their guns clattering on the metallic floor.

Branson twisted round and there was a pistol in his hand: Revson was too far away for his tipped needles to carry. Branson took careful aim, squeezed slowly and steadily, then cried out in pain as the President's cane slashed across his cheek. Revson threw himself to the floor of the aisle, his right hand clamping on the butt of Giscard's gun. By the time Branson had wrenched away the President's cane and swung round again, Revson was ready. All he could see of Branson was his head: but he was ready.

They stood in a group, isolated but not twenty yards from the ambulance, the President, the Vice-President, the seven decision-makers and Revson. Revson had a firm grip on April Wednesday's arm. They stood and watched in silence as the shrouded stretcher was lowered from the helicopter and carried through the dozens of armed police and soldiers to the waiting ambulance. Nobody had anything to say: there was nothing to say.

The President said: 'Our royal friends?'

Richards said: 'Can't wait to get to San Rafael tomorrow. They're more than philosophic about the entire episode. They're downright pleased. Not only has it all given America a great big black eye but it will make them national heroes at home.'

The President said: 'We'd better go talk to them.'

He and Richards made to turn away when Revson said: 'Thank you, sir.'

The President looked at him in incredulity. '*Me? You* thank *me?* I've already thanked *you* a hundred times.'

'Yes, sir. As a rule I don't like owing favours but I rather care for having my life saved.'

The President smiled and, along with Richards, turned and walked away.

Hagenbach said to Revson: 'Well, let's go to the office and have your full report.'

'Ah, that. What's the penalty for disobeying an order by the head of the FBI?'

'You get fired.'

'Pity. I quite liked my job. My proposal is that I shower, shave, change, take Miss Wednesday for lunch and *then* file my report in the afternoon. I guess you owe me at least that.'

Hagenbach pondered, then nodded.

'I guess I do.'

Two thousand miles away, among the higher echelons in the FBI headquarters, someone just came into a minor sweepstake fortune.

Hagenbach smiled.